Peril at Midnight

Published by Resurrected Press

This classic book was handcrafted by Resurrected Press. Resurrected Press is dedicated to bringing high quality classic books back to the readers who enjoy them. These are not scanned versions of the originals, but, rather, quality checked and edited books meant to be enjoyed!

Please visit ResurrectedPress.com to view our entire catalogue!

ISBN 13: 978-1-937022-89-1

Printed in the United States of America

Resurrected Press Books in A. E. Fielding's *The Chief Inspector Pointer Mystery* Series

Peril at Midnight

An
Inspector Reynolds
of Scotland Yard
Mystery

By Elaine Hamilton

Originally published in 1934

RESURRECTED PRESS CLASSIC MYSTERY CATALOGUE

Journeys into Mystery
Travel and Mystery in a More Elegant Time

The Edwardian Detectives
Literary Sleuths of the Edwardian Era

Gems of Mystery
Lost Jewels from a More Elegant Age

Anne Austin
One Drop of Blood
The Black Pigeon
Murder at Bridge

E. C. Bentley
Trent's Last Case: The Woman in Black

Ernest Bramah
Max Carrados Resurrected:
The Detective Stories of Max Carrados

Agatha Christie
The Secret Adversary
The Mysterious Affair at Styles

Octavus Roy Cohen
Midnight

Freeman Wills Croft
The Ponson Case
The Pit Prop Syndicate

J. S. Fletcher

The Herapath Property
The Rayner-Slade Amalgamation
The Chestermarke Instinct
The Paradise Mystery
Dead Men's Money
The Middle of Things
Ravensdene Court
Scarhaven Keep
The Orange-Yellow Diamond
The Middle Temple Murder
The Tallyrand Maxim
The Borough Treasurer
In the Mayor's Parlour
The Saftey Pin

R. Austin Freeman

The Mystery of 31 New Inn from the Dr. Thorndyke Series
John Thorndyke's Cases from the Dr. Thorndyke Series
The Red Thumb Mark from The Dr. Thorndyke Series
The Eye of Osiris from The Dr. Thorndyke Series
A Silent Witness from the Dr. John Thorndyke Series
The Cat's Eye from the Dr. John Thorndyke Series
Helen Vardon's Confession: A Dr. John Thorndyke Story
As a Thief in the Night: A Dr. John Thorndyke Story
Mr. Pottermack's Oversight: A Dr. John Thorndyke Story
Dr. Thorndyke Intervenes: A Dr. John Thorndyke Story
The Singing Bone: The Adventures of Dr. Thorndyke
The Stoneware Monkey: A Dr. John Thorndyke Story
The Great Portrait Mystery, and Other Stories: A Collection of Dr. John Thorndyke and Other Stories
The Penrose Mystery: A Dr. John Thorndyke Story

The Uttermost Farthing: A Savant's Vendetta

Arthur Griffiths
The Passenger From Calais
The Rome Express

Fergus Hume
The Mystery of a Hansom Cab
The Green Mummy
The Silent House
The Secret Passage

Edgar Jepson
The Loudwater Mystery

A. E. W. Mason
At the Villa Rose

A. A. Milne
The Red House Mystery

Baroness Emma Orczy
The Old Man in the Corner

Edgar Allan Poe
The Detective Stories of Edgar Allan Poe

Arthur J. Rees
The Hampstead Mystery
The Shrieking Pit
The Hand In The Dark
The Moon Rock
The Mystery of the Downs

Mary Roberts Rinehart
Sight Unseen and The Confession

Dorothy L. Sayers

Whose Body?

Sir William Magnay
The Hunt Ball Mystery

Mabel and Paul Thorne
The Sheridan Road Mystery

Louis Tracy
The Strange Case of Mortimer Fenley
The Albert Gate Mystery
The Bartlett Mystery
The Postmaster's Daughter
The House of Peril
The Sandling Case: What Would You Have Done?

Charles Edmonds Walk
The Paternoster Ruby

John R. Watson
The Mystery of the Downs
The Hampstead Mystery

Edgar Wallace
The Daffodil Mystery
The Crimson Circle

Carolyn Wells
Vicky Van
The Man Who Fell Through the Earth
In the Onyx Lobby
Raspberry Jam
The Clue
The Room with the Tassels
The Vanishing of Betty Varian
The Mystery Girl
The White Alley
The Curved Blades

Anybody but Anne
The Bride of a Moment
Faulkner's Folly
The Diamond Pin
The Gold Bag
The Mystery of the Sycamore
The Come Back

Raoul Whitfield
Death in a Bowl

And much more!
Visit ResurrectedPress.com
for our complete catalogue

FOREWORD

Peril at Midnight published in 1934, is the sixth of a series of mysteries featuring Inspector Reynolds of Scotland Yards' C.I.D. that appeared through the 1930's. Little information is available about the author, Elaine Hamilton beyond the list of books she wrote.

The Westminster Mystery, the first book in the series was written in the style that has become known as "Hum Drum" not because the books are lacking in excitement, but because they try to portray the reality of a police investigation. This style arose in the 1930's as a reaction against the more flamboyant style of detective fiction as epitomized by Agatha Christie's Hercule Poirot or Dorothy Sayers' Lord Peter Wimsey. In place of the eccentricities of these amateur detectives, this style revolves around rather somber police detectives who achieve their results by hard work, dogged attention to details and common sense.

By the time Hamilton penned *Peril at Midnight,* the series had evolved somewhat, becoming more melodramatic in nature, probably as a result of what the publisher thought would be popular. Inspector Reynolds is still at the center of things using the traditional tools of police detectives, surveillance, the searching of records, and the careful questioning of witnesses, but the story has been spiced up by the introduction of Mimi, a French woman with somewhat tenuous ties to the French *Surete.* Romance has been added to the mix, as well, not of Inspector Reynolds, who is happily married, but in the person of Linda Marchant, a young woman who finds herself caught up in a criminal conspiracy.

Peril at Midnight begins when Marchant, in Paris and broke, is offered a mysterious job in London through a newspaper add. Encouraged by Mimi, who had befriended her, she accepts the offer. Mimi is herself involved in the hunt for Zaldo, a mysterious and deadly international jewel thief, whose capers involve two singular traits, they always occur at midnight, and no witnesses are left alive to tell tales. Inspector Reynolds, who comes into the story when Zaldo moves his operation to London, had previously worked with Mimi on another case, though the cooperation between the two is not always what one might hope for.

While perhaps not as realistic as the works of some other mystery writers of the time, Hamilton tells her stories with a certain panache that is both witty and entertaining. There is plenty of action and suspense, and at least in the case of *Peril at Midnight,* more than a hint of romance.

Elaine Hamilton is today a nearly forgotten author, but during the 1930's at least nine of her novels were published though they are today hard to find. It is with pleasure the Resurrected Press offers this new edition of *Peril at Midnight.*

About the Author

Not much is known about Elaine Hamilton other than she wrote a series of mysteries in the 1930's featuring Inspector Reynolds of Scotland Yard. *The Westminster Mystery* published in 1930 was the first of these. Other titles in the series include *Murder in the Fog* (1931), *The Green Death* (1932), *The Chelsea Mystery* (1932), *The Silent Bell* (1933), *Peril at Midnight* (1934), *Tragedy in the Dark* (1935), *The Casino Mystery* (1936) and *Murder Before Tuesday* (1937).

Greg Fowlkes
Editor-In-Chief
Resurrected Press
www.ResurrectedPress.

TABLE OF CONTENTS

I. At The Grey Rat Cafe

Sunday night, October 15th

It was half-past eleven when the girl with vivid red hair crossed the brilliantly lighted Place Blanche and sank down wearily at a little table outside the café of the Grey Rat.

The Place Blanche, that queer shelf of gaiety, night clubs and music halls, which is below the heights of Montmartre and above the roofs of Paris! Charabancs, doing night tours, disgorge goggle-eyed trippers in search of nocturnal amusement. Orchestras and loud-speakers pour forth a medley of sound amid a thousand lights of hues that would surprise a rainbow.

The girl with the red hair might have been blind and deaf for all the interest she showed in night life as exhibited in the Place Blanche. Hat, newspaper, bag, gloves, lay as she had flung them on the chair beside her. One hand dangled loosely across the table, the other supported her cheek while her blue eyes gazed fixedly on the stone wall across the road.

Twice the waiter had approached her for orders, and receiving no sign that his question had been heard, had shrugged and given the job up until the unprofitable customer should come to her senses.

His third attempt was checked by an imperious signal from another client a few tables away. Obediently he went across to the small black-haired Parisienne who had beckoned.

"Leave her alone, Jules," she commanded. Jules scratched his ear.

"But, Mademoiselle Mimi," he began, "more than half an hour has she sat there and not even one small drink has she ordered. It is not good for the Grey Rat. I will tell her to go. Perhaps she is drunk or ill. "

"She is neither," Mimi retorted, with a flash of anger in her dark eyes. "Do not disturb her. Bring me a cognac, stupid one, *vite.*"

Jules hurried away. Mademoiselle Mimi's word was law in the Grey Rat. Not only did she attract many good clients to the café, and lived in a small flat on the top floor, but she was a friend of Madame, the proprietress.

Also, although Mademoiselle Mimi was so charming and looked no more than eighteen, it would seem that she had strange influence with the police.

At times expensive cars drove up to the café of the Grey Rat, and Mademoiselle would hold serious conversation with grave-faced people, who appeared to listen deferentially to the little Parisienne.

And there were nights when Jules was sure he had seen her go out disguised as a newspaper urchin. Madame had bade him hold his tongue when he had commented on the matter.

With the glass of cognac balanced on his tray, he was moving towards Mimi's table when a hand touched his arm. A young man whom he had never seen before stood beside him.

"Give this newspaper to the lady sitting over there," whispered the unknown in bad French.

Jules glanced suspiciously from the man to the lady who was to receive the newspaper. It was for the girl who had sat there so long.

Jules's temper rose. "Sacre bleu!" he exclaimed. "She buys nothing and she will not speak.. And now—"

"And now," interrupted the stranger, slipping a five franc note into the waiter's hand, "you will give her the newspaper, and you will say nothing. You understand?"

Jules understood perfectly, and indicated willing obedience by laying it on the girl's table at once. As she made no sign of having seen it, he thrust it nearer with a murmured: "For you, mademoiselle," and withdrew to deliver the cognac.

Who told you to do that?" Mimi asked him. Jules related the incident.

"The man has gone," he added, "so there can be no harm. It is the Paris edition of an English newspaper."

Mimi nodded, her eyes resting thoughtfully on the still figure of the girl. A few minutes afterwards three new clients arrived.

"This is the place," explained the eldest man, leading the way to a table that was situated between the two girls.

The men ordered drinks, expensive enough to cheer Jules's heart.

Under her long lashes Mimi surveyed them quickly. The two younger men were talking in English about her and the other girl.

"Good lookers, both of 'em, Fraser. That one with the auburn hair was singing at the cabaret across the road last week!"

"She looks miserable enough to be singing in the street now. Perhaps she's lost her job. Chance for your manly charms, Penley. I'll bet the price of the drinks that she turns you down. Personally I'm going to try my luck in my best French with the little black-eyed Parisienne. She's a peach. Which do you prefer?"

"The point is, which do they prefer? I've been here before, and am not going to risk the snub I'm sure you'll get," Blair replied.

Fraser adjusted his tie and with a wink at his friends approached Mimi, hat in hand. She looked up gravely. Before he could speak, she addressed him in English.

"I suppose betting has brought you to this, my poor young man," she said in pitying accents. "I am

sorry, for your misfortune. Go away and learn the wisdom." She dropped a coin in his hat and calmly turned her, back on him.

A shout of laughter greeted Fraser as with reddened cheeks he rejoined his friends.

"You were right, Blair," he agreed ruefully. "Snub it was. As for you, Penley, try your stuff on the other girl and perhaps I'll get a laugh out of it."

Penley swung his hand down in a contemptuous gesture.

"Watch me, boy. I'm a quick worker. Why, my style is famous in little old New York! Wow! See the statue come to life."

He sauntered across to the silent girl and, bending, kissed the white nape of her neck.

Her startled gasp was lost in another sound. Mimi, who had slid round behind, landed a stinging smack on Penley's face.

"*Va t'en*! Hop it! Scram!" she cried, using the vernacular of three countries to make her meaning trebly clear. Her dark eyes blazed with indignation.

Penley "scrammed."

"The famous style seems to be a little off colour," Fraser drawled,"' and the drinks would appear to be on you."

"Shut up," Blair put in. "Neither of you has covered himself with distinction, and as you don't seem anxious to apologise to those girls, I'm going to."

The opportunity which Mimi had sought to speak to the silent girl had come unexpectedly. She was sitting beside her now, talking in a low tone, when a tall man in rather shabby tweeds approached the table.

Mimi rose, placing an arm protectingly on the other girl's shoulder.

"Your two friends have annoyed us, so now you will make your evening complete, yes?" she demanded.

The man looked at her with quiet grey eyes.

"No, mademoiselle. I have come to say how sorry I am."

Mimi waved her forefinger with scorn.

"Sorry! That is easy to say." She lowered her voice. "*Ecoutez*. This girl—she is a stranger to me—is troubled. Anyone can see that. Your friend can find no better amusement in all Paris than to insult her!"

"And you also, I am afraid," the man added.

"That imbecile insult me!" Mimi's lip curled. "I can look after myself always. This girl—it is another thing. She is unhappy. I have no English words to tell you what I think of your friends who make the bets on such a subject."

"I should have stopped the young idiots." He glanced down at the girl. whose cause Mimi was championing and almost hesitatingly addressed her. "Please forgive them."

The girl raised appealing eyes and gazed at him as if vision did not focus accurately.

It doesn't matter," she said after a moment. "Nothing does when—"

"When things go awry," he finished. "I know. I've felt like that often. One doesn't know how to go on."

The girl looked puzzled.

"Go on with what?" she asked.

"With the job of living. I say, you'll think I'm talking like a parson."

"No. You're right." She paused and then asked a little breathlessly: "Why are you saying this? Are you a journalist or—or a detective?"

"Neither. You and I are both Britishers, I fancy. That's why I came over. I'm an author by trade and," he added with careful emphasis, "I'm not out to get copy."

"Thank you," she replied softly. "Good-bye."

On an impulse he drew a card from his pocket and laid it on the table.

"That address will always find me. I'm going back to London to-morrow. Meanwhile," he drew out his pocket-book, "will you let me—"

"No, no," she said quickly. "That would spoil it." He drew Mimi aside and spoke in an undertone. "Have no anxiety, monsieur," she replied. "I meant to look after her in any case. She interests me. Her fear is so terrible."

"What is she afraid of?"

"That I cannot say. But she needs courage more than money, I am sure. In a day or two I also go to London. I will persuade her to come with me. Until then she shall stay in my *appartement*. She will be safe."

"Will you let me know when you and she come to London?" he asked. "I too am interested." Mimi's eyes twinkled.

"That is easy to believe, monsieur. Mademoiselle is charming and beautiful." she added proudly, "You care to ask the good and famous Inspector Reynolds of your Scotland Yard about me, say that you have met Mimi of Montmartre."

"May I also say that I hope to meet her again?" he asked.

Mimi studied him for a moment.

"I think I like you," she observed in a serious voice. "Who knows, we may meet again one day. Especially," a glint of mockery came into her expressive eyes, "if you commit an interesting crime."

The man laughed. "Is that a threat or a temptation? And are you a detective or a gangster?"

"You who write books shall find out, monsieur. Please go now and take your so unpleasant friends with you. *Au 'voir*."

"What are you called?" she asked the girl when the three men had left the café.

"Linda. Linda Marchant." The girl was calmer now.

Mimi picked up the visiting-card which the man had left and carefully copied the name and address.

"He is nice, Linda, this man. Keep this card. He could be a good friend."

"I'm afraid of friends. They ask questions. Enemies are safer."

Mimi touched the newspaper that lay on the table. Was it a friend or an enemy who sent you this?" she asked.

Linda puckered her brow.

"I have no friends now and I don't know why the waiter brought it to me."

The French girl glanced through the pages. On one she saw an advertisement marked with blue pencil. Covering it with her hand, she changed the subject.

"Nearly an hour ago, Linda, I saw you come here and knew you were unhappy. You are English, I am French." She flicked a finger to and fro. "No matter: We are both women, and perhaps Mimi has a wiser head than you think. Will you trust me enough to see if I can help?"

For a second Linda's blue eyes looked searchingly into Mimi 's earnest face

"Yes. You were wonderful to come to my rescue as you did." She tapped nervously on the table.

"It's not a pretty story, Mimi. Somebody died— suspiciously. I ran away from London to avoid giving evidence against—a man whom I know. My words might have hanged him, though he was innocent."

"Was he or anyone else arrested?" Mimi's tone was hard and incisive.

"No one."

"So you came to Paris, took a job at the cabaret across the road and lost it, yes?"

Linda nodded.

"Four days ago. The manager—"

"I can guess," Mimi interrupted. "He is a fat pig, that creature; you are lovely and let him see that you hated him."

"I'm afraid I did. It gave him an excuse to send me away. I've tried scores of other places since, but it seems hopeless. I don't owe anything yet and—I don't mean to."

"Where is your luggage?" Mimi demanded.

"In a railway station cloakroom. I had to leave my room to-day."

"We will get it to-morrow. Meanwhile, Linda, you will stay with me until you go back to London."

"You're wonderfully kind But I can't go back, Mimi. I've no job, no money and I mustn't be found."

"London is a safe place in which to hide. I have enough money for both of us and have business there in a day or two. And," Mimi pointed to the advertisment in the newspaper, "I think someone means you to have a job. Read this."

> *Wanted immediately, for London, young woman, refined, medium height, auburn hair, blue eyes, age about twenty-two, for responsible position requiring tact. Knowledge of antiques preferable, but not necessary. Good salary guaranteed. Apply enclosing photograph, to: F. Yates, 27 Silver Square, London, W.1.*

II. The Mysterious Advertisement

Monday Morning

"There will be hundreds of applications from red-haired, blue-eyed girls," Linda said doubtfully next morning as she and Mimi discussed the strange advertisement over breakfast.

Mimi poured out another cup of coffee for her guest.

"Your unknown friend—or enemy—who sent you this newspaper must have thought that you had the good chance," she replied. "You are afraid to answer it because you think that someone of your past life has traced you to Paris? "

"That doesn't seem possible. I've never done cabaret work before and was only known as 'Lola' there. I had no letters from England, no one knew my address here and I lived alone."

"Maybe a friendly visitor to the cabaret knew that you had left and, noticing this advertisement, wished you to see it."

Linda accepted Mimi's solution.

"Probably. I wonder if it appeared in the London newspapers."

"I wonder," replied Mimi knowing that it had not done so, since she had already purchased and examined a pile of English dailies before Linda was awake. "*Alors*, you will make the go for this job, yes?"

A smile flashed across the English girl's face at quaint phrases.

"I'll have a go for it," she promised. For a while she gazed through the window at the view of Paris roofs and spires, blue hazed in the late October sunlight.

Then her eyes drifted back to the sitting-room alternately gay and sombre with its yellow-washed walls and dignified Breton furniture. Who was this Parisienne who had taken compassion on a stranger?

Linda studied Mimi's delicate profile, dark expressive eyes, and black hair cut in the style of a Florentine page. Here, she knew, was a girl of unusual intelligence with a cold, unclouded brain capable of clean-cut decision and reasoning.

"Why are you bothering yourself about me?" Linda asked.

Mimi lighted a cigarette and pushed the packet across to her friend.

"You interest me," she replied in cool, detached tones. "Also you are too lovely to be hopeless."

"My good looks never brought me any luck yet. Have yours?"

"*Certainement.* They are extremely useful in my work," Mimi stated gravely.

The English girl glanced round at the signed sketches and caricatures.

"Perhaps you are an artist, or an artist's model," she ventured. "And out of kindness you are allowing me to keep you from your work."

Mimi shook her head and gathered up the breakfast things.

"I never permit myself the luxury of sentiment as you English do. My work comes first. I am an artist's model sometimes; an artist in my work, I hope, always. Write your letter now. I will send it by air mail. In two or three days we shall get a reply, I make the bet of my shirt, as you say—"

Linda smiled at the Parisienne's assurance. "And then?"

"And then we go to London together," Mimi told her. "This morning I have business to arrange. Give me the ticket for your luggage and I will bring it back with me. Rest here quietly, Linda. No one will disturb you. Think a little of the kind author man we met last night. I fancy he will think more than a little of you."

Linda took the visiting-card from her bag and looked at it.

"He has a nice name. Stephen Blair."

On Wednesday morning the reply which Mimi had predicted arrived by registered post for her guest.

"Quick, open it," she cried. "If it does not make a rendezvous I lose the shirt."

The girls scanned the typewritten page eagerly. The communication was extremely business-like.

27 Silver Square, London, W.1.

DEAR MISS MARCHANT,

Your letter of October 16th duly received The photograph enclosed indicates that you might be a suitable applicant and we shall be glad of an interview at an early date. You mention that you can travel immediately.
Herewith we send you tickets for rail and boat, etc., to London, via Calais and Dover, dated Wednesday, October 18th.
Please wire immediately you arrive on stamped telegraph form enclosed, and fix appointment.

Yours faithfully,
F. YATES.
(Managing Director, Select Employment Bureau.)

"You were right, Mimi. There really does seem a hope."

"A hope!" Mimi exclaimed, examining the enclosures meticulously. "This Monsieur Yates who says that he is yours faithfully, must he send you a private aeroplane before you can do more than hope?"

The two days of rest, good food and Mimi's companionship had restored Linda to a frame of mind in which she could face the future once more with courage.

The sun shone on her thick wavy hair, turning its hue to glistening gold, and brought a radiance to the vivid blue eyes and lovely face.

For a second, compunction was in Mimi's heart as she saw the English girl's beauty and realised the risk that might be attached to the mysterious advertisement. That it was no fortunate coincidence, the French girl was convinced. Someone in London   wanted Linda to reply to it. And somewhere in the background of Linda's past lay the secret of an unsolved murder.

Mimi thrust sentiment aside. If there was a link between that secret and the advertisement she meant to discover it.

"*Alors,*" she remarked briskly, "we go to London at once. And, on arriving, we will send the paid-for telegram to your faithful Yates arranging the rendezvous for tomorrow, yes?"

Linda nodded. Suddenly she leaned across the table and gripped, the other girl's arm.

"You are so wise, Mimi. Tell me, do you think this is any trick of the English police to trap me?"

"*Surement,* no. If they want you and know where you are, why should they not come and see you? The man you believe innocent and for whose sake you ran away, are you going to see him again?"

An expression of horror shadowed Linda's face.

"I hope never! One day I will tell you everything."

"*Eh bien,* then one may perhaps be of assistance," Mimi remarked as she opened a letter bearing the London postmark.

Presently she passed it across to her friend.

"The nice Mr. Blair has not forgotten you."

The envelope was addressed to Mademoiselle Mimi, care of the Grey Rat, Place Blanche. Linda read the letter with interest.

DEAR MADEMOISELLE),

Your friend, Inspector Reynolds, sends you his kind regards and assures me that as a guardian you are without reproach. He hopes to see you very soon. I made his acquaintance while calling on a friend at Scotland Yard to-day. Please give wishes to the English girl whom you befriended and say that I trust you and she will let me have the opportunity of meeting you again. Could you both dine with me on Friday evening?

Yours sincerely,
STEPHEN BLAIR.

Linda pointed to a sentence in Stephen Blair's letter.

"That name may be of importance, if not dangerous, to me. How is it that you, a French artist's model, know a Scotland Yard detective well enough for him to give you a reference?"

'Surely it is to my—how does one call it—balance that he can do so." Mimi answered logically. "Permission to work in England is not easy for an alien to obtain. The inspector was amiable enough to arrange matters for me when I wished to model for an English sculptor. I behaved myself and he gives the reference. *Voila tout.*"

The English girl gave a sigh of relief.

"Mr. Blair lives in the Adelphi, I see, Mimi. Here's his address and telephone number. Do you think we might accept his invitation?"

"*Mais oui,*" Mimi replied with decision. "I trust he chooses his dinners better than he chooses friends. I will mention that point when I give him the works on the telephone."

"Please don't. I don't mind what I eat."

"I am French and I do. An army marches, one hears, on its stomach. I do not permit mine to be insulted. Be ready to leave in an hour, Linda. I will return for you in good time for the train."

Downstairs in the café Mimi called the waiter aside.

"You did as I ordered, Jules?"

"Yes, mademoiselle. All day yesterday I left the English newspaper on the table which the English girl had occupied. Late last night the young man who tipped me to give it to her came and sat down at that table."

"What was he like?" Mimi demanded.

Jules raised his hands with a deprecating gesture.

"The café was busy. I did not notice. Thin face and long nose: about twenty-five years, perhaps."

"Imbecile! What happened?"

"He opened the newspaper and asked me why the English lady had not taken it. As you instructed, I said that she had left it there untouched and had gone away, but that I could possibly give her a message."

"Of course he offered to pay you for her address," Mimi remarked.

Jules nodded and produced a note from his pocket.

"Precisely, mademoiselle. Again, as you ordered, I refused. Then he wrote this and told me to deliver it to the English girl and no one else. He also gave me five francs.

"Why didn't you come to my flat and let me know?"

"There are many stairs, it was late, and my feet were of a weariness."

Mimi patted his arm.

"I understand, my poor Jules. But this affair was important and I always pay you well."

"Always, mademoiselle," agreed Jules. "Well, this morning, only a quarter of an hour ago, the

man came again. 'Give me back that note,' he said, 'I have changed my mind.' He seemed agitated.

"What did you say?" Mimi asked eagerly.

"I told him that the note had been delivered to English lady as he had wished. He bit his lip and then went away. It is well, mademoiselle?"

"Very," Mimi told him. "Here are ten francs. Forget the affair, if you're asked about it."

"Jules's mouth widened to a broad smile.

"Merci, mademoiselle. It is entirely forgotten."

Tearing open the envelope, which was without address, Mimi read the message. It was written in block letters and attached to it was a newspaper cutting of the advertisement.

> *I KNOW YOU'RE DOWN AND OUT. TAKE THIS*
> *CHANCE. I'M SURE YOU'LL GET THE JOB.*
> *GOOD LUCK.*
> *A WELL WISHER*

It was now definite, Mimi reflected, that the ad-cut had been intended for Linda Marchant. Someone in London needed her urgently, and the man who had written this was merely making sure that she replied.

The ruse that Mimi had planned and Jules carried by deliberately leaving the newspaper on the table had succeeded. The stranger, fearing that she had not seen it, had left this message. This morning, probably hearing from F. Yates that Linda had replied, he had called in a hurry to get back the unnecessary message.

He had no cause for anxiety, Mimi told herself, as Linda would not receive it.

They were in the train a couple of hours later en route to Calais when she remembered a triviality that puzzled her.

"Your English argot—how do you say—slang, intrigues me *enorménment*, Linda. What does 'down and out' mean, please?"

"No money, home, friends or luck, Mimi," Linda replied with amusement. "I was a good example of the phrase when you found me last Sunday night."

"Thank you. I will remember," the student of English said earnestly.

III. INTRODUCING INSPECTOR REYNOLDS

Wednesday Evening

It was in the boat train to Victoria that Mimi first noticed the change in her companion.

Sunday night the English girl had been dazed and broken, without hope or interest. In Mimi's flat she had gradually recovered a measure of poise, but lacked force and initiative, accepting suggestions with amiable indifference.

This evening, as the train rushed towards London, Linda's blue eyes seemed full of fire, her lips were set to firm lines of determination. Even her slim fingers, which hitherto had seemed limp and nervous, were clasped tightly.

A queer smile twisted her mouth as she met Mimi's eyes.

"You've won, little French girl. Back I go into the fray. Only this time," she gazed through the window as if she addressed some bitter spectre of the past, "it's no soft-hearted Linda Marchant who tried to run straight and do the decent thing. It doesn't pay."

"Not immediately, perhaps. Once long ago," Mimi's voice became low and reminiscent, "when I had suffered badly and felt as you do, someone very wise said to me: 'It must be rather wonderful when you get to the end of life to be able to look back and know that you have done nothing to be ashamed of.' I shall never forget.

"This situation," Mimi went on, "be careful before you take it. If you like, I will ask Inspector Reynolds to make inquiries about the man Yates."

"No. Tell him nothing, Mimi. I can look after myself."
Linda's tone was hard as steel. "There are plenty of
crooked jobs to be had. I've been offered and have refused
them before. Probably Yates wants me as decoy duck for
a gang of tricksters, or hostess in a gambling den.
Whatever it is, I mean to take it—at a good salary."

Mimi lighted a cigarette.

"English juries are not sentimental over a woman as
in my country, Linda, and to go to prison is not at all
amusing."

"I'd as soon go there for my own sins as shield others,"
was Linda's unguarded retort. She bent forward and
grasped Mimi's hand. "Please believe that I shall always
be grateful to you. You protected me, a stranger, fed and
housed me and lent me money. That will be the first debt
I shall pay."

"That will be the last debt you need be anxious about,
Linda. I earn good money and spend little. Your past
trouble, is it likely to affect your future life?"

"Not if I see it coming and can avoid it. In Montmartre
I felt I must tell you everything, ask your advice. Now,"
Linda clenched her fists, "I mean to stand on my own feet
and keep my secret. Forgive me if you can, but when we
arrive at Victoria I mean to leave you. Don't worry! I'll go
to a man whom I once helped out of a pretty tight corner."

The French girl shrugged lightly and flicked the ash
from her cigarette.

"As you wish. There is nothing for me to forgive,
Linda. You are free to go where you please. We are not
the twins from Siam. But," she glanced up mischievously,
"what about our dinner with Monsieur Blair?"

"I'd go, but maybe by Friday evening—" Linda
hesitated.

"You will be employed by a band of thieves!" Mimi
finished. "What does that matter? Monsieur Blair is an
author and wide in the mind, I am sure. He may find you
even more interesting than in Montmartre. This is
Wednesday. I will make the date with him for Friday at

eight o'clock. Since I am not to know your address, where shall we meet?"

"Swan and Edgar's corner at seven-thirty."

"*Bon*! It is understood. We part at Victoria presently. You will telegraph to your faithful Yates, and I," Mimi blew a kiss to the air, "will ring up Stephen Blair who is sincerely mine."

Mimi picked up her suitcase as the train slowed into the station and wished Linda good-bye.

"You want to hide yourself, so I go now; *Bonne chance!*"

The train had barely stopped when Mimi jumped out and hurried along to the ticket barrier. Before she reached it a woman greeted her.

"*Chère madame*, how fortunate that you could meet me," Mimi cried, embracing the newcomer. "Will you please help me? I will explain later. Keep your eyes on that girl," she indicated Linda, who was just alighting from a compartment and giving her bag to a porter. "I must follow her in a taxi. She has a big trunk in the van. You are clever, and she does not know you. I will conceal myself here until she is ready to go"

Mrs. Reynolds nodded in understanding. Blest with keen intelligence and as the wife of one of Scotland Yard's inspectors, she knew how to deal with a situation such as this.

"Right. I'll see to it Mimi," she promised. "There's my husband at the barrier. He had business this way so came along with me. Get into a taxi with him and wait. He's over-working, underfeeding and dreadfully solemn these days."

Near the gate where tickets were being collected Mimi found the inspector, a tall, broad-shouldered man with a genial face and a mouth that could be grim or humorous according to circumstances.

Dragging him behind a pile of luggage she sketched in voluble French a brief outline of her meeting with Linda, making a few reservations.

His grey eyes twinkled.

"So that's why a certain Mr. Stephen Blair wanted information about you," was his comment. "What am I expected to do? Turn the entire Scotland Yard force out to watch over the lovely Linda or play a lone hand and do the job myself?"

Mimi turned a well-simulated look of scorn on him.

"This affair will need brains, monsieur. You shall have a nice thinking part to-day and Madame and I will show you the real detective goods!"

"Minx!" retorted the inspector with a cheerful grin. "I suppose you've come over here to annoy me with your muddled versions of English idiom and slang."

"My English, he is greatly improved and extended," Mimi informed him loftily. "Also, I speak American with a fluency. Listen to this, big boy, I'll give you the workings," she added in nasal tones. "How's that?"

"Awful" pronounced Reynolds "Here's my wife. Hop into this cab, Agnes. This conceited imp promised me a lesson in how a detective should work."

Mrs. Reynolds smiled with content to notice that her husband's depression was drifting away under the influence of Mimi's banter.

No one knew Mimi's brilliant brain and courage better than Mrs. Reynolds. On several occasions the little Parisienne had helped the inspector to bring daring murderers to justice, and she had once saved his life by shooting his assailant. Inside the cab Mimi turned to the inspector.

"The driver will obey you better than me Please tell him to follow Linda's taxi," she. coaxed. "See, it is just going."

Reynolds gave the order and the pursuit began.

"Bound to call in the police to help you after—" He stopped abruptly as he caught a warning signal from his wife.

Mimi was staring ahead, dark eyes, grown suddenly tragic in her white face. Suppose she had allowed Linda to go into unknown danger!

"Imbecile that I am," she muttered.

The inspector caught the murmured phrase and guessed the reason.

"Remember that if your great detective genius fails you, Mimi, you've got a humble inspector for a friend," he remarked. "Tell me more about Linda. All I know is that she was sad when you first saw her."

"Sad! *Ma foi.* She was," Mimi paused to recollect the new phrase, "she was 'out and down.'"

"That," complimented Reynolds, "is a really original version. What is the matter, Agnes?" he asked. They were going at a steady pace through Hyde Pak and his wife gazed in perplexed fashion after a small car that passed them.

"The man driving that car was at Victoria Station," Mrs. Reynolds replied. "I noticed that he followed Linda from her compartment to the luggage van, but kept at a discreet distance. It might be nothing but my silly fancy, Tom."

"You've never indulged in them before," her husband remarked. "Look, Mimi, the man drove past us in a hurry. He has now deliberately slowed down and is keeping behind your friends taxi." The inspector put his head out of the window and spoke to the chauffeur. "Keep behind the car that is between us and that taxi."

A few minutes the little procession was going up Baker Street and took a left-hand turning into a street that seemed composed of apartment houses.

"Keep out of sight or she'll spot you," Reynolds warned.

Mimi obediently slipped to the floor of the cab.

Ahead of them Linda's taxi pulled up at a house and she got out. A little behind her the small car and the man who had been driving jumped and opened his bonnet.

"Shall I make a dee-tour and get the number of house coming back, inspector?" asked the driver of Reynolds's taxi.

"Yes. You know me, eh?"

"Often picked you up at Scotland Yard, sir," the man called back as he executed the little manoeuvre.

When they passed through the street again both the small car and taxi had gone.

"I think the house was number thirty-five," Reynolds observed. "It looks as if your bird means to stay, as the taxi has been paid off. And now what?"

"Will you and Madame Reynolds please be my guests at my favourite Soho restaurant?" Mimi asked. "I have cabled this morning to the patron commanding a dinner superb. You will permit me?"

"We'll love to come," Mrs. Reynolds replied.

"Sure you wouldn't like the Chief Commissioner himself to keep watch outside Linda's house tonight?" Reynolds inquired. "Lovely English girl answers to queer advertisement, so needs Scotland Protection! He was deliberately baiting Mimi, hoping to learn more.

Mimi tossed her head.

"So that is all you think it is! Perhaps if you knew that behind Linda is an unsolved—" she ended abruptly and laughed. "Oh, la, la, monsieur. I know your tricks. Almost you caught me."

"Almost," agreed Reynolds, inwardly deciding to look up the records of recent unsolved murder cases and see if a girl named Linda had been involved.

"By the way," he asked with a casual air, as he lighted a cigarette, "what did you say Linda's surname was?"

"I didn't say," was Mimi's calm retort. "So, *mon ami*, to employ your golf expressions, this is my hole, I think."

"Ever heard of a gentleman called Stephen Blair?" questioned the inspector lightly. "He mentioned that he was interested in Linda and a funny little French girl, and meant to ask them to dine with him on Friday.

Maybe he will invite me also. If so, I fancy that you and I will halve this hole, young woman."

As their taxi stopped outside the restaurant in Soho, Mimi's lips curved to a mischievous smile.

"I wonder," she replied.

IV. AN ANONYMOUS LETTER

Wednesday Evening

At the door of the restaurant the proprietor, a stout, middle-aged Frenchman, met them. His cheerful face beamed as he saw Mimi.

"Monsieur Antoine is the brother of Jules, who is waiter at the Montmartre café where I live," she explained, introducing him to the inspector' and his wife.

Reynolds wondered, why such relationship should cause the Frenchman to treat Mimi as if she were a minor deity. He did not know that, thanks to a tip from Mimi, Antoine had stocked his cellars with the finest Burgundy, bought at a "give-away" price from a bankrupt Bordeaux wine merchant.

Neither did he know that Mimi had discovered the identity of the unknown thief who for over a year had robbed Antoine of goods and money, after two private detectives had failed to find out.

You are very welcome, monsieur and madame," Antoine said now in fluent English "Any friends of Mademoiselle Mimi shall receive the best that my establishment can offer."

The Frenchman led the way to a table.

"I reserved this on receipt of your cable, mademoiselle. Here is the menu I suggest."

Mimi scanned it critically.

"Excellent! Alas! Me, I must eat simply. To-day I have travelled on your so odious Channel!" She waved her hand up and down. "So while Monsieur and Madame Reynolds take the cocktails I will telephone, if they will excuse me."

Reynolds's lip twitched.

"To your dear Linda? I am afraid that 35 Kenford Street is not in the telephone book, Mimi."

"I too noticed that there were no telephone wires," she flashed back. "My call is not to Linda, but to Stephen Blair, monsieur."

She strolled up the restaurant, chattering gaily to Monsieur Antoine. Reynolds watched her thoughtfully.

"Exactly what mischief is that imp planning?" he demanded of his wife.

"Let Mimi handle that in her own way," advised Mrs. Reynolds.

"I'll get Linda's surname before I'm much older. If she knows anything about an unsolved murder—and Mimi isn't out for small game in crime—then it's my job to find out. I should look a fool if I let the chance slip."

"You'll look a bigger fool if there's nothing in it. And remember, Tom," Mrs. Reynolds's tone became more earnest, "if you butt in Mimi will outwit you. Wait til she asks for your help. Forget it and enjoy your dinner, for once."

Reynolds rather grudgingly obeyed her, though his eyes watched the little French girl who was now in the call box near the cash desk. His wife's counsel might be wise. Nevertheless, immediately when Mimi had finished telephoning, he intended to ring up the Yard have a man sent round to Linda's address to ferret out her name somehow.

Unfortunately for him, Mimi was one jump ahead. Her apparently joking conversation with Antoine as he had conducted her to the telephone was deadly serious.

"Listen, Antoine, my friend the inspector must not telephone until dinner is over. Can you arrange it?"

"Before you leave the instrument I will see that someone is there waiting to use it," Antoine promised instantly. "It will be a trunk call, I think."

"*Bon*! Now, directly the next course is served, ask me to come at once and see your wife who has a heart attack."

Antoine looked bewildered.

"But Marie is at the cinema and is in perfect health."

"A heart attack," repeated Mimi. "You will take me to her for a little minute. You understand?" The Frenchman bowed.

"Perfectly!"

Reynolds was moving towards the telephone as Mimi hung up the receiver when he saw another client enter the call box and begin a laborious search through the directory.

"Stephen Blair sends you his compliments," Mimi told the inspector. "Would the Trocadero grill room at eight-thirty on Friday suit you?" she asked sweetly.

Reynolds raised his eyebrows.

"It would, but as I'm certain that you and Blair and Linda would not be there, the idea lacks point."

"Let Mimi eat her dinner, Tom," Mrs. Reynolds put in, and kept the conversation going on general topics while their hostess ate large quantities of hors d'oeuvres.

When the delicately prepared sole arrived so also did the proprietor.

"Mademoiselle, a thousand pardons!" he exclaimed in an agitated voice "My wife begs you to come to her. A sudden heart attack. Calm her while I send for the doctor."

In his office a moment later Antoine, at Mimi's dictation, wrote a hurried note.

"You understand, my name is not to be mentioned," she instructed.

"The man I shall send immediately on this errand does not know of your existence," Antoine assured her.

"Excellent! Let the call box be occupied until he returns. If all is well and my friend Linda promises to do as requested, come to my table and as a signal say we must taste your famous brandy. Then, my good friend," Mimi drooped an eyelid. "the inspector may ring up his Scotland Yard or the Palace of Buckingham if he likes."

She was subdued and full of concern for Antoine's wife when she returned to the table.

"It is very sad." Reynolds agreed sympathetically. "Does the lady understand English as well as her husband?"

Mimi thought hard before she made a guarded reply.

"About the same, monsieur."

"That's good. Otherwise she might find the English 'talkies' a little difficult to follow."

The French girl pursed her lips.

"You make the snoopings," she commented.

"Merely a polite inquiry to the waiter after madame's health," Reynolds remarked airily. "If you must use slang, try to be grammatical. We use 'snooping' as a verb, not a noun. Also, concerning madame and to continue in your golf expressions, I believe this is my hole."

"It might have been, but—" Mimi paused for effect, "unfortunately you are stommied."

"'Stymied,'" corrected Mrs. Reynolds softly as her husband rose, shaking with laughter, and walked to the telephone box.

It was still occupied by the same man, who said he was waiting for an important trunk call.

They were drinking coffee when the proprietor came to their table and begged them to try his superb liqueur brandy.

"It will square off a perfect dinner," Mimi agreed.

"By the way, Antoine, your stupid waiter told Inspector Reynolds that your wife was at the cinema."

"She intended to go, but this sudden attack prevented her," he explained. "I have not told my staff, naturally. The call box is vacant, monsieur, and at your disposal."

"Thank you. It may be a little too late for my call," Reynolds remarked, with a stern look at Mimi's innocent face, but one can always try."

Half an hour later a man rang the door bell at 35 Kenford Street and asked to speak to the English lady who had arrived from Paris earlier that evening. The landlady appeared puzzled.

"You must have come to the wrong house, sir. My lodgers have all been with me for ages and nobody arrived this afternoon from Paris."

The man consulted a crumpled scrap of paper.

"A Miss Linda Somebody," he persisted. "I can't make out the name, but she is an actress, I believe. I come from a theatrical agency and want to see her on business."

"The only Miss Somebody that I have is over sixty and crippled with rheumaticks."

The man rubbed his chin and seemed worried. "I'll get into trouble with my boss. He was sure she'd arrived to-day?"

"Perhaps you'd like a look through my rooms. All my folks happen to be in, although it's only ten o'clock"

The landlady tapped at each door upstairs and down, mentioning to the occupants that the caller was a prospective lodger. Even the kitchen was not omitted, where a smutty-faced maid was frying sausages.

"That's the lot," the woman remarked as she conducted her perplexed visitor to front door. "No, it's no trouble at all. Sorry you've had your journey in vain. Goodnight."

A little later the man tapped at the door of Reynolds's office at Scotland Yard and entered. Seeing that Mrs. Reynolds and a young girl in black were with the inspector, he began tactfully "About that little job in Limehouse, sir—"

"Ah yes, Foster," Reynolds said, and leading the detective out on to the landing, closed his office door behind him.

"Must have been the wrong number, sir. The landlady bit on to my story beautifully. There's no Miss Linda who-is-it in the house. I saw everybody from the skivvy upwards. The only woman lodger there under fifty is married and ugly as sin."

In the basement of No. 35 Kenford Street, meanwhile, the "skivvy" removed a black fringe and side curls and wiped the smears from her face.

"Phew! That was a close call, Kate. Thanks for lending me your best toupee," she observed to the landlady. "I wonder, who he was."

Kate poured out a glass of beer and took a generous drink.

"I don't, Miss Linda. He was a Scotland Yard gent, I'll bet. All that talk of theatrical agencies didn't fool me, with thousands of pretty, actresses sitting on their doorsteps begging for jobs. It's the first man who brought the note that puzzles me. Have you any idea who he is?"

Linda shook her head.

"I'm worried because it means that two separate parties know where I am."

"The writer of this letter means kindly, anyhow," Kate comforted her. "All the anonymous letters I've ever heard of have been fair horrors. I've never had one in my life, while you, half my age, have an unknown friend in Paris send you a newspaper advertisement for your good, and another unknown here sends you a warning note to-night" She drained her glass with a sigh for lost romance. "It beats me, dearie."

"I don't want help or pity. All I want is to be left alone, and not have people trying to dig out the past." Linda clasped her hands desperately. "Kate, where am I to go? You know about—about everything, and I feel safe with you. With a stranger I should never know a second's peace."

Kate patted the girl's arm.

"You leave any ferrets to me: I'll deal with 'em. My back door opens into a lane that runs through to two busy side streets. They can't very well watch both ends of it and my front door too. Stop worrying and let me see the queer message again that you've just had. It couldn't be from that French girl, could it?"

"Mimi doesn't know my address," Linda said, as she passed over the note.

It was in large angular writing and bore no superscription.

"You were followed from Victoria Station to Kenford Street. Your surname is unknown. Warn your landlady to prepare for immediate inquiries and deny that you are in the house.—A Friend"

V. THREE OF A KIND

Wednesday Evening

Mr. F. Yates, of 27 Silver Square, stared moodily up at his feet which were on the mantelpiece of his sitting-room.

His spirits were not damped by the fact that they were particularly ugly feet. Having owned them for over thirty-five years he was used to the sight of them and only a tiresome corn made him aware of their existence from time to time.

Twenty-past seven. That fool Tyler ought to be back. The boat train was due at Victoria three-quarters of an hour ago.

A double rap on the front door made him spring up and hurry into the hall.

"Telegram, sir."

Yates snatched it from the boy's hand.

"No reply," he said after a glance at the message.

Back in his easy chair again, he re-read the message carefully. The girl had well and truly taken the bait, she was actually in London, and the first part of the complicated business was over.

This wire contained her promise to call at ten-thirty to-morrow morning. He rather wished she'd put her address on the telegram, but if Tyler had done his job properly that didn't matter.

Things were looking up and Mr. Yates decided to treat himself to a stiff whisky and soda. Standing in front of the mirror he raised the glass with a knowing wink.

"Here's to you, Mr. Yates," he remarked jovially, "wishing you success, a long life and an open door." He added the last words with a grim smile of remembrance for the time when doors had been closed on with a clang.

Standing on tiptoes, he was able to get a longer vision of himself. A suit of rather large check; a trifle baggy round the knees, he noticed, but cut in with a natty effect at the waist. Pin striped shirt showing a pleasing display of cuff; fancy tie, centred by a horseshoe ruby and diamond pin almost as good as the real thing.

"Nothing wrong about that, my boy," he remarked to the reflection in the glass.

His dark beady eyes had a trick of darting to and fro in a snake-like manner. They were set close together above a bent nose and thick lips. Mr. Yates's enemies were wont to use the adjective "shifty" in speaking of his eyes. He himself preferred to think that they were keen.

His face, he pondered now, was perhaps not his strong suit, but Clark Gable was no oil-painting and *he* could get away with it. Mr. Yates was therefore without hope of attracting Miss Linda Marchant during their interview to-morrow, and winning her confidence sufficiently for his purpose.

Tyler, his assistant, whom he was now expecting, had had a public school education and imagined that he knew how a gentleman should dress and conduct himself.

Mr. Yates pulled down his over-tight waistcoat with a jerk and laughed aloud as he thought of his own early career at Borstal. He had risen from that humble start by his own ingenuity. Like a Finnix, or whatever it was called, from the flames, he thought.

Whereas Tyler, who had begun life with every social advantage, had had a spot of trouble and drifted down until he was now working for the Select Employment Agency, which, in short, meant Mr. F. Yates.

At times Tyler protested against his employer's dress and manners, and made suggestions that caused resentment but were usually adopted, Mr. Yates had to admit, with success.

"Well?" he called out as a key clicked in the lock and the front door was opened.

"Extremely well, thank you, but thirsty," Tyler replied, helping himself to a drink. His voice had a tired cultured intonation that Yates ached to imitate.

In appearance Tyler was almost the antithesis of his employer. Clad in a well-made and rather shabby serge suit that threw into relief his pale face and finely cut features, he had a quality which, Yates had proved, impressed clients.

"I don't care a hoot about your health," rasped Yates irritably. "How's the girl?"

"She seems very fit too, thanks," Tyler replied in his usual unruffled tone.

"Talk sense. What d'you think I keep you lazing around for? Where is she?"

Tyler surveyed his exasperated chief over the edge of his glass.

"By the way, Yates," he observed, "that rig-out of yours is ghastly. It would shock any refined mind at a hundred yards range. Has she wired you yet?"

"Yes. She'll be here. Ten-thirty to-morrow. Mind you're early. Once more, where is she?"

Tyler glanced at the dock.

"A nice girl would probably be in a bath after that journey."

"Are you telling me that you missed her?" Yates demanded with rising temper.

"Have I ever missed following a charming woman?" Tyler asked in pained accents. "Linda, in perfect taste and complete with red hair, as scheduled, left Victoria in a taxi. Gallantly I darted after her in defiance of 'Stop' and 'Go' lights through the Park, along Oxford Street." He gazed at each hand alternately. "Let me see, which side did we turn? Never did know right from left."

Yates thrust his jaw out aggressively.

"Look here, Tyler, if you try to pull any funny stunts on me with Linda Marchant it'll be the worse for you. You know her address right enough."

"Course I do," Tyler agreed. "In a road off Oxford Street, number thirty something. It was a poor light so I can't be sure. Anyhow, what does it matter? She'll be here to-morrow."

"Suppose she doesn't come, you prize lunatic?"

"Why should she fail now, having come so far and at once? Remember, she's not seen that suit yet or it might indeed make her think twice." Tyler's face suddenly became serious. "Just what is this advertisement business about, Yates?"

The other man sneered. "Cold feet, eh?"

"No, I enjoy taking risks. But there are one or two little things that I draw the line at. Murder is one, and robbery with violence another."

"Your neck's safe, Tyler, if you do as you're told and don't attempt to squeal. Then—"

"Don't stop just as you've got me interested," the younger man entreated.

"Then I might make use of a certain cheque I hold, drawn by you on someone else's account."

Tyler raised his eyes to the ceiling.

"After all my pure devotion, my fat little friend still doesn't trust me." he remarked sorrowfully. "When you denounce me, as a good citizen should, Yates, I'd love to know what name and occupation you would give."

Mr. Yates changed the subject.

"Hope Wentworth didn't appear too anxious in Paris and make the girl suspicious."

Tyler stretched his arms and yawned.

"That chap's always inclined to over-act," he commented "What instructions did you give him?

"To insert the advertisement and send her a copy of the newspaper. The fool got the wind up and sent her a note as well."

"H'm. How'd you know this, Yates?"

Had a letter from him to-day. I cabled and told him to come back at once. He was probably on the same train as the girl. Did you see him?"

"No I'm not swivel-eyed. My job was to look for the girl, not Wentworth. His uncle, Keble Wentworth, owns an antique shop off the Haymarket and buys crown jewels and that sort of stuff as a hobby, doesn't he?"

"What about it?" demanded Yates.

"Nothing. I wondered why you sent his nephew to Paris. Do I now see the link? He's been forging cheques too and come under your guiding hand, I suppose. Where does the fair Linda fit into the pattern?"

Yates looked curiously relieved at Tyler's words.

"That's my business, my boy," he said jovially. "She won't come to any harm, young Wentworth's under control but not for the same reason that you are. There he is," he exclaimed as the bell rang. "Let him in."

Tyler opened the front door to a weedy-looking youth in whose face the nose seemed to be the predominating feature.

"Hello, Yates. Gimme a drink. I've had a foul crossing," the newcomer said huskily, sinking into a chair.

"You deserve it," Yates snapped. "One day you'll learn to obey my orders. That note you sent the girl might have busted the whole business. You've had one or two over the eight, haven't you?"

Wentworth wiped his forehead with a shaking hand.

"Yates, I'm scared. Working on your business may be nasty, but it isn't dangerous. This affair is for—"

"Shut up!" Yates warned him.

"Pull yourself together, Wentworth," advised Tyler in his cool, lazy tone. "A prospective burglary on your uncle's premises isn't a hanging matter. And anyhow I don't suppose you'd be chosen for the task."

Wentworth twisted round and stared at him. Who said it was burglary?" he demanded sullenly. "Yates talks too much."

"It was only a guess on my part," Tyler crushed out his cigarette. "I'll push off. You two bright lads probably want to have a heart-to-heart talk on matters that I'm too young to hear about. See you at ten ack-emma to-morrow, Yates."

"Sharp," Yates ordered. He lowered his voice as he went to the door with Tyler. "Er—these things will be all right for to-morrow, won't they?"'

"No," Tyler tersely replied. "Wear a dark suit, plain tie, white shirt and no jewellery."

On the hall table was a crumpled newspaper that Wentworth had thrown down. It was the Continental edition of an English daily and was folded open at the advertisement pages. Tyler picked it up and scanned the columns.

"Knowledge of antiques preferable but not necessary," he read aloud. "No wonder you wouldn't let me see this advertisement, Yates. I swallowed your yarn that Walderstein needed a girl of Linda's description for his revue!"

Yates squared his shoulders.

"She will do as I say and you won't interfere, Tyler."

The younger man flung down the newspaper, and pulled on his overcoat.

"Won't I? You watch me, my lad," he remarked pleasantly. "You may have a hold on me but you've nothing against Miss Marchant."

"No?" There was a menacing expression in Yates's eyes. "There are worse things than forged cheques, Tyler. I fancy Linda Marchant will be most reasonable and obedient."

Tyler turned up his coat collar and opened the front door, his face calm and unperturbed as usual.

"Myself, Wentworth, and now Linda. Three of a kind, eh" he observed with a chuckle. "You're a lovable little soul, Yates, but I hate the smell of your brilliantine. Good night"

VI. DEATH AT MIDNIGHT

Thursday Morning

At eight o'clock next morning Inspector Reynolds was having breakfast with his wife and their guest from Paris.

"It's a curious coincidence, Agnes," he observed, "that neither of you seems able to give me an intelligent description of the girl I only know as Linda. Usually you and Mimi take a one-second look at a woman and know everything from the quality of her stockings to the face powder she uses."

"Victoria Station is not exactly flood-lit, Tom. The girl had her back to me and I had to keep out of sight."

"You managed to recognize the man who had been watching her, when his car passed us in the Park," her husband said in an acid tone.

"I was lucky enough to see his face," Mrs. Reynolds explained. "Won't you have some bacon, Mimi?"

The French girl shook her head and took a piece of toast.

"It is not good for the so clear brain early in the day, thank you," she replied politely.

The inspector's grey eyes twinkled.

"Is your so-clear brain efficient enough this morning to remember the colour of Linda's hair and eyes?"

Mimi closed her eyes as if concentrating on the question.   .

"Brown hair, I feel sure," she murmured. "Her eyes, ah! they are difficult to remember but," she lowered one eyelid in Mrs. Reynolds's direction, "her squint is very small and by the profile she is quite pretty."

"A generous description—Linda would feel flattered. You won't tell me her surname?" Reynolds pursued.

"Always I have given you the goods on a case, monsieur. Linda is not a criminal, or of course I should place you wise on the affair. She answered a not ordinary advertisement, I was uneasy and made the donkey's nest out of nothing. I was an idiot to be anxious. You understand?"

"Not yet, but I shall," Reynolds assured her. "You're usually uneasy about nothing and unfortunately for you, you French baggage, I know most of your wiles." He scanned the pages of a couple of newspapers, and stared hard at a paragraph.

"I see a lot of the Euralian Crown jewels have been bought by three London connoisseurs," he remarked. "Private collectors who buy that sort of thing are looking for trouble" He paused for a moment thoughtfully. "It wouldn't surprise me if that slippery rascal Zaldo cropped up"

Mimi smiled into his abstracted face.

"Is Zaldo perhaps a singer who makes the gramophone records?" she inquired.

"Zaldo is—" Reynolds began and broke off abruptly.

"What colour are the hair and eyes of this slippery rascal?" tormented his guest.

"I'd give something to know." Reynolds's thoughts were far away as he spoke.

The French girl's expression changed to one of deep seriousness.

"Will you promise to leave my poor Linda alone?" she asked.

"Linda!" Reynolds exclaimed. "My time may be too occupied to bother about her and her trivial secrets. This piece of news," he tapped the newspaper, "means that Zaldo and his confounded gang will probably soon be at work over here. Who he is, where he lives and what he looks like, nobody seems to know. So don't try to be funny, infant, and tell me that you met him in your Montmartre café."

"Three years ago I met a man in Notre Dame Cathedral in Paris, monsieur," Mimi stated in clear tones. "Afterwards I was, told that he was Zaldo."

Reynolds stared in astonishment.

"What was he like?" he demanded.

He seemed interested in architecture. His eyes are—it is a promise about Linda?" she asked anxiously.

"A promise," Reynolds agreed. "Go on."

"This is not officially confirmed information," Mimi continued. "Monsieur Bernard, head of the Paris Sureté, told me that in his heart he believed the man was Zaldo. His eyes are dark brown, large pupils; brows that overhang. A thin nose, firm mouth, clean-shaven. Age about fifty. Head well-shaped, hair grey at sides." Mimi rose with curious dignity. "I will tell you the rest at Scotland Yard, monsieur. This is not the place to talk the shopping as you say."

An hour later in the inspector's office at the Yard Mimi, grave-eyed, greeted Reynolds's assistant, Sergeant Jenkins. This C.I.D man's work was always conscientious, but his highest and most ingenious efforts were of a personal nature and devoted to aiding Reynolds in any case upon which that officer might be engaged. Jenkins would have slaved cheerfully night and day for the inspector, and often, in attacks of zealous energy, he had been guilty of exploits more usually connected with a burglar than a detective.

Reynolds told him now about Zaldo.

"Excellent work, mademoiselle." Jenkins's tone held a touch of patronage. He knew Mimi well and respected her keen intelligence. Nevertheless at times he was a little jealous because she had assisted his chief so successfully. Mimi, perfectly aware of this, often retaliated by badinage that occasionally caused the bashful young detective considerable embarrassment.

"*Merci bien*, my good Jenkins. Keep the news about this criminal to yourself and do not tell your landlady."

Mimi turned to Reynolds again.

"Be careful of Zaldo," she urged. If I am right—and I believe I am—he is a Greek with English blood in his veins, cunning, clever and full of courage"

"I'll be wary, my child. Several times in the last year or so when jewels of immense value have changed hands, they have been stolen immediately afterwards," Reynolds said meditatively. And it is believed that these thefts were committed by this man. It is a queer thing, but unlike most crooks, he kills his victims, presumably to conceal his identity."

"Yes. Another queer thing, monsieur, is, that the crimes are always committed at midnight."

Reynolds nodded.

"Well, Mimi, first I find out the names of the three London collectors who bought up the Euralian Crown jewels, and then I'll spread a net for our Greek friend before he can get on the scene."

"He speaks perfect English," the French girl told him.

"I'll remember that. Meanwhile we're ahead of him. The jewels were only sold a day or two ago, and the names of the three purchasers were not given in the Press."

Mimi's face became anxious.

"Monsieur, yesterday at Victoria a second before I met your wife," she said earnestly, "I noticed a man who reminded me of Zaldo. His coat collar was turned up and I only saw his eyes. He met a young man who got off our train. They drove away together. I forgot the incident, but now I am worried."

"I'll have the air ports and boat trains watched to-day," Reynolds assured her. "My bet is that Zaldo is in Paris or Berlin. What is it, Jenkins?" he asked as his assistant entered.

Jenkins laid the first edition of the Evening Record on his chief's desk and pointed to a few lines in the stop press.

Mr. James Carr, the well-known connoisseur, was found dead early this morning at his home in Hampstead.

"Maybe it's a natural death and coincidence," Reynolds commented, "and maybe it's—"

"Zaldo," interrupted Mimi softly.

The inspector drew the telephone on his desk nearer.

After a short conversation with the dead man's butler, he replaced the receiver.

"Mr. Carr suffered from high blood pressure," he said. "The butler found him at his desk in the library at seven o'clock this morning and sent for his master's medical attendant. Mr. Carr is a widower with no children and lives alone except for the servants who have been there for many years. His valuable collection of jewels in glass cases appears to be intact. The butler has telephoned for Mr. Carr's lawyer."

"Will there be an inquest?" Jenkins asked.

"That depends on many things" Reynolds bit his lip and drew triangles aimlessly on his blotting pad. "You heard me ask the man if his master had recently made any addition to his collection or received any visitors late last night. He knows of no purchase and there were no visitors up to ten-thirty last night. Jenkins, we must trace the three collectors who bought the Euralian Crown jewels"

"I know a Jew in your Whitechapels called Vernstein," said Mimi. "He is a big fence and I suspect he sells stones for Zaldo. Vernstein thinks I am connected with a French gang of crooks and is friendly towards me. I might find out something there."

"It's a chance," the inspector agreed.

"I will go there with Jenkins," Mimi continued, "and introduce him as my fiancé, if he will promise to hold my hand en route."

"The only way I want to touch your hand is to slap it good and hard," Jenkins interposed. "All the same, it's a good idea to go."

"At once," Mimi agreed. "Are you troubled about Mr. Carr's death, monsieur?"

"Yes," Reynolds answered. "It seems normal except for one thing."

"What is it?" Mimi asked eagerly.

"A clock in the library had stopped. And," Reynolds added, "the hands pointed to midnight."

"The hour that Zaldo always chooses," said Mimi.

"Exactly," Reynolds agreed, rising. "I'm going to Mr. Carr's house. The lawyer might be there by this time. It's ten-thirty."

"Ten-thirty," Mimi repeated to herself. Linda was probably with Yates now. Mimi had meant to keep an eye on Silver Square in case there was a sinister side to Mr. Yates and his queer advertisement.

Mr. Carr's death and the possibilities of Zaldo being connected with it were, however, of greater importance.

With a sigh for Linda's safety, Mimi directed her attention to the more urgent matter.

"Have the Press any idea who these three connoisseurs are or if Mr. Carr was one?" she asked.

"None," Jenkins replied gloomily. "I've rung up half a dozen newspaper offices."

Mimi opened her bag and powdered her nose with care.

"*Alors*, we will go to see my Jew friend."

VII. Diamond Cut Diamond

Thursday Morning

In Silver Square that morning Mr. Yates was busily preparing a suitable background for his expected visitor, while Tyler smoked and made cynical suggestions.

Over the mantelpiece a large card in rather shaky lettering announced that this was the Select Employment Bureau.

A desk, cleared of its usual impedimenta of bottles and siphons, had been pulled across the middle of the room and furnished with office equipment and a mass of correspondence.

Mr. Yates surveyed his efforts with pride.

"I shall, be writing when she comes in and of course I shan't rise. Looks smart and business-like, eh?"

Tyler's eyebrows shot up.

"The pile of letters was a pretty touch," he commented. "If the lady is bright, she may notice that they all begin in the same way. 'Sir, If we do not receive payment by return,' etc. Also, it might be wise to let in some fresh air and eat a couple of cloves. The smell of whisky so early in the day might prejudice a sensitive mind."

His employer turned the top letter over and pushed up the window.

"I'll thank you to remember, Tyler, that during Miss Marchant's call you're my clerk and I'm doing the talking."

"Life for me shall be one long 'think' during the red-haired siren's visit," Tyler promised with a yawn. "Here she comes," he added as the bell rang.

Yates flung the end of his cigar into the fire and seated himself hastily at the desk, pen in hand.

"Do I look all right?" he asked.

"The suit is doing its best for you but you're a bit too clean to be natural," Tyler replied. "A bath always seems to give you such an air of 'spit and polish,' Yates. I'll show the damsel in."

"Miss Linda Marchant by appointment, sir," he announced a moment later.

Mr. Yates's decision to remain seated and immersed in correspondence changed as he saw a graceful, well-dressed girl enter the room. He struggled to his feet while she composedly took the chair opposite his own.

"Good morning. You are Mr. F. Yates, I expect." Her voice was clear and a trifle curt.

Behind her Tyler grinned in amusement at his employer.

Mr. Yates pulled himself together, murmured a 'good morning" and consulted a list of imaginary clients.

"Ah!" he said 'You must be Miss Linda Marchant."

"I've not had time to change my name since I was announced two seconds ago." The girl's tone now was definitely terse. "Suppose we come to business."

Mr. Yates's face registered consternation. Tyler, if only he had been told everything, would have handled this affair much better, he reflected. By raised brows he telegraphed an SOS to his assistant for help while his client was opening her handbag.

Tyler, remembering instructions to be silent, ignored the appeal.

"Here is your letter," Linda said, placing it on the desk. "What do you want me for?"

Yates cleared his throat and began nervously.

"I—we fancied that your description and photograph resembled the type of girl we required for a certain post, Miss Marchant. Of course," he went on warming to his subject as his courage returned, "it will be necessary to interview the numerous other applicants before a decision can be made."

The girl's blue eyes had a steely glint.

"You're not fooling me for a minute, Mr. Yates. Your advertisement did not appear in the English newspapers. I've looked through the files in the Public Library this morning. You took pains to see that I should receive a copy of the Paris edition by ordering someone to give me one that was marked. Now, do I give you back the price of my ticket to London and walk out, or are you going to tell me why you want me? "

Mr. Yates leaned forward in his chair and sucked in his breath.

"You're a clever young lady, Miss Marchant. It's rather difficult to explain."

"It needn't be," she retorted. "I'm hard-boiled and can't afford to be squeamish. Go ahead with the plain facts. I'll try to stand them."

"I—we rather expected you to be of a more timid disposition," Yates explained apologetically, with another silent appeal for aid to Tyler.

For the first time Linda smiled.

"A day or two ago you might have found me so," she admitted. "Yesterday I forced my delicate feelings through the sieve and the result is what you see."

"May I say that it is both attractive and interesting?" Tyler interposed in his lazy, cultured voice.

Linda twisted round and looked at him over her shoulder.

"Are you the 'we' in this Select Employment ramp?" she demanded. "Or does Mr. Yates play a lone hand?"

Tyler rose and bowed.

"I'm Nick Tyler, Mr. Yates's confidential clerk, and very much at your service," he said as he took a seat near the desk and offered her a cigarette.

"You know who I am, Mr. Tyler, so now we can get on a bit faster, perhaps." Linda accepted a light and glanced up at the other man. "Shoot the works, Mr. Yates. What am I to be? A smuggler of cocaine? If the pay is adequate, I'd consider the post, new though it will be to me."

Mr. Yates's face wore a pained expression. "Nothing so crude, my dear Miss Marchant," he assured her. "The position I hope you will obtain calls for tact and silence. Nothing worse. Before I explain more fully, may I—"

The girl turned to Tyler with a sigh.

"Can't you make him stop dithering and come to the point?" she asked.   "I'll hold my tongue whether I get the job or no."

"Spill the beans, Yates, whatever they are," advised the younger man.

The mask of suavity slid from Mr. Yates's face and revealed his normal expression of artful shrewdness.

"I'll spill 'em," he promised. "Now then, Miss Marchant, take off your hat, please. I want to see if that hair is faked."

"Colour and wave natural, hair grown on the scalp," Linda said promptly.   She dragged off her dark blue velvet cap and bent forward. "Pull!"

Mr. Yates pulled.

"Right.   Got any parents, brothers, sisters, or husband?"

"My parents died when I was a baby. I was an only child and am not married."

"Relatives?"

"None."

"Any 'sweeties' or close friends who'll be hanging around asking where you are and what you're doing?"

Linda shook her head.

Yates bit the end off a cigar and spat it out.

"Now, listen carefully.   Your   mother   was   called Eleanor Heath, if you're asked. She married a chap by the name of Marchant; makes it easier for you to keep your own surname, see?"

"I always wondered how genealogical trees were made," Tyler murmured.

"Shut up," Yates ordered. "Well, Marchant and his wife Eleanor died in Australia when you were a baby, Miss Marchant."

"I'll try to remember," she said with twitching lips.

"You'd better or," there was an ominous note in Yates's tone, "I might remember that there's something queer in your life, Linda Marchant."

The girl stared straight into his eyes.

"And that, Mr. Yates, is the first and last time you'll try to intimidate me," she replied. "I've seen things such as you crawling under large stones They're nasty, but I'm not afraid of them. You can come into the open or mind your own business. I don't care which. Make up your mind."

Tyler choked suddenly and hid his face in his handkerchief, while his employer mumbled confused excuses.

"Ah! right," Linda agreed. "We'll forget it. You need my services, and I need money, Mr. Yates. Go on with my family history."

Yates wiped his moist forehead.

"That part's finished," he said. "There's a rich old crank called Keble Wentworth. He runs an antique shop near Pall Mall. He's a bachelor. The shop is a blind for his hobby, which is buying and hoarding valuable jewels of historic interest."

Linda laughed softly.

"What am I supposed to do? Marry him or burgle the jewels?"

"Neither," Yates retorted. "He's only got one relative, a nephew, and hates him. Nephew knows he won't get a cent if his uncle dies, so—" Yates paused, and waved his hand vaguely.

The girl helped him out.

"Enter Linda Marchant, complete with late mother called Eleanor Heath," she continued. "It's a very thin yarn. All the same, Mr. Yates, even with that family background, whatever it may mean, I don't see how the nephew will benefit, unless you expect me to murder the cranky old gentleman. I do rather draw the line at that, you know."

Mr. Yates produced an expansive smile that showed some nice dental work in gold relief.

"You will have your little joke, Miss Marchant. Old Keble Wentworth is only cranky on one point. Long ago he was in love with a girl called Eleanor Heath. She married another man and was the facsimile of you. Red curly hair, bright blue eyes, same height and colouring."

"How do you know this?" Linda asked with interest.

"Old Wentworth's nephew works for me," Yates replied. "A few weeks ago he saw his uncle gazing at a miniature, saying it was his beloved Eleanor and lot of rot of that kind."

Linda puckered her brows.

"You surely don't want me to pretend I'm the spirit of the poor old man's dead love or that sort of nonsense?"

"Course not," Mr. Yates negatived promptly. "He needs an assistant to look after the antique shop and give him more time to mess about with his jewellery. His nephew wanted to take on the work but the old man said he didn't trust him and preferred to have a woman and a stranger. So we thought as you were so like the dead Eleanor, you might get the post and kind of soften the old man's heart towards his nephew."

Mr. Yates moved uneasily under the girl's steady gaze. Even to his unimaginative mind the story wasn't very convincing. It was the best he could think of, however. He had expected this red-headed, penniless girl to be humbly thankful to carry out his orders without dispute. Instead she had turned out to be a person of spirit, who asked far too many questions for Mr. Yates' comfort.

"There you are, Miss Marchant. Neither murder nor robbery, you see. A very simple affair."

Eyeing her vanity he was relieved to see that the girl's expression seemed to be that of awed admiration.

"Both simple and beautiful!," she murmured "I had no idea that businessmen worked for motives of pure philanthropy. It shall be my one aim in life to live up to

your high standard of altruism and soften the heart of old
Mr. Wentworth towards his nephew."

She had spoken in an almost reverential tone and Mr.
Yates was soothed by the reflection that she was certainly
more of a fool than he had thought.

Unfortunately at that moment he noticed that she
cast a significant glance in the direction of his assistant
who laughed outright and then put in a tactful word.

"Miss Marchant is not taken in by your pretty piece of
fiction, Yates," Tyler remarked, "but she's a wonderful
actress, as you observe, and can, I think, be relied upon to
do her part. Why not take her into your confidence and
tell her that of course you will benefit by her help?"

Yates accepted the hint.

"You're right, Tyler. I was only pulling your leg to see
how sharp you were, Miss Marchant. I've got to live. My
commission will come," he hesitated, indirectly. "Tyler
will take you along now to the address. You've heard old
Wentworth wants a girl for the antique business; you're
broke. Never mind about his nephew. Forget that part."

"Suppose he doesn't take me?" Linda questioned.
Yates tapped the side of his nose.

"Your looks will do the trick if you play your cards
right. Don't bring out the name of your supposed mother
too soon. Take any salary he offers, however small."

"It may be insufficient for me to live upon," Linda
objected.

Yates placed a document on the desk.

"I'm paying you five pounds weekly, Miss Marchant.
You can live on that, can't you?"

The girl nodded.

"Certainly. What strings are attached to your offer?"

"You sign this paper promising to give me everything
that you receive from Mr. Keble Wentworth, alive or
dead," was Yates's reply.

Linda read through the document and picked up a
pen.

"For the first time you're talking horse sense, Mr. Yates. You're gambling that the old man might leave me his fortune. Well, this is how much I value your chance," she said and signed her name.

VIII. A "GENTLEMAN" CROOK

Yates locked the paper away in a drawer with a satisfied smirk. In spite of one or two slight hitches, the business had gone off smoothly, he decided.

"Go down and get a taxi, Tyler," he ordered, "and bring me back the first edition of the *Evening Record.*"

Yates gave the girl a few final instructions while Tyler had gone on his errand.

Presently the younger man returned.

"Here's your newspaper, Yates. Never known you interested in racing before. Taxi's waiting, Miss. Marchant."

Tyler and the girl were curiously silent during the journey, as if both shrank from comment on the strange venture before her.

"Yates told me to wait," he said. "You'll find me in the café at the corner. There's Wentworth's antique shop." He paused and looked at her. "Good luck!"

"To the dubious schemes of the Select Employment Bureau or to me?" she inquired.

"To you. You've got pluck," Tyler replied. Linda pushed open the door of the shop and hear a bell give a warning tinkle.

She stood there in the semi-gloom, glancing round at the dusty furniture and china jumbled together in hopeless confusion. There was something pathetic and helpless about this place that appealed to her.

Suddenly she had an absurd desire to tidy and straighten up the muddle before its owner arrived.

She studied the medley of antiques: Jacobean oak, Adams and Chippendale should be grouped according to period.

As no one seemed to be there to question her movements, she proceeded to tug the cabinets and bureaus about and arrange the pottery and china more suitably.

After half an hour of strenuous effort, the collection had a totally different appearance. A trifle hot and breathless she stepped back to view the general effect and was astonished to see a man of elderly appearance with a pointed beard watching her. His dark eyes twinkled with amusement through horn-rimmed spectacles while he looked her up and down.

"You seem to be an enthusiast," he remarked "I've been watching you with much interest and must congratulate you. You have excellent taste."

The girl, who had shed hat and coat, thrust back a heavy wave of hair and began a stumbling apology.

"I'm afraid it was terribly impertinent of me. No one was here and I couldn't bear to see these lovely things in such a soiled and muddled state. And so—"

"And so you acted the part of guardian angel," the old man suggested gently. "I am Mr. Keble Wentworth. Did you want to see me?"

Linda bit her lip in desperation. Why on earth hadn't she waited to interview him in a normal manner instead of behaving so impetuously?

"I love antiques and called to see if you wanted an assistant," she said in rather shamefaced tones. "This," she waved her hand towards her work, "'looks as if I wanted to show off, doesn't it?"

A smile flickered on the man's grave face.

"On the contrary, you have unconsciously provided yourself with a good reference. Let us have a little talk on the matter."

Linda followed him to the far end of the shop where light shone through a high glass dome on to a semi-circle of closed cabinets.

"I keep my smaller treasures here," Mr. Wentworth explained, drawing a chair forward. "Please sit down."

For a moment his eyes strayed to her gleaming hair. "What is your name?" he asked.

"Linda Marchant."

He repeated the name half to himself.

"Your parents are alive?" There was a curious note in his voice that made the girl detest the role she had promised to play.

"They died when I was a baby." She pressed her hand across her eyes. "Please don't ask me about them to-day, Mr. Wentworth."

"You are too tired with that furniture shifting to be annoyed by my stupid questions. Only," he spoke in a disappointed tone, "you reminded me of someone. Miss Marchant, I am accustomed to make quick decisions. If you think you would like to work here, I shall be pleased to engage you at once."

"Surely you will need to find out something about me?" she stammered. It was as though an inner force was fighting to prevent her from deceiving this simple-minded old man.

"Your ability is proved; your character I shall soon discover for myself. I can offer you a salary of three guineas a week, and a commission of five percent on any sales that you effect. You can start at two o'clock to-day. Would this be agreeable to you?"

"Perfectly. I will be here, thank you," Linda told him.

Ten minutes later she sat in the café facing Nick Tyler with stormy eyes.

"Well?" he asked calmly.

"I've got the job, if that's what you mean. I hope to heaven it is well. If any harm comes to that defenceless Mr. Wentworth through me, I'll choke your greasy employer and be proud to do it."

Tyler glanced at her quizzically.

"You'll end by marrying the old gentleman if you're not careful," he warned. "Sentimentality is your trouble. Let's have some food before this place gets crowded."

"I don't want anything," she declared.

"You're too hot and bothered to know what you want. I'm going to order a suitable meal. You must keep your strength up in case you have to choke poor Yates later on. I feel quite sorry for him."

"Naturally," she retorted. "He's your employer."

Tyler shrugged his shoulders.

"Why should I turn against the kind hand that feeds me? By the way, now that you've hooked the situation, I must carry out instructions and give you this." He took an envelope from his pocket and laid it on the table.

"What is it?"

"A fiver. One week's salary paid in advance by the Select Employment Bureau." He caught her arm as she flicked the envelope back and stood up. "Sit down, young woman. You can't afford to be melodramatic. You've earned the money. Why not take it? Unless—" he paused with provocative deliberation.

"Unless what?" she demanded, resuming her seat.

"Unless you wish to break your absurd contract with Yates wherein you agreed to hand over all you receive from Mr. Keble Wentworth. It wouldn't hold water in any legal court, you know."

"I should have kept my word," she blazed back.

"You hadn't met the nice old gentleman when you signed. Now that you see how easy it will be to win his favour and probably his fortune, I can understand why you wish to return this flyer to Yates and cancel the deal."

"I don't know whether I hate you or your employer most."

Tyler grinned cheerfully and put some lettuce on her plate.

"Think it out while you eat," he suggested. "Anyhow I'm sure your last remark was ungrammatical."

She watched him mix a dressing with deft lingers and pour it carefully on to her salad. Indignation melted before this young man's cool effrontery.

He noticed the change and the smile hovering on her lips.

"Made up your mind that it's no use trying to quarrel with me?" he asked. "Most people find that out sooner or later."

"Are you ever serious, Mr. Tyler?"

"Not if I can help it," he said, and slid the newspaper that he had been reading out of sight. "If you haven't an impediment in your speech, you might try to call me Nick, my sweet little pet name."

"I shall call you Mr. Tyler on the rare occasions upon which we are likely to meet," Linda said formally.

"Rare occasions!" Tyler chuckled. "We're fellow conspirators, remember. All members of crime gangs meet frequently and address each other by their first names. You'll be seeing Yates weekly when you hand over Wentworth's salary—according to contract, of course. And you may be seeing me much. oftener, Linda."

"That's rather a boring prospect."

"It may also be boring for me," he retorted. "But if Yates sends me to you with a message I shall have to put up with it. You asked for that smack didn't you?" he demanded. "I say. I blew my last shilling on our taxi. You'll have to settle for lunch, I'm afraid."

Linda pushed the five-pound note across the table.

"Pay the bill," she said indifferently. "Can I look at that newspaper you were reading when I came in?"

'It's only a racing edition." Tyler spoke with reluctance.

"I know that. Women have been known to make bets." She held out her hand, as he hesitated.

"Give up the evil habit while there is yet time," he pleaded solemnly. "Anyway I've lost the paper."

"If you get up you'll find it. I saw you hide it on your chair a few minutes ago."

He passed her a copy of the *Evening Record* with a worried expression.

"The racing news isn't there," he told her as she studied the front page.

"Thank you. I learnt to read."

Presently she raised her eyes and stared hard at him.

"What do you know about James Carr?" she demanded.

"Let me think. Does he train or ride for Lord Morehampton?"

Linda compressed her mouth.

"Now I know where you and I stand," she said coldly. "You were reading this page when I came in. What do you pretend to be, Mr. Nick Tyler?"

"It all depends on the point of view, Linda. Some people would probably tell you that I'm a gentleman crook."

"Why bother about the 'gentleman'?"

"Why indeed?" he asked languidly. "Here's your change. Better count it," he added, as she flung the notes and cash into her handbag.

"I will—later. You've not answered my question about James Carr. Look at this." She indicated the headlines on the front page of the *Evening Record*.

The two-line item in the stop press of the earlier edition had swollen into big news.

> *A "GENTLEMAN" CROOK*
> *SUICIDE OR MURDER?*
> *CLOCK THAT STOPPED AT MIDNIGHT.*

> *Scotland Yard detectives (the journal said) are puzzled by the mysterious death of Mr. James Carr, a wealthy jewel connoisseur. Mr. Carr was found in his library by the butler early this morning.*
> *The cause of death is unknown but foul play is suspected. Robbery may be the motive.*

> *A curious feature of the case is that a clock in the library had stopped at midnight, but on being moved it went perfectly.*

Tyler crumpled the newspaper and tossed it on to the floor.

"The deceased gentleman was neither a friend nor an enemy of mine," he stated. "His end is very sad but you can't expect me to burst into tears."

"Not if you benefit by his death," Linda replied with emphasis. "I suspected something was wrong when you concealed the newspaper and tried to stop me from reading it. Mr. Keble Wentworth is also a wealthy connoisseur, as Mr. James Carr was, and by a flimsy tale I have been thrust into his employment. I have yet to find out the real purpose of that."

"Wouldn't it be wise to think the worst since you already imagine that I have robbed and murdered Mr. Carr?" Tyler asked with a queer smile. "Forewarned is forearmed."

"I'll remember that," the girl told him as she rose.

"Good-bye."

"Good hunting, Linda. Thanks very much for my luncheon, and—and everything."

IX. The Poisoned Decanter

Thursday Morning

"Well, doctor, what do you make of it? Natural death, suicide or murder?" Inspector Reynolds was in Mr. James Carr's library when he put the question to Dr. Tempest, one of Scotland Yard's pathologists.

The doctor had just made an examination of the body with Mr. Carr's medical attendant.

"Not natural death, certainly" he replied "Suicide is not an impossible theory, though it is a highly unlikely one. It's a bit early to be positive, but Dr. Oliver agrees with me that poison was most probably the cause of his patients death. Isn't that so?" he asked, drawing his colleague into the conversation.

Dr. Oliver acquiesced, inwardly grateful for the distinguished pathologist's tact in including him in this statement.

"Mr. Carr had high blood pressure," he added, "and I have visited him weekly. When I was called here soon after seven o'clock this morning, I concluded that he had had a seizure."

"Naturally you had no suspicion of foul play," the inspector said. "Was Mr. Carr depressed or worried about anything?"

"He was a singularly cheerful man, intensely interested in his collection of precious stones and, from what I gathered, untroubled by money worries," was Dr. Oliver's reply.

"What about the staff?" asked Reynolds.

"A butler and his wife looked after him, with perhaps extra help. They seem to be superior servants who were devoted to their master," Dr. Oliver told him.

"Thank you. I'll see them presently." Reynolds glanced significantly at a decanter and wineglass on the desk and turned to the pathologist. "Is this wine under suspicion?"

Dr. Tempest tilted the decanter and tasted the contents.

"Grave suspicion, inspector. I fancy we shall find a strong dose of Fleming's Tincture is in it. You know what that is?"

Reynolds nodded.

"Aconite. It might be mistaken for sherry, I suppose."

"Easily, taken as Mr. Carr always took alcohol," Dr. Oliver interposed. "He had acquired the American habit of tossing down a drink at one gulp. I tried in vain to persuade him to sip it slowly. His reason, so he said, was that he drank wine for the effect and not for the taste."

"If anyone knew of this habit and had access to the decanter, it would therefore be simple to assume that Mr. Carr would drink the poison before the strange flavour warned him of its presence," Reynolds summed up. "What is a fatal dose?"

"One to three drachms," Dr. Tempest replied. "I can tell you more after the autopsy, inspector."

"I think that's all I need detain you gentlemen for," Reynolds said.

Mrs. Lang, the butler's wife, appeared to be deeply shocked by her master's death, but was of no assistance. Her duties were in the kitchen, she said, and she rarely saw Mr. Carr as her husband waited at the table, acted as valet and received all household instructions.

"A kinder master no one could wish to have, sir," she added. "I can't believe he'd wish to kill himself, for only last evening before dinner I heard him singing in his bath as happy as a bird. And he had the wireless on until past ten o'clock."

Lang corroborated his wife's statement.

"How long have you been with Mr. Carr?" Reynolds asked, studying the man's refined face with interest.

"Ever since the War, sir."

When did you last see your master alive?"

"At ten-thirty p.m. As usual I took the decanter of sherry and a wineglass to the library at that hour, and asked him if he required anything more, and then locked up and went to bed."

"He seemed in good health and spirits last night?" Reynolds inquired.

"Yes, sir. He said: 'Nothing more, Lang, thank you. Leave the French window open; it's a warm night. Tell Mrs. Lang that I like her cheese soufflé more than it likes me, but indigestion won't stop me in eating it another time.' We both laughed at his joke."

"Did he, to your knowledge, have any visitors before or after you went to bed?"

"None up to half-past ten, sir. If anyone came after that they can't have rung the bell or I should have heard it. I'm a light sleeper. The French window in the library was unlatched this morning."

"What visitors have been to the house recently?"

Lang thought for a moment.

"No one since last Sunday night when Dr. Oliver was here to supper."

"Any workmen?"

"A young fellow calls every month to inspect the wireless. He came last Monday."

"H'm. And this is Thursday," the inspector said reflectively. Surely Lang or his wife could have no reasonable motive for poisoning their master, and yet who else had had an opportunity to touch the decanter? The butler, too, was speaking frankly and not attempting to pretend that Mr. Carr had had a late visitor, as he might have done had he been guilty. "Is there a gardener?"

"No, sir. I do the little that is necessary."

"Sewing woman, window cleaners, chauffeur, charwoman?" Reynolds persisted.

"My wife does the mending, I clean the windows and drive the car. My master rarely used it. We have a charwoman once a week—Tuesdays."

A flash of hope came to the inspector's heart. Here at last was an outside person who had access to the household.

"Tell me all you can about her," he said.

Lang gave a rueful smile.

"Afraid there's not much to tell. She's a queer old bird called Mrs. Nunn, very deaf and drinks like a fish. I have to lock away the wine and spirits before I go out."

Either Lang did not suspect that his master had died from unnatural causes or else he was acting remarkably well, Reynolds reflected.

"Go on about Mrs. Nunn," he urged. "How old is she and how long has she worked here?"

"She's about sixty and has worked for Mr. Carr for nearly twenty years; long before we came here. He insisted upon her being kept on, although my wife declared that she was more bother than she was worth."

"What were the charwoman's duties?"

She was supposed to scrub the hall and kitchens, and polish the parquet floors in the dining-room, library and lounge."

"Did Mr. Carr talk to her at all?" Reynolds asked.

"He didn't see her for months at a time," Lang explained. "My wife paid her, and kept her out of the master's sight as she was such an untidy old object. It was lucky for her that I didn't see her either or I'd have told her what I thought of her slovenly ways and drunken habits!"

The inspector looked puzzled.

"But if she was here for a whole day once a week surely you saw her frequently?"

Lang shook his head.

"There are a lot of valuables in the house and the master liked me to be in from dusk onwards. So I had every Tuesday off from half-past nine in the morning until five or six o'clock. It suited me as I could get a long tramp in the country. Mrs. Nunn didn't up until ten and left about five. That's why I never saw her: it's been a good 'miss.' My wife takes Friday afternoon and evening. We can't both leave the house."

"I understand," Reynolds answered. It seemed improbable that a deaf and tipsy old charwoman, who had been employed there for twenty years, would poison the sherry, even if the decanter had been left out. "Was Mr. Carr a heavy drinker?"

"Not at all, sir. He rarely drank anything but sherry. I opened about three bottles a week for him." Lang paused and bit his lip. "That reminds me, I forgot to lock the decanter away on Tuesday morning before I went off for the day. I bet that old woman had a 'go' at it, confound her."

Somebody undoubtedly had had a "go" at it, Reynolds thought, but not in the way the butler imagined.

"We are none of us infallible, Lang. Where is the decanter usually kept?"

"On the sideboard." The man's expression altered suddenly as if a terrible idea had just occurred to him. "Excuse me, sir, but there's nothing wrong about Mr. Carr's death, is there? I mean, he died of a seizure, didn't he?"

The inspector evaded a direct answer.

"We shall not know what the cause of death was until the autopsy has been made," was his careful reply. "Tell me, Lang, did you notice anything curious or unusual in the library when you found your master this morning?"

"The unlatched window was unusual but Mr. Carr must have died before he could fasten it," the man explained. "I mentioned on the telephone that the grandfather clock had stopped at midnight. That seems curious. It runs for eight days, is wound regularly each Saturday and has not stopped before in the middle of the week. My wife thinks it's a supernatural touch. I've been too worried to decide what it is."

Reynolds looked up as Mrs. Lang came into the room and said that a young lady who would not give her name wished to see him.

In the dining-room the inspector found Mimi waiting for him.

"What are you doing here?" he asked severely. "I thought you and Jenkins were going to Whitechapel two hours ago?'

"The Jew was out. I have made an appointment to see him at five o'clock," Mimi explained. "Monsieur, do you know that a strange charwoman worked here last Tuesday?"

"How did you find that out?" Reynolds demanded.

"From the milkman. I told him I wanted work as a sewing maid. We had a chat, he and I. He saw

the woman two days ago scrubbing the kitchen. She was about fifty years of age, dark, sharp nose, a heavy build. As he thought she was foreign I felt you ought to know."

"I certainly ought!," Reynolds agreed with emphasis. Wait outside. I won't be long."

"A few minutes later he joined the French girl, and, hailing a taxi, gave the driver Mrs. Nunn's address.

"The butler knew nothing at all about the change of charwoman," Reynolds explained. "His wife says Tuesday morning a stranger appeared, saying that Mrs. Nunn was ill and had sent her instead. She was a quiet woman who worked well and said nothing about herself. Mrs. Lang didn't tell her husband when he returned in the evening because he might have been angry that she had broken Mr. Carr's rule by allowing a stranger to come into the house."

"Has anything been stolen?" Mimi asked.

"That we can't say until the lawyer arrives. He will unlock the safe. The counterfoils in Mr. Carr's cheque book may tell us if he has recently drawn any large amount."

"The result will be interesting," Mimi predicted. "I wonder if Mr. Carr bought some of the Euralian Crown jewels. And as the clock stopped at midnight I wonder whether Zaldo has stolen them."

X. Three Bottles of Gin

Thursday afternoon

The taxi pulled up at a dingy house in one of the back streets of Marylebone, and Reynolds, after discharging the driver, asked a small boy where the charwoman lived.

"Hi, mum," yelled the urchin. "Here's a genelman and a gal wants Mother Nunn."

A woman leaned from an upper window and inspected the callers.

"Fourth floor back," she shouted down. "I ain't seen the drunken old hag for a couple o' days."

Mimi made a grimace as she walked daintily up the staircase behind Reynolds.

"What is an 'ag, monsieur?" she inquired.

"That's one," the inspector told her as the slatternly creature who had called out to them appeared on the landing and offered herself as guide

"I'll go in and make her cleanup a bit if you'll wait here," she volunteered A crafty look came into the woman's eyes when her offer was rejected.

"What d'you want her for? she demanded "If you're giving away bottles of gin like the other bloke, I want 'em as bad as that old hussy. At times I come over that queer with the pain in me stummick—"

Reynolds interrupted the diagnosis.

"I'm afraid that I'm not giving anything away," he said significantly. Who was the 'bloke' who called on Mrs. Nunn?"

"How should I know? Santa Claus, p'raps," the woman retorted with bitterness as hope of liquid gifts from this stranger died. "Came here larst Monday night he did, and, would you b'leeve it, brought her three bottles of the best! The mean old hound locked her door when he went, and I haven't seen hide nor hair of her since."

"What an 'ag!'" Mimi agreed in sympathetic tones. "Why did this handsome young man bring presents to a woman so greedy as Mrs. Nunn?"

"Arsk me another," the woman replied gloomily. Walking into the trap Mimi had set she added: "You made a mistake, miss. He wasn't young nor handsome. Oldish he was, and had eyes as black as your hat."

"Perhaps the bottles were not meant for Mrs. Nunn," Mimi ventured.

"Yes, they was. I was downstairs shouting for my Alfie to come in as 'twas past nine o'clock and pitch dark, when along comes Father Christmas all covered up so's you could only see his long nose. 'Where does Mrs. Nunn live?' ses he. I took 'im up to her room out o' kindness, and banged on her door."

"Can you be sure it was last Monday night?" Reynolds interrupted.

"Yes. Washin' day. I'd got me arms full o' clothes when he come. Well, Mother Nunn wanted to know who was there and said if 'twas the Queen of Sheba she wasn't getting out o' bed to let her in. The man whispered: 'Say I got a present for her."

"Of course she let him in then," Mimi prompted.

The woman sneered at the girl's apparent ignorance.

"She did not. Called me a blinking liar and told me to prove it. So he pulled off the paper and showed me the three bottles. There wasn't no trouble to get her to open the door after I'd shouted in that news." She swallowed indignantly. "A bob's all I got for me trouble and he ordered me downstairs as if he was a lord. I must ha' been in the pub when he went."

Mimi slipped a coin into the woman's hand. She glanced demurely at the inspector when they were alone.

"One day, when I have time, I will teach you the elementals for obtaining information," she promised.

"Let's see what the lady has to say on the subject," Reynolds replied, knocking at her door. "I wonder if she's still in bed!"

Mrs. Nunn was not in bed but her attire indicated that her rising had been so recent as to be an affair of moments.

Without apology or embarrassment she bade her visitors enter but instructed them, with a hiccough, to leave the dogs outside.

"Dogs!" Mimi whispered in bewilderment that turned to a grin as she caught Reynolds's warning signal.

"Welcome lil shtranger," Mrs. Nunn chanted, and lurching forward, embraced the inspector. He disengaged himself and placed her on a chair in a corner of the room where she lolled back and gazed at him affectionately.

"Pretty hopeless, I'm afraid," Reynolds said in an undertone to Mimi as Mrs. Nunn broke into song.

If there had been any previous doubt as to her vocal talent there was none now. She did not, however, allow that obstacle to restrain her. Fixing Reynolds with a glassy eye, she inquired, in a piercing soprano, if he would love her in December as he did in May.

The song ended a trifle abruptly and Mrs. Nunn patted her chest with a coy request for pardon.

"Cough miksher gone wrong way. Li'l drop o' gin'll put me right." She stumbled towards the table where two empty bottles and one half full indicated that the gift had been thoroughly appreciated.

"Sit down, Mrs. Nunn," Reynolds begged in persuasive. accents. "I want a chat with you."

The lady tried to focus her eyes upon the owner of the voice; locating him with some difficulty.

"Course, dearie. Shtay 'n have a bit o' shupper," She urged hospitably.

Considering that it was barely an hour after noon the invitation was rather premature. Still, as his hostess seemed to be amiably inclined towards conversation,

Reynolds decided to wait. Time might clear up Mrs. Nunn's blurred elocution.

The door was opened with a bang and the slatternly neighbour appeared bearing a large cup of strong tea.

"Drink this," she ordered, thrusting it under Mrs. Nunn's nose "It may bring yer to yer senses a bit"

With a scornful glance at the gin bottles she added: "It's a miracle you ain't dead."

Mrs. Nunn drank obediently.

"Brought your lil girl too," she remarked, noticing Mimi for the first time and giving her a beaming smile. "The very spit o' yer pa, ain't you, dear?"

The phrase was unknown to Mimi but she grasped the sense of it.

"*J'espere que non,*" she murmured devoutly, favouring her "parent" with an impish moue. "That would be insupportable."

"It would,' snapped Reynolds. "Be quiet!"

"Don't tease yer pa, lovey," advised Mrs. Nunn. "Can't you see he's irritable 'n upset?"

"Tell me," Reynolds asked, "who was the woman who did your work at Mr. Carr's last Tuesday?"

The charwoman gazed at him in blank astonishment.

"What?" she almost shouted. "Some woman went there an' took my job! I scratch her blinking eyes out!" She calmed down and waggled a finger at the inspector. "Garn, dearie, you're trying to kid me. Mr. Carr wouldn't have a stranger in the house! I have me faults, but he knows I'd never touch a pin as wasn't mine. What day is it? "she demanded, with a touch of anxiety.

"To-day is Thursday. A dark, middle-aged woman went there on Tuesday morning. She said that you were ill and had sent her in your place. Mr. Carr did not see her."

Mrs. Nunn appeared to be dazed by the tidings. "I never sent no woman, dark or fair," she declared in solemn tones "That job was too good an' easy. I dunno a living soul I'd trust. It's true I was bad and mistook the day I was due there, but nobody went by my orders."

"Do you know the man who brought you the gin on Monday night?"

"No." Mrs. Nunn raised her eyes to the ceiling. "A stranger an' a gentleman he was, Heaven bless 'im"

"Would you know him again?" pursued Reynolds.

The charwoman shook her head dubiously.

"It was late when he come and I'd only got me candle. No, I'm afraid I wouldn't know the gentleman again. But," she exclaimed brightly, "I can tell you somebody as does know him."

"Who?" Reynolds asked eagerly.

"Why, Mr. James Carr," was Mrs. Nunn's answer. "The gentleman said that Mr. Carr had sent along a little present as it was his birthday and I was to drink to his health. I did too, long life to him!"

"I'm afraid I have bad news for you, Mrs. Nunn. Mr. James Carr was found dead in his library early this morning."

Reynolds expected to have a torrent of morbid questions coupled with wild exclamations of horror. To his surprise the charwoman sat still, her cheeks ashen white.

"A dear good gentleman!" she faltered. "Never forgot a kindness. That's why he kept me on. Eighteen years ago, when I wasn't so free with 'lifting me elbow' so to speak, I spotted that he had a crook for a butler and told him so. He watched and found the man trying to open his safe one night." She screwed her face into a worried expression. "Did Mr. Carr die natural?"

"What makes you ask that question?" Reynolds parried.

"Them jools of his. He had a king's ransom put away in cabinets and a safe. What's more," she went on, "he was thinking of buying another lot, more valuable than all the rest."

"Why do you think that, Mrs. Nunn?"

"I don't think; I know," she retorted in triumph. "When I ain't in drink I'm sharp enough. Last Toosday week when I was washing the veranda outside Mr. Carr's library window, he had two gents inside with him."

"Had you seen these men I before?"

"No, sir, an' I wasn't supposed to see them then. Or *hear* them either," the woman said with a significant smirk. "The butler and his wife thinks I'm very deaf! Saves me a lot o' trouble; I needn't talk, and I can listen in peace when I wants to."

Reynolds nodded. That explained Lang's statement.

What did you hear?" he inquired.

"Mr. Carr and the two gentlemen were going to buy the Crown jewels of some funny country."

"Euralia," Reynolds suggested.

"That's it. They must have had a list of 'em 'cause one of the gents was reading out about emerald and di'mond tyras and necklets of rubies an' things. And Mr. Carr an' the other gent kept saying which bits they wanted. They was jool collectors, I fancy. One gent was going to Paris to buy for the three of 'em. I heard Mr. Carr say: 'It was a good to meet. At least we shan't be bidding against each other."

"Did you tell anyone about this, Mrs. Nunn?" Reynolds asked. "Mrs. Lang or her husband, for instance?"

The woman shook her head.

"Not one word to anybody," she declared. Would you recognise either of those gentlemen who were with Mr. Carr that morning?"

"I don't think so." Mrs. Nunn's tone was dubious. "One was about Mr. Carr's age and the other much younger. I'm no good at describing folk."

There was a wry smile on Reynolds's face as he and Mimi drove away from the house.

"Don't worry, monsieur. That woman can perhaps identify the other two collectors."

"If we don't have to identify their dead bodies first," was Reynolds's reply. "Unless Lang and his wife know their names, Zaldo may be on their track with his murderous games before I know who they are."

"It is half-past. one. Let us eat," Mimi suggested. "Me, I have a little hunger and a large thirst for pale beer. I go to lift the elbow." She stopped the taxi at a restaurant.

"I'll join you when I have rung. up Lang," Reynolds promised. "Mr. Carr died on Wednesday. If the strange charwoman, put poison in the decanter on Tuesday, why did he not die that night?"

A few minutes later Reynolds returned with the result of his call.

"Lang says that Mr. Carr was out on Tuesday night and, on returning, went straight to bed. So he did not touch the decanter until Wednesday night. That saves us further complication in that direction, which is about all that can be said of a pretty bad business. Neither Lang nor his wife saw the two men who were with Mr. Carr in his library last Tuesday week. It was Lang's day off, and his wife says that her master must have admitted his visitors and seen them out later. Mr. Carr's lawyer will be there at five o'clock."

"I shall then be with Vernstein, the Jew in Whitechapels." Mimi raised her glass of ale. "Here's luck and courage."

"It's sporting of you to give up your time to helping me, infant."

"You may have all the time there is with pleasure until these mysteries are solved. Excepting tomorrow evening when," Mimi said airily, "I have the date with my sweetie, Mr. Stephen Blair"

"Congratulations. But," Reynolds said with a chuckle; "if you wish to preserve the secret of your meeting place, be sure no one is following you." He glanced meaningly over his shoulder

"Oh, la, la! That man was standing near Mr. Carr's house this morning," the French girl observed, looking in the direction Reynolds had indicated.

He was also in the street where Mrs. Nunn lives. I saw him there when we came out!" The inspector's tone was grave. "Mimi, he musn't follow you to Whitechapel. I ought not to let you go there without me. You can twist Jenkins round your finger and he'll perhaps allow you to get into danger that I could avoid."

There was a reassuring steadiness in the French girl's dark eyes as she replied softly in French.

"I have learnt to be wary long ago. Vernstein knows me, or he thinks he does. If he can and will tell me the names of those other two collectors who bought the jewels, we may be in time to save their lives. It is a chance that you dare lose."

"Very well," Reynolds agreed. "I'll draw off the man at that table. Remember, I shall have no peace until I know that you're all right. Ring me as you leave Whitechapel."

XI. Tea for Two

Thursday, 4p.m.

At four o'clock that afternoon the door bell of Mr. Keble Wentworth's antique shop tinkled. Its sound was so prolonged that Linda Marchant hurried down from the back of the long shop to satisfy the demands of the impatient caller.

Her lips met in a disapproving line as she saw the back of a tall young man who was pushing the bell casually with his stick.

" Well?" she demanded in an unpromising tone.

He swung round.

"Better than I've felt for months, Thanks."

"I'm not in the least interested in your health, Mr. Tyler."

"Business girls should cultivate good memories. Only a few hours ago I said you may call me Nick. Of course," he added kindly, "if you really have an impediment in your speech and find it difficult to say, I'll let you substitute something easier. You might try 'darling' or 'sweet one', though it's a little early to begin that yet."

The girl looked at him with stormy eyes.

"If you only knew what I thought about you, you'd—" she began.

Tyler held up his hand.

"Sh! I do, and—you don't. Sounds complicated, but it's quite simple. Think it out. Pull down the storm-cone, Linda. You look adorable, but girls with ginger hair can't afford to get red at the wattles."

"You've no right to come here. I'm employed by Mr. Wentworth now. He'd be extremely annoyed if he saw me wasting my time chattering to you."

"Not he. Being a sentimentalist at heart, he'd waggle a shaky finger and say: 'Bless you, my children. Get on with the good work,' or something classical to that effect. Unfortunately he may not have that pleasure. I've just seen your old genelman slip out, and, by the determined look in his eye, I think he's making for some spot where he can get a 'quick couple.' I heard him tell a taximan to drive to his club."

"Why have you come?" Linda demanded.

Nick perched himself on an old oak dresser and started to tear the paper from a parcel he had brought.

"My master, one Frederick Yates—bless his sweet soul!—ordered me to convey his love and congratulations on your conquest of old Wentworth. It wasn't exactly 'love' that he sent. I'd have choked him if he had. To be accurate, he said: 'Tell the girl she's a good egg. She's to keep her mouth shut and her eyes open, and report to me weekly on the day that Wentworth pays her.'"

"Yates is a detestable creature," Linda muttered. As for you, you're the most conceited pup I've ever met."

Nick grinned imperturbably.

"Glad I'm 'placed' anyhow. Have a chocolate," he offered, extending the box he had unwrapped. "Those are hard ones. Don't risk 'em if your teeth are not your own."

They are," the girl retorted, taking a hard chocolate and crunching it defiantly. "Are yours?"

"Lady, you're touching on ugly secrets that should be known only to man and wife. But, things being as they are between us, I own to two 'crowns' on the left upper floor. I'll chance a hard sweet and eat on the other side."

Linda eyed the expensive box speculatively.

"For a man who couldn't pay for his luncheon three hours ago, you've managed rather well, haven't you?"

"I've—er—come into a little money quite recently," Nick mentioned. "Or perhaps I should say I've acquired some."

"A distinction with a difference?"

"You grasp my meaning perfectly though I shudder to hear a cliché fall from your fair lips." He bit a chocolate in half, regarded it with a frown, and pushed it into her mouth. "I hate marzipan."

"So do I," Linda flared at him with her mouth full.

Nick drew her head forward and patted her back.

Spit it out like a little lady. I won't tell the old genelman your nasty habits." From a table near, he picked up a small jade elephant, exquisitely carved. "That's nice. What's his name?"

"Be careful. It's valuable."

"I know. What I asked was the name of the animal."

Linda forced back a smile.

"It hasn't got one, idiot."

"Well, it's going to," Nick told her. "I like elephants. We'll christen him 'Percy."

The girl pulled the curio from his fingers and placed it on the top of a tallboy behind her.

"Why did you do that?" he asked peevishly. "I was getting very fond of Percy."

"I'd noticed that." There was a decided hint in her tone. "Are you going?"

Nick opened his eyes in wide astonishment.

"Lord, no! I've only just come. What about a cup of tea, lass? I'll need it to get my strength up for your boss."

The girl appeared to be staggered at the idea. "You can't possibly stay and see him."

"I intend to meet my rival, with or without your permission, Miss Marchant. It may be a tiresome wait. The dear old creature may be drawn into a hot game of ludo at the club, forgetting the cares of his shop and the snares of his lovely assistant."

"I don't want your company in the meantime."

"I don't particularly want yours, young woman, unless you can be bright and amusing. Can you sing, or do any parlour tricks? That might save me from boredom. Or can I play with Percy?"

"You certainly can't," she retorted. "And I'm not here to entertain unprofitable callers."

Nick Tyler raised his eyebrows.

"Girl, you forget yourself," he replied haughtily. "How much is he?"

"How much is who?

"Percy, of course. Who else could I mean?"

She took down the jade elephant and looked at the price marked on it.

"Two guineas, Mr. Tyler," she replied with scorn. Nick stretched out his hand.

"Pass him over. Percy's mine."

The girl grasped the piece of jade firmly.

"I'm responsible for Mr. Wentworth's goods. You'll show me your money first, please."

Nick took a note-case from his pocket and drew out three one-pound notes. Adding a two shilling piece, he gravely gave her the money.

"That will 'larn' you to be polite to customers in future," he said severely. "I shall not give you a tip."

"Do you mean this?" she said, holding out a note to him. "I said two guineas."

He closed her fingers an it.

"Either you have defective sight or you can't count. The amount is correct," he replied.

"Two guineas equal two pounds two shillings, Mr. Tyler."

"Thanks so much; you know quite a lot, don't you? Nevertheless, what I've given you is correct. Arithmetic is evidently a weak point of yours. I suppose that is why you didn't count the change that I gave you from the fiver at our luncheon. One naturally doesn't like to expose one's ignorance."

"How clever of you to guess," she said with the suspicion of a smile.

"Did you count it, Linda?"

"No."

"Delicious little liar!" With a deft movement he tucked the note into the neck of her frock and kissed her cheek lightly. "Receipted with thanks. Now do I drag you out to tea by the roots of your red hair, or do we make it here? Percy likes his food punctually."

She looked at him in comic despair.

"What am I to do with you?" she asked. "There are cups and saucers and a gas ring. You shall have tea if you will be good and go away immediately afterwards."

"Any intimidation, madam, and I shall return Percy. It would be a pity, for I was taught to be kind to animals, and already the little fellow is showing signs of affection for his new master."

"Come along and boil the kettle."

Nick Tyler followed her to the far end of the shop where, under the glass dome, there were facilities for preparing the meal.

His eyes wandered curiously over the strong black cabinets which lined the walls.

"What does your boss keep in these?" he asked.

"How should I know?" She set the teapot on the table. "There's nothing to eat, I'm afraid."

"I brought a box of cakes. You'll find 'em beside my hat near the door. Run and fetch 'em."

"You badly lack confidence, don't you!" was Linda's comment as she obeyed.

Returning, she regarded him suspiciously.

"What were you doing at that cabinet?" she demanded.

Nick strolled back to the table and sat down entirely at ease.

"I can't put a ten-foot cabinet in my pocket," he complained, "and considering that it's locked, I haven't been able to acquire its contents during your short absence. Of course, given time—"

"I don't trust you, Nick Tyler."

He placed the jade elephant solemnly beside the box of cakes.

"You must have learnt 'The Gipsy's Warning' when you were an infant and taken it to heart now you're old. Buck up! Percy wants a drink. He takes two lumps, please."

Linda cast a worried glance towards the door. "I'm sure there'll be trouble if Mr. Wentworth comes back and finds you here," she said.

"What's the betting that he won't be charmed to see me?" Nick asked. "I'm told I have beautiful manners."

"They're so well disguised that one would never recognise them. Have you met Mr. Wentworth before? If so, it's not a fair gamble."

"Never saw him in my life until this afternoon. If your old gentleman doesn't say that he's pleased to make my acquaintance within three minutes of my meeting him, I promise not to come here again. If he does succumb to my powers of fascination, you must promise to dine with me very soon. I take soup in perfect silence, so don't be afraid."

'I'm not, for I shall not be there to judge," Linda replied firmly.

"Yes, you will, if I win. Not to-night, because I've dirty work to do at the cross roads after dark."

"And, in any case, not to-morrow," she flashed, "because I have an engagement."

Tyler's face became stern.

"Go steady, Linda," he warned. "An engagement implies that you have friends who know where you are living and working. You told Yates that you had none. It was part of the bargain. Queer, no doubt, but you agreed to it. I wouldn't try to 'double-cross' him if I were you."

"Please allow me to mind my own business," she said hotly. "The friends I am meeting do not know where I live or anything about me, and will not do so. I shall keep my share of the bargain, but I've yet to learn that it includes supporting visitations from you, Nick Tyler."

The young man bestowed upon her the smile of a proud father.

"Bless the child!" he exclaimed, "who said she had a stutter? She can pronounce 'Nick' well enough to become a B.B.C. announcer." He rose swiftly as the door bell tinkled. "Ah! Here comes your boss. Tune in to the conversation, and get a few hints from me. We'll fix Saturday for our dinner. I'll let you know the time and place."

Taking "Percy" with him, he advanced to meet the elderly man who had just entered.

"Ah, good afternoon, sir," Nick said in a tone of genial respect. "You are Mr. Keble Wentworth, I think. After making my little purchase," he showed the jade elephant, "I was so attracted by your place that I thought I should like to wait and meet the owner."

Mr. Wentworth bowed.

"That's very nice of you," he replied in pleased tones. "I always enjoy a chat with my clients. I hope you were not bored in the interval."

Nick glanced over his shoulder and discovered that Linda was within earshot.

"The articles here are beautiful," he said clearly, "but, as they are dumb, I must admit that your description of them will add greatly to their interest. My name is Tyler," he added.

"I'm very pleased to make your acquaintance, Mr. Tyler," the old man answered. A reply that caused Nick to risk a triumphant grin at Linda.

"Have you time to look around? If you care for tapestries that is a fine example on the wall. I call them the 'soft goods' in the antique business."

To the girl's astonishment Nick promptly named the period and assessed its merits in technical terms. "I pride, myself on my knowledge of soft goods," he ended.

It is agreeable to discuss antiques with one who understands and appreciates them," Mr. Wentworth remarked. Lowering his voice he added. "You must make allowances for my assistant, Mr. Tyler. She is new to the business. I hope she gave you satisfaction."

"I found her quite capable for my requirements," the young man assured him in a voice calculated to reach across the street, "A trifle formal in manner, but perhaps that is wise in dealing with clients. After all, Mr. Wentworth, one never knows! Oh, by the way, I hope I did not trespass. Your assistant kindly offered me tea and I gratefully accepted."

The old man smiled with approval at Linda.

"Quite right. I'm delighted that she thought of doing so," he said.

The two men strolled round, chatting about the various pieces of furniture.

They paused at last under the glass dome where Linda was clearing away the tea things.

"You are perhaps a collector, Mr. Tyler?" questioned the connoisseur.

"Only of currency, I'm afraid, in these hard times," Nick replied. "Though, when I can manage it, I dabble mildly in precious stones. That is not in your line, of course. It's getting late. I must be off."

The older man's eyes twinkled behind the horn rimmed spectacles.

"Come in again, Mr. Tyler. I may have other things to show you that I think will be of especial interest. I shall be here every morning but, now that I have an assistant, I may slip off to my club most afternoons for an hour or so. Miss Marchant, will you give Mr. Tyler his hat, please?"

Linda preceded them to the door, opened it and, with an icy expression that would have made a heat wave work hard, handed Nick his hat and stick.

He nodded graciously. "Thank you, Miss—?" he hesitated as if he had not heard the name.

"Marchant," she snapped.

"I mustn't forget, for future occasions. You did very well this afternoon; very well indeed," he said in a tone of kindly patronage.

Linda swallowed the words she longed to utter.

"Your praise is gratifying but undeserved, I fear," she replied.

"Not at all, Miss Marchant."

She thrust a parcel into, his hands.

"This is yours, I believe."

"Ah, yes. A few chocolates. I meant them for my fiancée, but I've bought the wrong kind." Nick turned to the connoisseur. "May I give them to Miss—er—Marchant, sir, in memory, of a very pleasant afternoon?"

"Please do. I'll take them for her," Mr. Wentworth offered as he noticed the girl's reluctance. "Good day."

"A very pleasant afternoon!" she muttered, as her new employer moved away. "I could murder you, Nick."

"And so I win my bet," was his irrelevant remark.

"Nothing would induce me to dine with you," she vowed furiously.

"Saturday, if not before. The Berkeley. Eight o'clock," Nick told her. "Good-bye angel."

XII. Mimi Turns Crook

Thursday afternoon, 5 p.m.

Mimi was unusually serious as she and Jenkins left the Tube station in Whitechapel.

"Gunner's Court is up a turning about two hundred yards from here," she told him.

"What do you know about Vernstein?" Jenkins questioned. "And why, exactly, are we going there?"

"He is a fence in a big way clever enough to have evaded the law so far. I want to find out if he is working, as I suspect, for Zaldo. Vernstein knows that I am coming. If he is alone this afternoon, well and good. If he smells a rat and has anyone else there to protect him and watch us, he—" She broke off and her eyes widened as she noticed a man who had got out of a taxi just ahead of them. "There is the answer," she added. "That man is almost certainly one of Zaldo's confederates. He is an American called Kent. Wait here a minute, please."

Hurrying back to the Tube station she rang up Stephen Blair from a telephone booth. He listened gravely to her request.

"I understand," he replied over the wire. "You have given me Linda's address to be used only if you cannot dine with me to-morrow night. You think she may need a friend. Are you in any danger? I can look after two people as well as one, you know."

Mimi meditated for a moment. The man she had just seen going towards Vernstein's house might try to detain her. It might be wise to ask Stephen Blair to stand by.

"Thank you," she said. "It is now five o'clock. If I do not meet you in three-quarters of an hour, in this Tube station, come to number four, Gunner's Court, and ask for me."

"It will mean quick work, but I'll be there," Blair promised.

She joined Jenkins with her usual nonchalant air.

"We'll be late," he complained. Noticing that she looked inside her handbag, he added: "Hope you've not forgotten your lipstick!"

"I've forgotten nothing."

"You seem nervous, Mimi."

"Nervous! *Ma foi!* I who have hidden in the cellar of Apaches, and have mixed with criminals to discover their secrets! In comparison, this will be a picnicking. But, one must be careful."

"I will," Jenkins promised.

"*Bon.* I shall call you 'Joe.' First, you must appear to be shy and awkward; second, speak with a wide Cockney accent. Third, look like a fool. *Entendu?*"

"I understand." The' detective's voice was sulky. "Why you want me to come along and pretend that I'm your fiancé beats me. What excuse are you going to make to Vernstein for calling on him?"

"You will see. Have you any money?"

"About thirty shillings."

She thrust a five-pound note into his hand. "You'll need that," she said.

"What's the idea?"

The French girl gave his arm a warning pressure.

"There is Vernstein's window," she whispered.

A moment later she knocked at a door. Her voice rippled on in a stream of gay chatter until her summons was answered.

"Good afternoon, Mademoiselle Mimi. What do you require?" came in suave guttural accents from a grey-bearded man in his shirt sleeves.

Mimi greeted him warmly.

"May we have the little talk, please?" she asked. "This is my young man, Mr. Vernstein."

The Jew flashed his teeth at Jenkins and appraised him with suspicious eyes. "Will you both come in?" he invited.

Mimi drew the Jew back into the passage.

"Joe *thinks* he is my fiancé," she whispered. "He wants to buy me a ring. Perhaps you can make the little business with him."

The Jew nodded in understanding.

"So that's why you've brought him" He leered at her meaningly. "I don't usually do such small deals. How much has he got?"

"Five pounds. You will please give me good value. Also for me, I will take ten per cent for bringing you a customer."

Vernstein pinched her ear.

"Cunning little monkey!" he remarked. "All right. You shall get a commission. I'm an honest man."

Mimi laughed softly.

"Dear Mr. Vernstein, only fools need be honest. You are far too clever for stupidness. My gang in Paris say that no one can make such smart arrangements as you with stolen jewellery. Sell me a nice ring, and perhaps I can do you the good turn with very—big business."

"I'm doing very big business myself these days," he boasted. "One likes to do more, of course. What is it?"

"We will first buy the ring." Mimi said firmly, and went into the sitting-room. Near the door sat Jenkins, twirling his cap, and looking as vacant as Mimi could possibly have wished. He cast a tender smile at her as she came in.

"I told you Mr. Vernstein would sell you jewellery cheaper than anyone else, Joe. My young man is in the fruit trade," she added to Vernstein, who was staring hard at the stranger.

It was the first Jenkins had heard of it, but he rose nobly to his new occupation.

"That's right, guv'ner. Covent Garden, Market," he supplemented, with the desired Cockney accent. "Blimey,

I got a thirst on me. Let's see that ring for my gal and we'll be off."

Vernstein's expression relaxed a little. Taking out some keys, he opened a cupboard and unlocked a safe inside it. The instant the Jew turned back Mimi slid her fingers into the pocket of his coat hanging on a chair. A second later she withdrew from that pocket a letter and two or three slips of paper. Like lightning her eyes ran over the things, and she slid them all back into the pocket except one sheet. This she passed to Jenkins, who tucked it into his shoe.

That was something accomplished, anyhow, the girl thought. Meanwhile, she remembered the figure of Kent whom she had seen entering Gunner's Court and wondered if, for once, she had not been too daring.

"These rings are worth twice as much as you want to pay," the Jew said, placing a small tray on the table.

"*Magnifique!*" exclaimed Mimi. "Come and look, Joe."

Jenkins obeyed, and did not doubt the truth of the Jew's words.

Mimi examined the stones with the air of an expert.

"I like this one," she decided.

"Ah, ha, you are sharp to choose the best," Vernstein exclaimed.

Mimi twirled the large cabochon ruby gleaming on her finger.

"Joe, please pay Mr. Vernstein."

She talked airily while the financial transaction was being arranged.

The Jew locked away the other trinkets.

"One minute, please," he said. "I have something upstairs that I want to show you." There was a crafty look in his eyes.

As the door closed on him, Jenkins turned to the girl.

"Let's clear out, sharp!"

"No. I've been waiting for this," she replied. "Tranquil."

The door was opened softly and a man came in.

"Put your hands up and keep them there," he ordered.

"Do as you're told, Joe." Mimi's tone was sharp and unmistakable.

Jenkins relinquished his instinct to fight and obeyed in surprise as Mimi corroborated the stranger's command, and drew a small revolver from her handbag.

"I've got him covered, Kent,' she said. "Search him if you're nervous. He's only a porter and too stupid to do any harm."

"I've only got your word for that," Kent replied, with a strong American accent.

"Don't you see I'm fighting on your side?" she demanded.

"Going to make me keep me 'ands up till Christmas?" Jenkins asked in sarcastic tones. He was cursing inwardly, for letting himself be caught in this trap. What the deuce was Mimi's game? He swallowed his indignation as he remembered the inspector's instructions to act as the French girl ordered.

"You lay a finger on my gal, yer blinking coward," he said, "and I'll do yer in."

Kent sneered.

"Your girl, you fool! She's got as much use for you as I have. We're old pals, eh, Mimi?"

The girl rippled with laughter.

"That is right," she admitted. "I'm sorry I cheated you, Joe, but I was—how you say—hard up and you were so easy. Forget all about me. I play for big money."

Jenkins took his cue and played up admirably;

"A dirty trick if ever there was one," he grunted. "Serves me right for trustin' a forriner. If I wasn't so fond of you, blimey, I'd go straight to the nearest copper. Strewth, I thought you was on the level, Mimi."

"The level, it is too dull a life for me," she replied. Her mind was working rapidly. She had dealt with this situation of Kent's appearance in the only possible way. But there was one difficulty that had to be overcome. She had not told Jenkins of her telephone call. In less than fifteen minutes Stephen Blair, who was now waiting in the Whitechapel Tube station, would call here for her!

If he did so, his life, together with hers and that of Jenkins, would probably be at stake, for Kent would realise that she was spying upon him and Vernstein. Somehow she must arrange with Jenkins to keep Blair away! The chance came unexpectedly.

Kent opened the door and called up the stairs.

"Is it O. K. to let this chap go?"

Swiftly seizing the opportunity Mimi whispered to Jenkins. .

"Stephen Blair is at Whitechapels Tube station. Tall, thin man. Stop him from coming here."

"Stephen who?" asked Jenkins with a puckered brow.

But it was too late for Mimi to reply. Kent had swung round towards them.

"Scram!" he ordered.

The girl hoped for the best. Jenkins would probably manage somehow, though her spirits sank a little as he disappeared, leaving her alone with Kent.

Apparently undisturbed, she seated herself on the table.

"Give me a cigarette," she said. "Where's Vernstein?"

"Upstairs," Kent replied. "He prefers other people to do the dirty work. That's why he sent for me when he heard you were coming. He doesn't trust you, baby."

The girl shrugged and blew out a cloud of smoke.

"Why should he?" she inquired. "We're all ready to cut each other's throats for the sake of money. By the way, how do you like working for Zaldo?"

Kent gave a startled jump.

"He's in Cairo, so far as I know."

Mimi raised her eyebrows and smiled.

"Then you don't know much, *mon ami*. A man called James Carr recently bought some jewels that were— interesting. He died last night." She leaned nearer Kent. "Zaldo was in London yesterday. I guessed Vernstein was selling stuff for him. So I kill two birds by bringing that stupid porter with me to-day. I get the ring and *voilà!* You arrived!"

"Very clever!" Kent commented. "What do you think you'll get out of all this?"

"Something more than a ring." Mimi flicked the from her cigarette and looked Kent full in the eyes. "I, too, am working for Zaldo!"

XIII. Stephen Blair Goes Quietly

Thursday afternoon

Considerably worried, Jenkins walked down the Court and turned towards the Tube station. As he did so, he almost collided with a tall man of distinguished appearance.

"Can you tell me where Gunner's Court is?" the stranger asked in a cultured voice not usually associated with visits to the slums of Whitechapel.

Jenkins eyed him up and down and bit his lip It was only a guess that this was the man Mimi had meant, and yet the circumstances pointed that way.

"Do you want to see Mr. Vernstein?" he demanded.

The stranger frowned.

"I want number four, Gunner's Court," he said curtly.

"Do you know a French girl called Mimi?" Jenkins pursued in his best imitation of Inspector Reynolds's crisp style.

Unfortunately Jenkins's coster attire rather detracted from his assumption of authority, and this did not commend him favourably to Stephen Blair. Mindful that Mimi had admitted on the telephone that she would probably be in danger, he took this roughly-clad individual with the domineering manner to be someone sent to prevent him from rescuing her.

"That is no business of yours, my man," he said in sharp tones. "Let me go," he added indignantly as Jenkins caught his arm.

"Is your name Stephen Somebody?" Jenkins asked in desperation, holding the stranger's arm firmer.

Undoubtedly, Stephen Blair decided, the man was a scoundrel—one who had heard his Christian name. "Take your hand away," he ordered, "or I'll call a policeman and give you in charge."

Jenkins glanced round in the fervent hope that such a threat might be fulfilled. At least it might prevent this insistent idiot from upsetting Mimi's plans and possibly imperilling her life. Jenkins tightened his grasp on Blair's arm.

"Listen to me," he said in a peremptory tone. "Mimi told me to send away a Stephen Somebody who was waiting at the Tube station. She said you mustn't call at Gunner's Court."

Blair by this time was convinced that the man was not only a scoundrel but a dangerous one. If Mimi had sent any message it would have been clear and definite, he was positive, and she would not have chosen this disreputable ambassador.

Suddenly Jenkins made an imperative signal with his free hand. Blair's chin set; the fellow was beckoning to an accomplice, was he? He struck Jenkins's hand a smart blow and tried to wriggle free. Two other hands caught Blair's arms from behind and he turned to confront a police constable.

"Hang on to him, officer," urged Jenkins. "I'm a detective from Scotland Yard and this man is obstructing me from my duty."

"Confound your impudence!" the captive raged. "Officer, this man attacked me and refused to let me pass."

"Where were you going?" the officer asked.

"To make a call at four, Gunner's Court," Blair replied.

The officer looked at him dubiously, but did not release his hold. Gentlemen of this class were rare birds in the neighbourhood, and their errands were of a doubtful character.

Whereas the man dressed as a coster who had beckoned to him and announced that he was from Scotland Yard, had spoken in a tone with which P.C. Gordon was familiar.

Jenkins pulled something from inside his sock, where he had hidden it early that afternoon.

"Here's my warrant card, officer," he said.

"Right," replied the constable as he read the wording. "What do you want me to do?"

"Help me with him until we get out of this street and then call a taxi," Jenkins ordered "I'll take him to Scotland Yard."

"Where I shall have much pleasure in telling Inspector Reynolds what I think of you," Blair retorted warmly.

Jenkins's face wore a pleased smile

"The inspector is my chief," he replied, "and I am here to-day by his instructions, Mr.—"

"Blair. Stephen Blair," his prisoner snapped. "I'll go quietly."

"Thank you. On we go, constable. You needn't hold Mr. Blair's arm."

Stephen Blair lighted a cigarette as they drove apparently to Scotland Yard, and glanced at his captor. Anger was fast fading into amused resentment. After all, this detective was only doing his duty. Blair flicked open his case.

"Have a cigarette, and let's call it a day," he proposed. Seeing Jenkins hesitate, he added with a chuckle: "Your disguise is so good that you can't blame me for resisting."

Jenkins accepted the cigarette and the olive branch.

"You've no idea how serious it might have been if I hadn't prevented you, Mr. Blair."

"Well, it's your party. Where are we going now?"

Jenkins ruminated on the question. Actually he had no idea of going to the Yard. He had gained his objective by preventing Blair from calling at the Jew's house. The next thing was to be sure that he did not return there.

"That depends on you, Mr. Blair."

"What about releasing me on parole with a caution?" the prisoner suggested.

"Very well, sir. Will you undertake not to go back to Gunner's Court unless Inspector Reynolds gives you permission? He knows Mimi is there trying to obtain certain information."

Stephen Blair screwed up his face in surprise.

"So serious as that, eh? All right. You have my promise. But why does Scotland Yard call in a little French girl to procure information? Hang it all, man, she's only a kid."

A broad smile widened Jenkins's mouth.

"Mimi's not such a kid as you fancy, Mr. Blair, and is very capable of looking after herself. As for aiding the Yard, it's entirely by her own wish and unofficial," he added loyally. "She thought she could find out something and begged us not to interfere in any way."

"I'm delighted to know that. What's her real job?"

The question cornered Jenkins for a moment. Mimi preferred to keep her detective work in Paris a secret.

"An artist's model sometimes, Mr. Blair. Occasionally she acts as a mannequin in London dress shops and has met many strange characters in Paris cafés. Once or twice she has been able to assist Inspector Reynolds. She is very friendly with the inspector and his wife and often stays with them." He looked at Blair as a thought struck him. "How did you meet her?"

"In a Montmartre café. I was befriending an English girl who been annoyed by two youngsters. They were with me and I apologised on their behalf. It was inauspicious introduction, but both Mimi and the other girl were very nice about it. The two girls came to London together and—" Blair broke off, remembering Mimi's wish for him to be silent. "I hope the English girl has obtained work," he ended lamely.

Jenkins noted the constraint in Blair's closing sentence and drew his own conclusions. The inspector had been very interested in this girl, he remembered, and had tried vainly to trace her at a house in Kenford Street, thinking that she knew something about an undiscovered murder case. He resolved to do a little deft questioning.

"Let me see, the girl's name was Linda, wasn't it?" he inquired with a casual air.

"If so, it probably still is," was Blair's unhelpful reply.

Subterfuge having failed, Jenkins resorted to bolder methods.

"Do you remember her surname?"

"She never told me," Blair answered with meticulous truth. "Our interview in Montmartre was of the briefest nature; apologetic on my side, and mainly monosyllabic on hers." Thoroughly alive to Jenkins's scheme, Blair was now enjoying himself. This detective owed him a bit and he meant to get it back.

"You seem fascinated by Mimi's friend, sergeant. Have you met her?"

Baffled, Jenkins said more than he intended.

"Not yet, but I mean to," he retorted.

Thereby putting Blair well on his guard. No such meeting should take place if he could prevent it. Whatever Linda's secrets were, she should keep them so far as he was concerned.

"You'll find her charming," Blair said lightly. "Any more questions, officer?"

The detective reddened. Blair was more astute than he had anticipated.

"I was a bit curious about your visit to Gunner's Court," he admitted. "Do you know Vernstein well?"

"No," Blair replied, guessing that this must be the tenant of the house.

Frustrated in that direction, Jenkins tried fresh tactics.

"Inspector Reynolds didn't say you would be calling there."

"The inspector knew nothing of my intended visit," Blair answered. "You will doubtless inform him of your brave efforts and my subsequent arrest. The first blot on my copybook!"

The C.I.D. man surmised that Blair knew a great deal more about Linda than he pretended.

"You will be seeing Miss Linda soon, I believe," he said.

"Pardon me," Blair interrupted, "are you asking a question or making a statement?"

A little nonplussed, Jenkins admitted that it was a guess on his part.

"Ah, that's different." Blair adopted a profoundly legal manner. When you can produce facts, come and ask me the questions that seem to feel are necessary concerning my movements. We're passing near my rooms now. I'll make a bargain with you, officer. Let me get out here on parole and I'll pay this taxi."

"Thank you," Jenkins agreed, a little sheepishly.

XIV: The Hand of Zaldo

Thursday. 7:30 p.m.

"You don't appear to have covered yourself with distinction, my lad," was Inspector Reynolds's dry comment after he had listened to an account of the episode concerning Stephen Blair.

Jenkins agreed humbly.

"I was trying to get a 'line' on the mysterious Linda, sir. You thought she was mixed up in something suspicious."

"It's far more important that we concentrate on the James Carr murder case," Reynolds told him in caustic tones. "Also, I'm frankly uneasy about Mimi's safety. I feel half inclined to throw away our chance of getting information and get a search warrant to raid Vernstein's house to-night."

"She seemed to be handling the situation very well, sir, when she sent me away. Both Vernstein and the American called Kent, were eating out of her hand."

"She has brains and knows how to use 'em," the inspector remarked. "If only one can forget the risk she is running there's humour in the picture of Mimi joining a band of Continental crooks!"

His assistant gave a wry smile. He had seen Vernstein and Kent. If they were fair samples of the crowd, he didn't envy the French girl her task.

He pulled from his pocket the slip of paper that she had taken from the Jew's pocket. With the air of one about to bring out an unassailable trump, he now placed this on his chief's desk. It had always been a favourite trick of Jenkins's to play his worst cards first and reserve his ace.

Reynolds stared at it and whistled softly.

"Look at this," he exclaimed. "It's definitely a list of the Euralian Crown jewels, divided into three sections. *A* was purchased by James Carr. Here's his name. *B* and *C* were probably bought by the men that Carr's charwoman overheard talking in his library." He banged his fist on the desk in exasperation. "If only *B* and *C* sections had borne the names of the other two men, our task would have been easy.

"It's the worst possible luck," Jenkins gloomily acquiesced. "There's a date for the *A* section. What does it mean, sir? October the eighteenth was last night."

"That was the date on which James Carr was robbed and murdered." Reynolds's voice had a tragic note in it. "If we cannot find out who B and C are, they will probably meet the same fate."

"Shall I go back and keep an eye on Gunner's Court, sir?"

"It's a good idea. Mimi must be safeguarded somehow. Disguise yourself thoroughly and don't let Vernstein or his confederate see you in the neighbourhood."

Jenkins promised that he would take every precaution.

"I've been interviewing well-known collectors all this afternoon," Reynolds said. "Not one of them could give me any help. They had heard vaguely of James Carr, but had never met him or any of his associates. The only bright spot was that I was followed everywhere most faithfully."

Jenkins expressed violent indignation at the news.

"I'd like to get my hands on him!" he exploded.

"It was a novel experience for a C.I.D. man to be shadowed! This chap did it so well that I felt like telling him to join the police force. I drew him off after I had had luncheon with Mimi. He must have seen her with me, which may be dangerous for her if he is one of Vernstein's bunch."

"Did you get any information from Mr. Carr's lawyer, sir?"

"Not yet. He has been in York on business. He was wired for and will meet me at Carr's house at half-past eight to-night."

Jenkins scanned the inspector's tired face.

"It's half-past seven, sir. You've plenty of time to get a meal first. I expect you've had nothing since breakfast."

"Not much," Reynolds admitted, drawing the telephone towards him. "I'll ring up my wife and break the news that her guest has joined a crook gang and then I'll get some food."

He replaced the receiver presently and looked at Jenkins with rather a blank expression.

"That's funny. There's no reply. Well, off you go to Whitechapel. I'll see you here to-morrow morning."

"I'll ring you up at your home to-night," promised his assistant.

Reynolds reached the late Mr. Carr's house nearly a quarter of an hour before his appointment. One often learnt something of value by arriving before one was expected.

"Has the lawyer turned up yet, Lang?" he asked the butler.

"No, sir. A Dr. Tempest telephoned a few minutes ago and said he would be glad if you would ring him up.

Reynolds moved towards the library.

"I'll use the extension in here. Had any callers to-day, Lang?"

The butler pursed his lips.

"Dozens. Mostly newspaper men who got nothing from me."

"Show the lawyer in here when he comes, please," Reynolds requested, dismissing the butler.

A minute later Dr. Tempest answered his telephone call.

"They told me at the Yard where I could find you, inspector," the pathologist said over the wire. "The post-mortem on James Carr proves that he died of poison: Flemming's Tincture, as I suspected. The exact quantity he took has yet to be ascertained, but that's enough for you to get on with."

"Quite. Thanks very Much, doctor. The inquest is at ten-thirty to-morrow morning."

"Right. I'll be there. By the way," Dr. Tempest went on, "your wife is here waiting for you in your office. She asks me to tell you that she will stay there until you come. Also that the apples have arrived."

Reynolds laughed.

"I'm afraid she will have a long wait," he replied. "It may be very late, tell her, as I've two more appointments this evening. I don't know what she means about the apples. I've ordered none."

"A present, perhaps," chuckled the medical man. "Good night."

The inspector had barely finished telephoning when Lang ushered in an elderly gentleman.

"Mr. Ingersant, sir," the butler announced and withdrew, leaving the two men together.

"Lang told me who you were, inspector. This is a melancholy business," the lawyer said in a harassed manner. "Mr. Carr and I were old friends. I'm very shocked."

"When did you last see him?" Reynolds asked. "I shall be greatly helped by any details you can give me."

The lawyer consulted his pocketbook.

"Last Monday week at three o'clock in my office," he said precisely. "Our interview was less agreeable than usual. Mr. Carr had previously ordered me to sell a large number of securities although it was a bad moment. He requested me to have the amount turned into French currency. I did so reluctantly and gave him the money in thousand franc notes. That was why he called on me. I told him that he had lost heavily on the sale of shares and conversion into French money, and he told me to mind my own business. He took the notes away with him, for what purpose I cannot tell you."

"What was the amount?" Reynolds inquired.

"Four million francs; about fifty thousand pounds sterling. He probably meant to buy jewels of immense value." The lawyer spread his hands. "I have no patience with such purchases. Of what use are they? It is unsafe to have them in a house."

"Mr. Carr probably insured his collection," Reynolds suggested.

"He did nothing of the kind," was the lawyer's retort. "He said that money could not replace his treasures if they were stolen."

"Did you ever see his collection?"

"Once, some years ago," Mr. Ingersant replied. "My attitude was unsympathetic, I'm afraid, for the reasons I've stated, and Mr. Carr never repeated the invitation nor mentioned his purchases to me after that. Has he been robbed, inspector? If so, I suppose the shock caused his death."

"Mr. Carr was murdered," Reynolds said quietly. "I am hoping that you can help to show us whether he was also robbed, Mr. Ingersant. I have his keys, but preferred to wait until you came before examining the safe, as I thought that you might have some what jewels he owned."

The lawyer appeared to be staggered by the news.

"Murdered!" he repeated. "How could he have been so foolish as to keep priceless things in the house?"

"Collectors rarely like to part with their treasures, Mr. Ingersant. That known fact makes them easy prey for thieves. Here are the keys."

The lawyer glanced at a safe standing on the floor but went towards a bookcase that occupied one side of a wall.

"There is another safe behind this, inspector. Help me to find the secret spring. I've only seen it worked once, years ago."

It was quite ten minutes before Reynolds discovered the tiny knob that, when twisted, caused part of the bookcase to hinge forward, revealing a large safe behind it.

Mr. Ingersant unlocked it and uttered an exclamation.

"Mr. Carr can't have been robbed, inspector. Every drawer is full and appears to be untouched"

Consulting the list that Mimi had obtained, Reynolds compared the various items thereon. Not one was in the collection before him!

Mr. Ingersant unlocked the door of the other safe. It was empty, except for a small silver clock.

The lawyer took it out with a puzzled frown on his face.

"This used to stand on Mr. Carr's desk. I gave it to him years ago," he said. "It's neither valuable nor antique. Why on earth did he put it in his safe?"

Reynolds opened the clock face and extracted a slip of paper that had been wedged beneath the hands. The paper contained a list of jewels was an exact copy of those in the *A* section on Mimi's paper.

"Mr. Carr was undoubtedly robbed of jewels that he had recently purchased and had locked in this safe," the inspector said slowly.

But he did not tell the lawyer that he could guess who had placed the clock in the safe. There was no doubt in his mind that this was Zaldo's work, for the hands had been wedged at the hour of midnight.

XV. A Case of Apples

Thursday, 6 p.m.

Mimi was in a tight corner and realised it fully.

Jenkins—her quondam fiancé—had gone, and with him all hope of outside help, even if she desired it. Her quick brain had got her out of dangerous places before and might do so again if she kept calm, she decided.

Meanwhile, having been rushed into this strange situation in Vernstein's house by force of circumstances, she meant to find out all she could before considering escape from it.

She appeared to be entirely at her ease as she sat on the table, swinging her legs and smoking a cigarette.

"You're a cool customer," Kent told her. "It gives me a pain to hear a pretty kid like you talking of sharing in future burglaries as if they were sweepstakes. You must have been born without a heart."

"I have all my organs, thank you," Mimi assured him primly, "but my heart is worked by my head and not by silly sentimentals. Also you are wrong about sweepstakes. If one buys a ticket in a lottery, perhaps one wins. If these burglaries take place, I surely win. Money is useful and pleasant, and when one is poor, one mustn't be too particular."

"Do you draw the line at something worse than burglary?" questioned Kent, trying to appear casual.

Mimi raised her shoulder in a gesture of indifference.

"Personally I dislike violence, but if one cannot get money without it, what will you?"

Kent's eyes narrowed. He determined to test her nerve.

"Ever been mixed up in murder cases?"

"Several, though of course I never committed the crime," was Mimi's prompt reply. "I suppose the burglaries may include something of the sort."

"Zaldo's maxim is that dead men tell no tales."

He may be right," the girl agreed. She lighted a fresh cigarette. "Carr's job seems to have gone off well. When is the next?"

A wily expression flickered across Kent's face.

"If you're also working for Zaldo, as you say, you'd know." He frowned as a knock was heard on the front door. "Is that your boy friend again?" he asked in a fierce whisper.

"Of course not. Joe's a harmless fool but he won't come back here to be bitten a second time," Mimi asserted with a laugh that she hoped sounded natural. Suppose it was Jenkins; or worse still, Stephen Blair! "Perhaps it's the great Zaldo himself," she added.

"He's too clever to move far from the West End. I believe he hangs out in a posh hotel." Kent rose and fitted a knuckle-duster on to his hand. "If it *is* your 'sweetie,' he'll get this."

The moment Kent left the room Mimi hurried to the window. Drawing aside the blind, she could see the man who stood in the court waiting for admittance. The gas lamp shone full on his face; there was no possibility of mistake.

It was the man who had been following her and Inspector Reynolds that morning.

Whatever danger she had been in before faded into insignificance before this. Kent would hear that she was in league with a Scotland Yard detective. He and the man were talking in low tones in the passage now.

Suddenly she had an inspiration. On the opposite side of Gunner's Court she could see a cobbler working in a window. A card with large lettering was hung against the pane; it showed her that his name was Pernot. A French name. Possibly he was a Frenchman. If necessity arose maybe her fellow countryman would help her, especially if adequately rewarded.

It was fortunate that she was well supplied with money. Even if Kent knew some French he would not understand the argot that Mimi could employ to one of her own race.

Taking off her shoe, she cut the lining with her penknife and resumed her seat on the table, a little cheered.

A moment later the door was opened. A man put his head in, stared hard at her and went out again.

"That's her," Mimi heard him say.

Without a second's hesitation she called out:

"Bring in your friend, Mr. Kent. I saw him following me this morning."

Kent's face was black with rage as he and the newcomer entered.

Mimi had had two good rules firmly grounded in her, one being that when you didn't know what to say it was wise to retreat to high ground and preserve an aloof silence. The other was that when you knew you were going to be attacked it was wise to get in the first blow.

She chose the latter method now and led off in fierce offensive.

"You did your work disgracefully this morning;" she informed the stranger. "Zaldo has no use for idiots and knows how to deal with them. If I tell him that both I and the detective that I was trying to get information from observed your clumsy efforts, he will be furious. What do you want here?"

The man appeared staggered at the outburst and gazed at her speechlessly.

"Stop a minute, my girl," Kent put in. "Taking the whip hand too soon, aren't you? Perhaps you'll explain what you were doing tailing around with a 'tec this morning and having lunch with him."

The French girl's eyes blazed.

"Certainly I will explain—to Zaldo and no one else."

"When? "Kent demanded with a cynical smile.

"To-morrow evening," Mimi deftly invented, remembering her dinner engagement with Linda and Stephen Blair, and realising that she might be detained here otherwise. "I am dining with him. Perhaps you also are going, and your friend here."

Kent shook his head in a puzzled fashion.

"No, we're not. And neither will you unless I'm convinced that your talk to this detective was with Zaldo's knowledge."

"Ring him up and ask," Mimi suggested with bland impudence, while inwardly she wondered how long her bluff would hold good.

"I will. Give me his number."

The French girl smilingly shook her finger to and fro.

"That is an old trick, my good Kent. You don't know Zaldo's address or his telephone number; and if you did, you would not dare to disturb him. In short," she ventured boldly, "I doubt if you and your friend here have ever seen him. If so, you will please describe him to me."

By the baffled expression in both men's faces she knew she had scored a point.

"Your actions to-day need explanation," Kent said. "I'm not satisfied about the Scotland Yard man. Who is he, Dan?"

"An Inspector Reynolds," replied the newcomer. "He's a darned sight too hot on the James Carr trail for my liking. He's been round to old Carr's charwoman to-day."

"And I heard all that was said," Mimi declared. "Reynolds is dull and stupid. I can twist him round my fingers."

"Maybe she's telling the truth, Kent," Dan said, adding in an undertone that was perfectly audible to Mimi. "Besides, it don't matter a row of beans about this Reynolds fellow. He's worried us once too often. I delivered a case of apples at his private house an hour ago."

Kent gave a low whistle.

"Zaldo must have got the wind up badly."

"It's no affair of mine. The balloon goes up at midnight," said his companion. "I've done my bit, and am going to the movies. If you don't want the little French miss I'll take her too."

"Me, I am too largely occupied," Mimi declared.

No evidence of the fear she was experiencing was visible in her face or manner. Two phrases were beating like hammers in her brain. A case of apples had been left at Reynolds's house and the balloon would go up at midnight! By that hour the tired inspector and his wife would probably be asleep, unsuspecting danger. Somehow she had to warn them, though she was convinced Kent would not let her out of his sight. She pulled off a shoe. "I must have this mended at once. See, the lining is torn; it hurts my foot."

"All right," Kent agreed after he had inspected it. "There's a shoe-mender opposite. I'll take you across to him."

Mimi shook her head.

"Not one inch can I walk. Bring him here and I will explain what is necessary."

Kent eyed her speculatively while his companion fetched the cobbler, an elderly man.

Speaking in English, Mimi showed him the shoe and opened her handbag. With a gesture of vexation she turned to Kent.

"Go up and ask Vernstein for the commission he owes me on the ring, please," she ordered. "I have no money."

Leaving Dan on guard, Kent went upstairs.

Instantly Mimi broke into rapid French, pointing to the shoe as if it were the subject of her conversation, but actually she was giving him a message for Reynolds saying she feared there was a bomb in his home, timed to, go off at midnight.

The old cobbler nodded and, pocketing the money that she slipped into his hand, promised to be back in a few minutes with the repair finished.

"What were you two gabbling about in French"? grumbled Dan.

"It was simpler for me to explain in his own language," the girl replied.

Her mind was easier now. One half of her problem had been solved. She felt sure that the old French man would deliver her message.

The cobbler brought back her shoe remarkably quickly.

"It is well it was only a small repair or I could not have done it to-night," he said, looking straight into Mimi's eye's. "I am just going out to do an important job. Good night."

"Don't think that you're leaving here," remarked Kent to Mimi when they were alone.

"If there is a woman in this house I think I will stay," she agreed at once.

"Vernstein's housekeeper sleeps here. She's a vile tempered woman but respectable."

"*Bon*! I will share her room. My temper also can be vile if required," Mimi remarked. She glanced at her watch, filled with fear for Mrs. Reynolds, in case anything went wrong with her message. "Take me to a telephone box at once."

Kent pulled on his overcoat.

"Off we go, baby. I'm sticking right beside you. Going to ring up your hairdresser?"

The light of battle was in Mimi's dark eyes. Courage had returned.

"No. I am going to ring up—*Zaldo*," she announced.

"Suits me fine. I shall hear all you say over the wire and I've always wanted to know that elusive brute's telephone number."

That was the last thing he would learn, Mimi reflected. Kent led the way down Gunner's Court and turned into the street.

Her heart was pounding when at last they entered the Tube station. With a surly expression Kent opened the door of a telephone booth, evidently intent to go inside first.

It must be now or never, Mimi thought. She stumbled, clutched wildly at his legs apparently to save herself and pulled him off his balance. In falling the man hit his head on the pavement and before he had recovered she asked for Reynolds's home telephone number. Kent staggered in and stood beside. her.

XVI. The Midnight Peril

Thursday evening

Mrs. Reynolds was in a restless mood. It was five minutes past seven, the daily maid had gone and the inspector wouldn't be home in all probability before half-past ten. He was nearly always late when working on a murder case. She was wondering whether she'd wash her hair or go to the movies when the telephone bell rang.

Lifting the receiver, she became engaged in a peculiar conversation.

"Who is there?" asked a voice that seemed: familiar.

"Mrs. Reynolds speaking. Is that you, Mimi?"

"Yes, Monsieur Zaldo. I thought you would recognise my voice," came the queer reply.

At once Mrs. Reynolds's brain leaped to the knowledge that the French girl wished to send her a message and could not speak openly.

"I understand, Mimi," she replied "I'll try to guess at your meaning. Go on"

"It is imperative that you go to the Dogs Home at once," Mimi continued.

Again the girl's seemingly cryptic, words were clear to Mrs. Reynolds. "The Dogs' Home" was her nickname for her husband's office at the Yard, and Mimi knew it quite well.

"I will do so," she promised. "Am I to give my husband a message?"

"No. You must wait there for him." Mimi's tone was urgent. "He knows the reason."

"I'll leave at once," Mrs. Reynolds replied firmly. "Don't worry about that. Take care of yourself. Are you all right?"

"Oh yes, thank you, Monsieur Zaldo. I am being well looked after," came Mimi's answer. "I will see you at dinner to-morrow night as we arranged. *Au 'voir.*"

An hour later Mrs. Reynolds was sitting comfortably before a big fire in her husband's office, engrossed in a book. The inspector, she learned, was at the late Mr. Carr's house. She had just decided not to disturb him when Dr. Tempest looked in.

"Hello, Mrs. Reynolds," he said. "I'm going to get through to your husband presently on the wire."

"When you do," she replied, "tell him I shall wait here until he fetches me to-night."

It was nearly nine o'clock when a constable came to her.

"There's an elderly Frenchman downstairs, ma'am," he said in worried tones, "who has made an extraordinary statement. Something about a bomb being in your house."

Mrs. Reynolds dropped her book.

"Bring him up at once, please," she begged. Presently the old cobbler was ushered in, and told her of his interview with Mimi.

"I ought to have been here long ago, madame," he explained, "but there was a breakdown in the Tube."

Mrs. Reynolds pressed some money into his hand and thanked him.

In a very short time the Highgate police had been notified and a Flying Squad car was racing towards her house.

*   *   *   *   *

Mimi replaced the receiver with a smile at Kent baffled expression.

"I'm sure you feel much better for hearing my conversation with Monsieur Zaldo," she observed.

"I shan't forget your side of it," was his reply. "Let's go back to supper."

"I'll buy some burgundy to put you in a good temper," Mimi told him.

The meal in Vernstein's sitting-room was scarcely festive. Vernstein was uneasy, despite the respectful courtesy that Mimi elected to show towards him.

Kent watched her furtively while he drank glass after glass of wine. She rewarded him by mocking banter, hoping to goad him into an outburst of temper. Anger often unlocked secrets. Mimi was not wasting her brilliant repartee and two good bottles of wine merely to give Kent a pleasant evening.

"So you think I'm a fool and know nothing of Zaldo's plans," burst from him at last.

"It would take more proof than you can give me to make me think otherwise," Mimi retorted. "You may have known about James Carr, but I wager that Zaldo has not told you what coup is arranged for to-night."

Her taunt melted the man's caution.

"To-night's affair I haven't heard of, unless you mean the Reynolds blow-up. But I know the affair that is to come off to-morrow night and the one after that too," he boasted. "And that's more than you do."

"Careful, Kent," Vernstein said warningly.

"He need not be," Mimi put in with a supercilious smile. "I helped to make the plans, and the final details Zaldo and I will discuss-at dinner to-morrow evening."

Kent glared at her and refilled his, glass.

"Oh, you will, eh? Then you can tell him I'm not going to tackle the caretaker single-handed. It's not do easy to chloroform a man as he thinks!"

This was the first definite information Mimi had been able to obtain. She must feel her way delicately, she decided, and try to draw Kent into giving details.

"I told Zaldo so and he promised that you should have—" She paused and affected to think "I forget who was selected."

"That fool Dan who was here to-night," Kent cut in bitterly. "All he's fit for is delivering 'apples.' When it comes to doping a man, he's a wash-out. Why doesn't Zaldo see us, separately if he likes, and give us his orders personally instead of sending 'em through that greasy skunk in the Square?"

Before Mimi could devise a question that might lead to the identity of the "greasy skunk" being revealed, Kent had darted off at another angle.

"Zaldo's taste changes quickly," he said with a wink. "You're dark and small. He's just fetched a red-headed bit from Paris on some job."

A pulse leaped in the girl's brain. Linda, with her red hair, who had been drawn to London by the mysterious advertisement! The "greasy skunk' in the Square must be Yates of the Select Employment Agency in Silver Square!   If so, into what dreadful trap had poor Linda fallen?

Mimi forced a confident smile to her lips as she took a long shot.

"Neither you nor Mr. F. Yates," she said distinctly, "knows very much.   Me, I am Zaldo's confidant, not his doll."

Kent drew the cork of the second bottle, replenished his glass and drained it at one gulp.

"Maybe I've been misjudging you, my girl," he said more cordially. He glanced at the old Jew who was nodding with sleep, and lowered his voice. "I don't mind admitting that I've got cold feet about to-morrow's job and the one after it. Robbery is one thing, but murder makes me sick. Yates says that if there's any risk about chloroforming the caretaker I'm to use a spanner. You know what that means!"

Mimi nodded gravely.

"Yes, and I think Zaldo is wrong" A wild plan came to her. "How would you like me to go with you? You can hold the man while I use the chloroform. I'm very strong and not at all afraid. What have you got to do when the caretaker is quiet?"

"Nothing," Kent grumbled. "Go home—if I'm lucky. Go to jail if I ain't. Say, kid, there's something in your idea. You've got brains. Unless Zaldo objects—"

"I shall not tell him when I dine with him," Mimi interrupted. "The chloroform business will not take long. When and where shall we meet?"

"Top of Villiers Street, Charing Cross, eleven-thirty sharp. Sure you can get away from Zaldo by then?"

Since her dinner engagement was with Linda and Stephen Blair, Mimi was able to say with perfect truth that she could be free at that hour. With every art known to her she tried unsuccessfully to obtain the name and address of the next night's victim. Kent had drunk enough to make him pleasant but not unwisely communicative.

She made a desperate essay in another direction.

"Tell me,' she asked Kent, "about Zaldo's new red-headed girl. Is he in love with her or is he only using her as a decoy?"

"I dunno," the man replied. "Yates says she's a beauty, proud as Lucifer and smart with her tongue. You must see her."

"I must," Mimi agreed quietly. There was terrible fear in her heart. What fiend of curiosity had made her urge Linda to reply to that diabolical advertisement and send the girl into this mess? To warn her was impossible; to guard her with a detective, dangerous. For if Zaldo suspected he would certainly kill Linda. "She's in her new job, of course?" Mimi asked.

Before Kent could reply the door opened and a swarthy-faced woman of heavy build came in.

"Here's your stable companion," he murmured under his breath.

The woman cast a furtive glance at Kent and Mimi. Then rousing the Jew she spoke to him in a rapid undertone.

"This is my housekeeper, Mimi," the old Jew explained. "She has prepared a small bed in her room for you."

Mimi beamed graciously at the woman and murmured a polite greeting, while her pulse raced with excitement. Vernstein's housekeeper fitted in with the description of the woman who had taken Mrs. Nunn's place last Tuesday!

Somehow, Mimi realised, she must contrive to let Inspector Reynolds know of her suspicion and give him the news that she had learned from Kent.

By midnight the woman was snoring heavily and the house was silent.

Creeping cautiously downstairs, Mimi let herself out and ran to the nearest telephone box. With anxiety in her heart she rang up Reynolds's private house. To her great relief he answered her call.

"Thanks to your wonderful help, all is well here," he said. "Total damage is that a shed in the garden has gone up! My wife dragged the case of apples out there before she knew what it really contained."

"The bomb went off before midnight then," Mimi observed over the wire.

"Probably owing to the jolting," Reynolds surmised. "Don't you think you'd better give up your dangerous experiment and come back, Mimi?"

"No," she said decisively. "Listen, monsieur." In brief, vivid words she told him what she had discovered and of her intention to take an active part in the affair with Kent.

"Please let two of your best observation men be at the top of Villiers Street at half-past eleven tomorrow night and follow me," she requested.

"I'll be there myself," Reynolds promised. "Be careful, Mimi."

"I'm now going back to Vernstein's," she told him with a gurgle of laughter. "Wish me *bon voyage*."

XVII. A Page From the Past

Friday morning

Linda awoke with the pleasant feeling that something nice was going to happen that day though she was too sleepy to remember exactly what it was.

She stretched her arms in drowsy content, switched on the light and looked at her watch. Half-past seven. No need to get up until her early tea arrived. Her duties in Mr. Wentworth's shop did not begin until nine-thirty. Very agreeable duties under a charming and courteous employer, she reflected.

Her mind drifted back over the past unhappy months when she had hidden herself in Paris, living precariously on her earnings from cabaret engagements and never losing the feeling of being hunted to earth.

That had ended from the moment she met Mimi at the Grey Rat in Montmartre. The little French girl had infused new life and spirit into her. If Mimi hadn't insisted she, Linda Marchant, would never have answered that queer advertisement, never have buried the past by obtaining this new delightful post.

Also, but for Mimi, she would probably never have known Stephen Blair or that irrepressible idiot, Nick Tyler.

Ah, that was the "something nice." She was to dine with Stephen Blair and Mimi that very evening. It would be lovely to see them both again. Mr. Blair had radiated an impression of steady kindliness and good humour on their one and only meeting in Montmartre. An author, he had told her he was. Anyhow, his personality was totally different from that of the maddening irresponsibility of Nick.

She compared the two men critically. In age, voice and appearance they were not unlike. The resemblance finished there. In temperament Stephen Blair seemed the epitome of everything sane and reliable. Whereas Nick Tyler was as changeable as a barometer and besides admitting himself to be a crook—which might or might not be true—he was undoubtedly employed by a very objectionable person called Yates.

Yates, Linda decided, was a dangerous man and the less she had to do with him and Nick, the safer she would be. And instantly caught herself wondering if Nick would call at the antique shop that day on some ridiculous pretext.

She checked herself angrily and was working out a thoroughly efficient snub for him when her tea, borne by the landlady, appeared.

"Morning, miss. It's a bit parky this morning. I'll light your gas stove before you get up."

"Thank you, Kate. How d'you like my room? I 'lifted its face' last evening and made new curtains and cushion covers."

Kate surveyed with approval the changes that her lodger had effected.

"It looks grand," she declared. "All the same, it's not half good enough for you, miss. A beautiful creature like you deserves a palace. I don't know what the men are thinking of to let you stay single."

The girl smiled.

"There's been no noticeable rush up to now. And anyhow a palace somehow sounds rather draughty. I'm much better off in this cosy room. It's a haven of comfort and peace after the miserable places that I lived in in Paris."

A haven of comfort and peace! The words sang in her brain while she dressed, and formed a rhythm as she walked along Kenford Street to catch a bus to her work.

Outside Baker Street station a hand touched her arm. She swung around, half expecting to see Nick Tyler.

The gay little rhythm died and was replaced by a feeling of cold misery as she saw who it was; saw for the first time how mean and shifty this man's eyes were, how weak and sensual his mouth and chin.

"What do you want, Dan?" she demanded, trying to control the panic that had seized her.

The man's lips parted in a sneering smile.

"So this is how you keep your promise, eh, Linda?"

"I kept it and nearly starved," she retorted. "There was no reason why I should be exiled for ever, Dan. Even if I am in London, I am still capable of holding my tongue. Besides, the affair is dead and forgotten."

"It might easily be dug up, and you'd be the means of putting a rope round my neck if they got you as a witness and you said a bit too much."

"Innocent men are not hanged in this country." Linda tried to speak reassuringly, to comfort herself as much as the man. "You were innocent, weren't you?" she asked in a breathless whisper.

"Course I was, but that confounded chemist could cause a lot of trouble if you were found and the case re-opened. The verdict said that old Gillingham died from an accidental overdose of a sleeping drug."

"Accidental!" The girl shivered. "At first I believed you. Now I often wonder and worry about it all. Does a man ever take even a small dose of sleeping mixture when he is in his office in the City? Surely he would wait until he went home. And in any case Mr. Gillingham's heart was in too bad a state for him to risk taking such drugs."

"A bottle of veranox tablets was found in the pocket of his overcoat that was hanging up in his office."

"Yes, but I never saw him wear that overcoat all the time I worked as his secretary." She reminded the man. "Also it was a bottle of veranox that you bought from that chemist the night before."

"Thousands of bottles are sold of that brand. All would have been well if you hadn't been fool enough to come into the shop. Your red hair is so darned conspicuous."

"I've told you before that it was raining and I had no umbrella, Dan. You were the fool to tell the chemist that the tablets were for me! I was staggered when he told me to be careful not to take more than two."

"He was just closing his shop," Dan retorted, "and would have refused to serve me if I hadn't said they were for my fiancée. He wouldn't have cared about my neuralgia."

"And I shouldn't have cared if you hadn't made me go back to Mr. Gillingham's office soon after to fetch my umbrella. The rain had stopped by then." A tragic look came into the girl's blue eyes. "You picked up the little bottle of indigestion tablets he always kept on his desk and asked when and how many he took. I told you four or five after luncheon and dinner in a little brandy and water. You knew that he came back there nearly every evening after dining to do an hour or two of quiet work alone."

"Are you daring to suggest that I put some tablets of veranox into that bottle of indigestion tablets on his desk so that he would take them by accident?" the man blustered angrily.

"I am not saying so, Dan, but a jury might say there was strong circumstantial evidence against you, as you are aware. You had both time and opportunity to do it and slip the veranox bottle into his overcoat pocket while I was in the other office. You know that, else you wouldn't have made me swear to leave London and tell no one my address. "

The man nodded gloomily.

"Yes, it might have put me in a horrible hole. Lucky you overslept the next morning and that old Gillingham's clerk telephoned to tell you what had happened."

"It was strange that I overslept," Linda corrected. "Dan, did you drug the coffee I had that night?"

Any previous doubt she had held changed to certainty as she saw the man's expression. The shifty eyes were glinting with malice while his lips parted in a forced smile.

"You're imagining a lot of nonsense, my dear. What reason could I have for doing that?"

"None, unless you wanted to be sure that I was out of the way next morning and therefore need not be called as a witness at the inquest. How's your brother?"

The man gave a short laugh, considerably relieved that she had changed the subject.

"You're thinking of another sweetie, my girl. I never had a brother. Expect you to wonder why I'm up so early. I've been living in Baker Street, but this morning I had a row with my landlady and have cleared out. I've just dumped my luggage in the cloakroom before I take it along to rooms I know of nearer the City. Where are you staying?"

So he was leaving this district, Linda thought with thankfulness. At all costs he mustn't find out her address.

"I'm living near Kensal Rise," she invented hurriedly. "Nobody knows me in those parts, Dan."

"I'll come and see you—soon. There was an ominous note in his voice.

"As you please," she agreed with apparent indifference. "Though surely it would be wiser if we didn't meet again. You know I'll hold my tongue and we agreed to end everything before I went to Paris."

"I'm going to *see* that you hold your tongue. Remember that if I'm caught you'll be arrested too. Holding back information is a serious offence, Linda. Well sink or swim together. You're a spitfire but I'm fonder of you than I am of any other girl, so we'll begin again. Have you got a job?"

She fought down her alarm.

"I have one in view. What are you doing?"

"Working for a continental company, all sorts. of jobs. The last was delivering fruit. The pay is good though: enough for two, Linda," he added with a smirk.

"Thanks, Dan, but I like independence. Also," she said boldly, "before I shared a man's money I should want to be certain that it was earned honestly."

"You mean that I'm not straight, not good enough for your ladyship," he sneered.

"No man who threatens a woman is good enough for me, Dan. Also, you have a bad memory. Long ago you told me that you had a young brother who had once worked for Mr. Gillingham and had got into a bit of trouble over money he'd taken. You said Mr. Gillingham could ruin him as he refused to part with your brother's written confession that was locked in his safe. You asked me to let you have the keys of the safe, for your brother's sake. Naturally I refused."

"It was my cousin," the man interposed hastily. "You must have misunderstood me."

"There was no mistake on my part, Dan. In those days I loved and trusted you and was sorry for your young brother. So, although I wouldn't give you the keys, about a week before Mr. Gillingham died I opened his safe. There were no papers of any description there! Nothing but precious stones that seemed to me to be very valuable. That is why I wonder now if your present job is straight."

"You needn't, my dear." The man caught her arm. "Look here, let's go. I've some urgent business, and you're coming with me. After that we'll go to your nest at Kensal Rise and talk things over."

"I'm afraid you will think me mercenary," she said, fencing for time, "but why should I bother about you if you're hard up? Delivering fruit isn't exactly lucrative, is it? Perhaps you were only bluffing."

Her eyes went beyond him desperately, and twisting sideways, she made a signal that he did not see.

"Bluffing, eh!" He pulled a roll of notes from his pocket. "Look at this!"

Linda took the notes from him and let them fall apart from her fingers, praying that she had timed her action correctly.

With an angry curse Dan scrambled to pick them up as they fluttered along the pavement.

And at that moment Linda slipped into the taxicab that she had signalled.

"Drive anywhere. Fast as you can," she gasped to the driver.

The man let in his gear with a crash and swung off into the traffic.

"Leave it to me, lady," he called over his shoulder.

Linda drew a long breath as the taxi darted through the streets. She was quite sure now that Dan was a thief, if not something worse. If he had drugged her coffee that night he could easily have obtained the office keys from her bag and gone back to see whether Mr. Gillingham had already swallowed the drug.

She continued that chain of reasoning. Had Dan found Mr. Gillingham dead he might have stolen the key of the safe and taken all or some of the jewels that she had seen there.

The only report of the inquest that she had seen before her flight to Paris had made no mention of robbery. Somehow she must find out if Mr. Gillingham's safe had contained jewels after his death.

Then, if Dan found her and became an active danger, she too would have a weapon of defence.

XVIII. BLACKMAIL!

Friday morning

Mr. Yates wasn't feeling at all well.

He had had two or three ticklish bits of business to arrange yesterday which might easily have landed him in gaol had they gone awry. To forget his worries he had made a night of it and was now paying the penalty with the usual violent headache and rather more than the usual irritability.

The sight of his morning mail lying on the floor of the Select Employment Bureau office brought no soothing balm to his frayed nerves. He guessed only too well what the envelopes contained.

His guess was correct. The post yielded half a dozen bills, with imperious attachments indicating that they were for the third and last time of asking, and a circular full of ideas on how to treble one's income.

The suggestion was unfortunate for Mr. Yates's hope of tranquility. Already he had worked himself up to boiling point comparing the risks he ran with the money he received. This circular assured him that any man with intelligence could make big money safely and honestly.

That being so, by the simplest process of logic Yates decided that with his superlative brain plus the will to make money *dishonestly*, he ought to be receiving considerably more than he was given now from his mysterious employer, Zaldo.

For over three years Yates had been Zaldo's confidential agent and go-between. Yet only once had he ever met him!

That occasion had been at their initial interview in the private sitting-room of a Paris hotel. The future employer had sat in a dark corner, with his hat on and muffled to the eyes, while Mr. Yates had wriggled uneasily under a strong electric light and succession of pointed questions as to his past career.

Zaldo seemed to know all about Mr. Yates' periods of seclusion behind prison bars. Embezzlement and confidence trickster jobs had been his downfall. Apparently they were references for the work Zaldo required of him.

"This is the first, and will probably be the last time we shall meet, Yates," he had said, "though I shall be watching you closely. I will pay you a salary with bonus for special jobs. My orders will reach you by telephone or letter. You will obey them implicitly. Any disloyalty or trickery on your part will be severely punished."

Hence this flat in Silver Square, which was also his business office. Hence too, as work increased, his staff of Nick Tyler and young Wentworth who were used for outside duties.

Wentworth had been sent to him by Zaldo with credentials stating that he was the worthless nephew of old Keble Wentworth, the connoisseur. The report added that the young man had been caught cheating at cards in London clubs and was a weak fool.

"His services are to be retained, but he is not to be allotted work requiring tact and skill," Zaldo had written.

Nick Tyler was Yates's own selection, and supplied the tact and skill lacking in Wentworth junior. Yates had sufficient evidence locked away in his safe concerning Tyler's past to feel reasonably sure of the whip hand over this astute and illusive assistant.

Until recently Mr. Yates had run straight with his employer. Then, having some cash and leisure, he had proceeded to multiply both by wild card speculations. Within a few months only the leisure remained and an increasing pile of bills. No further financial aid would be granted by Zaldo, he knew.

Therefore Mr. Yates was seriously considering a little private business, known in the vernacular as "double crossing," to supply the tiresome deficit in his banking account. That such a venture was highly dangerous if discovered by Zaldo he was fully aware.

Mr. Yates's fertile brain was being severely taxed in finding a method that was foolproof. Last night, in a flash of inspiration, the method came to him: blackmail! The same flash revealed the possible object of his intentions: a gentleman with a sticky reputation known as Dan, one of Zaldo's outside men.

Kent, the American, and Vernstein, the Jew fence in Gunner's Court, were also employed by Zaldo, but to Mr. Yates they were little more than names. He had sent them messages but rarely had personal contact with them. Dan was the only one of the gang whom he knew well and it was Dan he was waiting for now, having sent him a peremptory message last night.

Where was the fellow? Yates demanded irritably. It was nearly a quarter to ten and he didn't want Tyler butting in on the interview.

The jarring note of the telephone bell made jump.

"Mr. Yates speaking. Who's that?" he snapped

"Morning, lovie. This is the one and only Nick Tyler calling," came across the wire. "You don't sound your normal sweet self. Suffering from 'hang over,' I suspect."

"What in blazes do you want?" rapped his employer. "I'm busy, and shall be all morning."

"A most unusual state of affairs but one that happens to suit me," Nick replied amiably. "Don't forget to take your Glaxo at eleven. Bye-bye."

That ensured freedom from Tyler's shrewd eyes anyhow, Yates reflected. He banged down the receiver and turned to see the grinning face of his expected visitor.

"You're late, Dan. I said half-past nine," he observed in a testy tone.

Dan strolled across the room, helped himself generously to a drink and sat down in an easy chair.

"Did you, indeed! What makes you think you can order me about, Yates?" He flicked a finger towards the telephone. "Had a row with your bird over the wire, I suppose, and think you'll take it out on me. Well, I happen to have just had a row with my bird, so that makes us quits." Dan clenched his jaw as the memory of his meeting with Linda returned and the ease with which she had slipped away in the taxi. "Also, at half-past eight this morning I had a first-class scene with my landlady and she told me to get out at once. So I'm in no mood for any of your funny stuff."

Yates swallowed his temper with difficulty. It was too early to quarrel with Dan.

"Where are you going to stay?" he asked. "I must make a note of your new address."

"Think I'll move in here with you; for a time anyhow," Dan replied coolly. "I may be getting married soon."

"Didn't know you had a regular girl. You'd better be careful. Women talk."

"This one won't," Dan asserted. "She daren't. D'you get me?"

Yates showed his teeth in a mirthless smile.

"I get you. Cunning brute, aren't you?" Dan's taste in girls was pretty good, he reflected. If this visitor stayed here the girl might be calling to see him. Also there would be a chance to search Dan's luggage and perhaps verify his own suspicions. "Well, I don't mind your sharing the flat for a bit if you pay your whack. Nice and handy for your girl to come in and see you too, when you make up your quarrel. What's she like?"

Unfortunately Dan knew Yates's taste in girls also; likewise his predatory instincts.

"Not much to look at," he said firmly, "but she suits me. Our row will soon blow over. She wouldn't come here, even if it were wise. I'll get my bags from Baker Street station right away. So long, Yates."

"Half a minute. Did you take the case of 'apples' to that flattie's address in Highgate last night?"

"Yes. Is that all you wanted me to come here for at half-past nine this morning?"

"Not all," Yates told him. "You're due to work with Kent to-night, aren't you?"

"Due or not due, no chloroform jobs for me," Dan stated. "I'd rather cut the whole business and go abroad. If the caretaker's got a weak heart he may die if we give him a drop too much of the stuff. And that would mean the rope trick with a tolling bell."

"You weren't so squeamish when you put veranox into Gillingham's bottle of indigestion tablets, were you?" Yates asked with a sneer. "By the way, it was odd that Zaldo found Gillingham's safe half emptied of jewels. I wonder who'd been there first."

"I neither know nor care," Dan answered with elaborate indifference. "I put the tablets in, and came away an hour before Gillingham went back to his office that night."

"How do you know what time he went there if you came away?" Yates's voice was silky.

"I don't, of course. It was only a guess."

"It would have been easy for you to have gone back again before Zaldo was due, wouldn't it?" pursued Yates. "You had the office keys from Gillingham's secretary."

"She and I left the office together about eight o'clock. I was with her until quite late. Look here, Yates, you can't fasten anything on me. I've got an alibi. That girl could prove I was in her room until nearly midnight."

"A girl must be really fond of you, Dan, to give away her reputation like that!" Yates gibed. "I never saw Gillingham's secretary. I must meet her and hear her story. Where is she now?"

A hunted look came into Dan's eyes. He must be very wary. Yates evidently was on the track of something. It meant blackmail if he found out the truth! At all costs Linda's identity must be kept out of it, for she would say, with truth, that Dan had not been in her room for more than a quarter of an hour. If only he had not suggested staying in Yates's flat! To back out now would show that he was afraid.

"How on earth should I know where she is?" he told Yates. "I don't keep a record of the movements of every girl I meet casually. Though I daresay I could find her if ever I needed an alibi. Which I don't. Sure I shan't be crowding you too much if I park here?"

"Not at all. I'm delighted, my boy," Yates replied warmly. "That's a smart suit you're wearing. Bet you didn't get it for a tenner."

"A Jew tailor made it very cheaply," said Dan, telling himself that he must rip the Savile Row label off before Yates spotted it.

"You might give me his address. A cheap tailor who can cut as well as that is a find." Yates's eyes hardened to artful slits "I'll see about finding Gillingham's secretary. By the way, Dan, I'm short of cash. You can lend me the thirty pounds Vernstein paid you for delivering the 'apples.'"

Dan hesitated for a moment. Then, with an inward groan, he handed over the roll of money that he had thrown to Linda. Yates had begun his blackmail tricks!

Mr. Yates rubbed his hands contentedly when Dan had gone. Jew tailor indeed! That suit had cost twelve guineas at least, and Dan's earnings did not justify that expenditure.

His suspicions about Dan were undoubtedly grounded on fact. If he had not taken jewels from Gillingham's safe and double-crossed Zaldo, he would never have parted with all that money so easily now.

The only delicate problem that harassed Yates mind was whether it would pay him better to inform Zaldo of what he had discovered, or blackmail Dan and keep quiet.

There was no necessity to trouble about finding Gillingham's secretary. That was merely a useful threat to frighten Dan. In any case the girl was probably hundreds of miles away by this time.

Mr. Yates treated himself to a nice little drink, ignorant of the fact that Gillingham's secretary was the

Linda Marchant whom, by Zaldo's orders, he had enticed to England and placed in Keble Wentworth's. shop.

XIX. NICK PAYS A CALL

Friday morning

As the crow flies Linda Marchant was not more than a mile from Yates's office and trying hard to forget her disturbing encounter with Dan.

It was fairly easy to do so in the peaceful atmosphere of the antique shop. Mr. Wentworth had told her that she could arrange the furniture and china as she liked. She was taking advantage of that permission this morning, partly to give herself no time to worry about Dan, partly to please her new employer who was so considerate.

The shop door opened with its preliminary tinkle of the bell and he came in.

"Good morning, Miss Marchant. Hard at work, I see." He glanced round appreciatively. "A very charming effect. Don't do too much though. You ought not to move the heavy pieces of furniture alone. You should get the charwoman to help you. Isn't she here?"

Linda shook her head.

"I'm sorry to say that I was a quarter of an hour late this morning, Mr. Wentworth. It shan't happen again. I'm afraid the charwoman was tired of waiting for me. She wasn't here when I arrived."

Mr. Wentworth smiled at the girl's confession.

"It is more probable that she never came at all. She's unpunctual and lazy. I think we'll try another woman who applied to me yesterday."

"With all these valuable things about I should be afraid to allow strangers to work in the place if it were mine." Linda's voice had a worried note in it. "I can't think why you took me on trust."

"Can't you? Well, put it down to my vanity, Miss Marchant. I like to pretend that I'm a clever judge of character."

"All the same, I think it is dangerous for you to be so trustful of me—and everyone," Linda said impulsively. Remembering Nick Tyler's words about the locked cabinets at the back of the shop, she felt she must warn this guileless man whose old-world ideas were more aged than his years warranted.

"I wouldn't rob you; you've been too good to me," she hurried on. "But—but other people may not be so scrupulous. Please be careful."

There was a cryptic expression on the connoisseur's face as he looked at the girl.

"Don't be uneasy, my child," he said gently. "I'm not such a simple old fool as I appear to be. I don't trust everyone. Still," he paused and gazed straight into her vivid blue eyes, "I do trust you. You strongly resemble someone whom I knew long ago. I think you may be like her in character and disposition. Tell me, are your parents alive?"

Linda's cheeks crimsoned. Bitterly she regretted the promise to impose upon her confiding employer's credulity and tell him the concocted fable concerning her supposed parentage. To appeal to Yates to release her from that promise would be useless. He could even show Mr. Wentworth the contract she had signed, agreeing to give Yates all that she received in return for five pounds weekly! She was certain now that Yates had evil designs on her employer's valuables.

Dare she throw herself on Mr. Wentworth's mercy and confess the trick that Yates had played to get her, into the shop? No, for not only would that betray Yates, but Mr. Wentworth would naturally feel he could never trust her again. That meant a repetition of the misery she had endured in Paris, without work, home, money or friends.

There was no way out. All she could do was to obey Yates's orders, and try her utmost to guard Mr.

Wentworth's safety and interests. Perhaps, indeed, she could serve him best by staying here, even if it involved deception.

No," she replied at last, thankful that this reply at least was truthful, "my parents died long ago."

"Do you resemble your mother or your father?" Again she could give an honest answer.

"They both died when I was very young, but the woman who brought me up said that I was like my mother."

The old connoisseur looked at her for a second and then turned away.

"Forgive me if I seem to be curious, Miss Marchant. What was her maiden name? I am—"

The shop bell rang violently before he could finish his sentence. Never had Linda welcomed an interruption more.

"Please, sir, can you change a pound note?" asked a boy.

Before that transaction had ended a customer had called to see Mr. Wentworth and the embarrassing conversation was over.

Shortly after eleven o'clock he approached her again.

"I may not be back again to-day, Miss Marchant," he said. "Should any client call on business that you find difficult to deal with, ask him to come in again to-morrow morning and see me about it. Lock up and go to your luncheon at one o'clock. And leave a little earlier to-night. You look tired. Good day."

Linda watched the connoisseur go. She felt a queer sense of loneliness that brought a rush of tears to her eyes. She appreciated his reserved manners and gentle courtesy, and longed to protect him from dangers that she was sure he never dreamed of. With all her heart she prayed that Dan might never find out where she was employed, or the locked cabinets at the back of this shop might be rifled as Mr. Gillingham's safe was!

If only she could confide in someone wise and understanding! Dare she tell Mimi everything and ask her advice? No, for complete confession would involve Dan and Yates. Perhaps even Tyler.

The door bell rang and a small boy entered, bearing a tray covered with a cloth.

"What's this?" she asked, as he put it on a table.

"Gent told me to bring it here, miss. Said he'd be coming along presently," the boy told her.

"Herewith kindly receive gent in person," remarked a man's voice brightly. "Good morning, Miss Marchant. I hope I see you well."

"If you don't, Mr. Tyler, you should wear spectacles," she retorted. "What are you doing here? Are you out of work or is espionage part of your routine?"

Nick put his head on one side and studied her solemnly.

"Health excellent, I observe; temper a trifle frayed. As for your kind inquiries about myself, I am happy to assure you that my sight is keen enough to observe signs of recent tears in your eyes and a high polish on your charming nose."

Linda made an indignant exclamation.

"Also," her tormentor continued, "I am neither out of work nor engaged in spying. Every working man gets a half day. This is mine."

"The morning is an unusual time for a half day off, isn't it?" Linda's tone was sceptical.

"All the best gentlemen crooks work late at night. In my dishonourable profession we take our well-earned leisure early in the day."

"I regret that I can't work up a suitable feeling of gratitude at being honoured by your spending your spare time with me, Mr. Tyler."

"You needn't bother. My appearance here is due solely to my kind heart."

The girl raised her eyebrows.

"Really! It is so well camouflaged that no one would know about it," she said acidly.

"Still sore that I mentioned your shiny nose, I see! No, madam, strange though it may seem, my benevolence is not being strained for your sake." He lowered his voice. "Percy is homesick."

"Percy?" .

"Percy." He produced the jade elephant from his pocket. "He's off his feed and moping badly. There seemed nothing else to do but bring him back here and tempt his appetite in his native haunts. Come along to the other end of the shop where he can get a tasty snack in peace. Here, you may carry him for a treat."

He lifted the tray and Linda followed him, protesting that Mr. Wentworth might return at any minute and what would he say at such unorthodox behaviour?

"He would say," Nick replied, "My dear Mr. Tyler, how kind of you to devote your time to training my rather raw assistant. She means well but is painfully ignorant. Come in as often as you can and give her a few easy lessons in general knowledge."

"You must be, a great comfort to yourself, Mr. Tyler. I've always wondered what a superiority complex was like. Now I know."

Nick poured out two cups of coffee and placed one before her.

"Have a sandwich?" he invited. "Percy can't eat until you do."

"I won't have a sandwich and I resent your abusive manners," Linda said irritably, and stirred her coffee. It had a fragrant smell, the sandwiches looked delicious, and she was hungry. "I've said no and I mean it," she added, pushing away the plate that he offered her.

"All right, lady. As you wish. If you won't eat, will you kindly open your face wide enough to admit a cigarette."

Her lips parted and closed upon a sandwich which Nick thrust into her mouth.

"And that," he said with a pleased smile, "is how the trick is done. I hope you'll give Percy a good home and make him happy. No, don't try to thank me; wait until your mouth is empty, I implore you."

"Anyhow, I'm not going to take that piece of absurdity that you call Percy," she said a little later when the coffee and sandwiches were finished.

"Indeed, you are. He never really loved me. Also," Nick lighted two cigarettes and put one between her lips, "incredible as it may seem, I always pay my gambling debts. You see, even the worst of us can still retain a shred of honesty."

Linda looked at him and was silent

"Go on, say it," he urged. "Or if you don't like to hurt my feelings, I'll say it for you. You're thinking that I'm maddening and rather fascinating because you can't understand whether I'm as bad as I appear to be. You wish that you'd never met me, and are glad I came this morning when you were unhappy and worried about something."

"Just that," Linda confessed. "Add also that I wonder what was the real object of your visit."

"Since we're being frank with each other, I'll tell you." Nick's eyes held a curious expression. "A desire to 'snoop' in general, and a greater desire to know in particular what Mr. Keble Wentworth keeps in the locked cabinets behind you. There was a third wish too that I won't bore you with," he added lightly.

Her lip curled.

"Hence this tray of coffee and sandwiches as excuse to call."

"No. I'd had no breakfast, happened to be hungry and thought it would be fun to bait you for a while. I love to see you get thoroughly angry with me. It's the easiest game I've ever played."

"A true sportsman!" the girl commented. "I expect you shoot tame rabbits when you're in need of real fun."

"That's an idea I hadn't thought of. Thanks, I'll try it one day. Let's get back to the subject of the cabinets. What's inside 'em, Linda?"

"If I knew I wouldn't tell you." There was a note of anxiety in her voice. "Why do you ask? Is it merely idle curiosity?"

"Curiosity of the most active variety," he assured her seriously. "After all, why should one man have a monopoly of riches that would keep me and a hundred others for years? I wouldn't rob a poor soul, but Mr. Wentworth is wealthy and I live by my wits. I warned you, but you didn't believe me, did you?

The girl stood up, her eyes wide with fear.

"You mean that, given the opportunity, you would take the jewels or whatever he has in those cabinets?" she demanded.

"I certainly would. What are you going to do about it, Linda? Ring up Scotland Yard and tell them that you've a potential thief here? Go ahead. I'll promise not to run away."

Suddenly he saw the colour drain from her cheeks, heard incoherent phrases tumbling from her trembling lips.

"The second time—the second. No, no I can't go through it again," she murmured brokenly.

"Sit down, Linda, and pull yourself together," he ordered, "or you'll be telling me things you don't want me to know."

His crisp tone braced her to self-control.

"Sorry I frightened you, my child," he went on. "But we were being frank with each other and I don't want you to have any pretty illusions about me. I think you must have come in contact with a lot of soft and rotten characters in your time. I like 'em a bit hard myself. They're safer. In all the best detective fiction the 'crook' usually turns out to be the gallant hero in the end, chivalrous to the point of nausea. I'd rather you thought too ill than too well of me, do you understand?"

"Yes. Thanks for being straight with me, Nick. I was a fool to crack up in that hysterical fashion. There was a reason though."

"I gathered that from your words. Now listen clearly. *There will be no second time* for you to worry about. Whatever happens, I promise that you shall not be involved in it in any way. Does that help?"

She nodded.

"A great deal. It's of no use begging you to give up this horrible wish to rob my employer," she said. "You're a determined man and are probably working for a gang. Maybe it's wicked of me, but I won't betray you to Mr. Wentworth. I'm not even sure that he would believe me."

"I know the rest, Linda," Nick interrupted softly. "You're rather a wonderful girl in case no one has ever told you so."

"Wait until I've finished and you may not think so," she replied. "I won't warn either the police or Mr. Wentworth, but, Nick Tyler, with all my power I'll try to circumvent you and protect my employer's property."

"Good!" Nick applauded. "That's the spirit! Attaboy! And now that the nice distinctions of our friendship and enmity are defined, you shall pay your gambling debt and dine with me to-night."

"It's impossible. I have an engagement."

He raised an eyebrow in comic despair.

"That's a pity. I'd set my mind on having dinner with you to-night. Ask me to join your party. You'd better agree. I'm an obstinate hound."

"That makes two of us," Linda flashed back. "I'm equally obstinate."

"All right," Nick agreed in crestfallen accents. "Anyhow please take Percy with you to-night, and tell me what you're going to wear."

She dropped the tiny jade object into her handbag.

"It's only a simple dinner party. I shall probably wear a plain dark green frock, if it interests you to know," she replied.

Nick picked up his hat.

"It does. Good morning."

XX. Mimi Scores a Trick

Friday morning

Mimi thanked her stars that she happened to be wearing a smart dress. Despite the nature of her work, she was wholly feminine by nature and to have met Stephen Blair and Linda that evening in garments a trifle worn would have spoilt the dinner for her.

Clad now in a clumsy dressing-gown lent to her by Vernstein's housekeeper, she examined her limited wardrobe. Piquant velvet cap made by a good Paris milliner, black cloth coat with Persian lamb collar in the latest style, black charmeuse frock designed by an artist friend and cut with a line that showed her dainty figure to advantage, neat shoes and fine silk stockings.

The result was satisfactory. She bought very few clothes, but always they were of the best quality and made in a style to suit her particular type.

When she wore them correctly she presented an expensive effect of *chic insouciance*. But, by a jerk of her hat and a slouching adjustment of her coat that effect could be altered at her will to produce a very different appearance It was a quick change Inspector Reynolds knew and marvelled at. It was one which Detective-Sergeant Jenkins did not know. Indeed, on their way to Vernstein's house yesterday day he had grumbled at her for being too smart when he himself was in the garb of a working man.

With an impudent grin she had turned her back for a few seconds. He was startled when she faced him again. Gone was the trim Párisienne. In her place was a slovenly looking little creature in ill-fitting apparel with her hat perched at an out-of-date angle.

She laughed inwardly now as she thought of Jenkins's surprised face, and of her plea of poverty to Vernstein and Kent while she was wearing a coat that had cost two thousand good French francs.

She drank the coffee which the housekeeper brought, demanded a hot iron to press her frock and proceeded to make a leisurely toilette. There was much to be thought about and the less time she spent downstairs with Vernstein and Kent the safer would she be from their awkward questions. They were both astute and suspicious, particularly Kent. The best way to throw them off their guard was to do the unexpected thing and stay upstairs.

There was a lot that she wanted to find out about them, but still more that she didn't intend them to find out about her. Her information could only be obtained by going down and watching every opportunity to spy and listen. Yet undue haste on her part might wreck her chance. At all costs she must find out the name and address of to-night's victim.

At noon the housekeeper came to her again.

"Aren't you dressed yet?" she asked. "Mr. Vernstein and Mr. Kent keep asking for you. Perhaps they want to see you on business."

"My compliments and say that I do not want to see them either on business or pleasure," Mimi replied. She handed the woman a slip of paper and some money. "Get me these things quickly and bring me a lot of hot water, please."

The woman read the list aloud.

"Toothbrush, sponge, powder, lipstick, cigarettes.' Special kinds too There are no smart shops near here and I've my work to do. What's the hot water for?"

"To wash my hair," Mimi explained. "If you are busy, tell the lazy Monsieur Kent to go. I need a quiet day. I am dining out to-night and have important matters to think about now. *Allez!*"

A few minutes later the woman returned with the hot water.

"Mr. Kent's gone out to buy what you want and a fine fuss he made about it too," she told the girl. "I can't waste any more time. I must go out and buy the dinner."

Mimi shampooed her hair quickly and then waited on the landing until she heard the housekeeper leave the house.

"Mr. Vernstein," she called out, "may I come down and dry my hair by the fire, please?"

The old Jew assented amiably. He felt almost fatherly towards the quaint little figure that appeared in a borrowed dressing-gown with a towel round her dripping hair.

"Where is Kent?" she asked timidly.

Vernstein chuckled.

"Doing your errands, much against his will. Come and sit on the rug, my dear. You're shivering." Mimi gave him an innocent smile.

"I'm glad we're alone, Mr. Vernstein. I don't like Kent very much. He thinks he is clever and knows more than you do." She curled up against the old Jew's knee and gazed into his face confidingly. "You have brains!"

Mr. Vernstein stroked his beard and beamed at the compliment.

"Kent tells me that you're dining with Zaldo to-night. A great honour, eh? But will you be able to get away in time to help Kent on the caretaker job?"

"I'll manage it," the girl promised. Suddenly she saw a chance to learn something. "In case I'm delayed by Zaldo, would it be quicker if I went direct to the place to-night? I arranged to meet Kent at the top of Villiers Street at half past eleven."

"It might save time," the Jew admitted. "Where are you meeting Zaldo?" he asked with a cunning smile.

"Dear Mr. Vernstein, I dare not tell you that." Mimi appeared troubled. "However, I can say it is not far from our job to-night. You know London so well. Please tell me my best way to get there from Piccadilly Circus. I can't afford a taxi." She held her breath in suspense while awaiting the Jew's reply.

"Good girl not to waste money," he said. "You could go by Tube."

He paused and Mimi's heart beat as she heard a key being inserted in the front door.

"I think a bus would be simpler," he went on. "Take one that goes along the Strand and get out at Harrington Street. Walk down there and take the second street on the left. You can't miss the place. It's a new block of flats painted grass green."

Mimi thanked him in a casual tone, her brain already leaping to the next move.

"Better not tell Kent that you've asked my advice about to-night, Mimi. He's got a nasty nature."

No suggestion could have suited her purpose better.

"I'll slip upstairs before he comes," she said.

In the bedroom she pondered over the problem before her. She knew roughly the address of tonight's victim. With skill she might find out his name or at least the number of his flat. The more knowledge she paraded before Kent, the more frankly he might talk on this subject.

It was nearly two o'clock when she strolled downstairs. Kent was finishing his meal.

"You have bought what I needed, yes?" she asked, helping herself to a fillet of plaice.

"Yes. Very much the fine lady, aren't you?" he growled. "Coming down at this hour indeed!"

"Mimi is my guest," the Jew said sternly.

Kent looked from Vernstein to the girl speculatively.

"You two seem very friendly all at once," he remarked.

"Not at all." Mimi's smile was disarmingly sweet. "We have known each other a long time."

"Are you funking the job to-night?" Kent inquired in an anxious tone as the Jew left them alone.

"Funking? It means afraid, I think." Mimi moved her finger to and fro. "I am not afraid, Kent. I meet you outside the place instead of Villiers Street?"

"You could if you knew the address," the man jeered. "But you don't, and I'm not going to tell you. Who knows, you might run to Scotland Yard with the news!"

"Let me think." Mimi contemplated the ceiling, ignoring his words. "My best way will be to take a bus along the Strand and walk down Harrington Street. Second turning on right, the new block of flats. In this smoky London I am afraid the bright, green paint will soon become soiled."

"You've already seen the place!" Kent exclaimed in surprise.

"Why not? Zaldo trusts me more than you do. Is the elevator at to-night's job working? "she chanced.

"Not yet, I'm told. That won't matter. The flat Zaldo wants is on the first floor and stairs are safer."

"Of course. No lift-man to notice too much." She glanced at Kent warily. "Of course you know the victim's name."

"No, I don't," he answered. "All I know is that he only moved in yesterday. Lucky for him if he goes out to-night and stays out until Zaldo's got what he wants."

"Have you seen the caretaker?" It was a vital question and much rested on the reply.

"No, I wish I had," Kent grumbled. "He maybe a heavy weight. Those chaps often are."

"Don't be alarmed," Mimi replied in comforting tones. "I have seen him. You will find that he is thin and not especially strong," she added, remembering Jenkins's build. "Of course you know his name?"

"He's called Quayle, but with any luck we shan't be on chatting terms with him, Mimi."

The girl laughed.

"I'm always lucky. Cheer up. I'm going for a long walk this afternoon."

"And I'm going to sleep," Kent said with a yawn. "You won't fail me to-night?"

"*Certainement* I will not."

"Thanks, Mimi. I wish you'd meet me at Villiers Street as we arranged first."

"All right," the girl agreed.

Her heart danced with joy as she walked down Gunner's Court. What did it matter now where she met Kent? She was free and had obtained news of tremendous importance. How best to make use of it was the decision that now had to be made.

Half-way along the street that lay at the bottom of Gunner's Court she caught sight of Jenkins, faithfully keeping guard in case she needed him.

Without a sign of recognition he followed her to the Tube station.

"Everything goes marvelously," she said when they met.

Hurriedly she related what she had discovered, and gave him his instructions.

"Two of Inspector Reynolds's men will follow me from Villiers Street to-night," she added.

"Aren't you going to tell him everything?" inquired Jenkins.

"If I do, he will certainly stop your part!" she replied. "Also, if he acts too soon, we may miss the big coup. I want to get Zaldo himself."

"Perhaps you'd like the sun, moon and stars as well. I'd feel easier, Mimi, if the inspector knew." Jenkins sighed heavily. "I've got a delicate stomach and even the smell of chloroform makes me sick."

"Then," retorted Mimi, "don't eat too much dinner."

XXI. Mimi's Problem

Friday

Inspector Reynolds was worried. Patient work, long hours, ingenuity, intuition all seemed to be in vain although he had called upon them to the point of physical and mental exhaustion.

Summing up the situation, the facts were that a clever criminal had a mania for robbing and, if necessary, killing jewel collectors, and a peculiar vanity for leaving his trademark by stamping the crime as being committed at midnight

Last night (his mental survey continued) a man by the name of James Carr had been murdered, one of three connoisseurs who had bought the Euralian Crown jewels.

Unless one could discover the identity of the other two men they also were probably doomed. The deal had taken place in Paris, but when or where the inspector could not trace, though the head of the Paris Sureté had made inquiries at Reynolds's request.

Every known buyer of precious stones in London had been interviewed. Not one of them could tell him anything useful. They seemed all to be elderly, eccentric, and secretive to a baffling extent.

Working from another angle, Reynolds had tried to locate Zaldo's hiding place. Hotels in the West been discreetly but thoroughly combed in search of an alien answering to the description that Mimi had given.

As a last desperate resource he was contemplating visit to Vernstein who was certainly working for Zaldo.

The flaw in this idea was obvious. Bribes would not induce the Jew to talk, even were such a course advisable. Vernstein was probably, receiving regular income from the arch-crook that he would not willingly sacrifice, and he would certainly risk being murdered for treachery, to his master.

It was useless to watch Vernstein's house in Gunner's Court. Zaldo probably never went there, and was unknown personally to the members of his gang. If there were the slightest suspicion that C.I.D. men were interested in the neighbourhood, Zaldo's associates would be transferred to a new locality and the trail would be lost.

Also, Mimi was there, possibly obtaining valuable facts, and probably running into danger that made Reynolds shiver to think about.

From his desk he drew the slip of paper that Mimi had taken from Vernstein's pocket. What he needed was not a list of jewels but the names of the buyers of them.

For the fiftieth time he turned the paper over and glanced at some nearly illegible notes pencilled on the back. They probably had no bearing on the case and appeared under his powerful magnifying glass to be a memorandum.

Suddenly he frowned as two words became faintly visible. One seemed to be "Dan" followed by the figures "£40" and "April 4." The other word was not so clear, and might have been anything of nine or ten letters beginning with a capital "G" and ending with a small "m." Two or three upward loops were indicated and the shadow of one downward loop.

It must be a proper noun, for it began with a capital "G" and might be a town or a name, he decided.

His grey eyes were alert as he opened a Gazetteer and prepared to wade through the columns in search of a long word containing tailed consonants for the middle letters.

To his surprise he found only one town that fulfilled the requirements: Gillingham, a small place in Kent. Why should the mythical "Dan" receive £40 on April 4th for work done in a country village? Nothing notable had occurred in that district so far as Reynolds could remember.

Perhaps the directory would be more helpful. He slid his finger down lists of names under the letter "G." At the recurrence of "Gillingham" he paused, a chord of memory awakening. An elderly man of that name had died rather mysteriously some months ago, he remembered. Suppose it was last April!

Ringing his bell, Reynolds ordered newspaper files of that month to be brought.

Presently he discovered a brief paragraph announcing the death of a Mr. Gillingham, a wealthy stockbroker who was found dead in his office on April 4th.

In a newspaper of a later date he read an account of the inquest. The deceased had suffered from a weak heart and had died from an overdose of veranox. A half-filled bottle of the drug was found in his overcoat pocket. An open verdict had been returned.

There was no mention of jewels and apparently no reason to suspect foul play or robbery. Nevertheless Reynolds stared at the newspaper account and wondered if Zaldo had played any part in this tragedy.

The door of his office opened and closed softly but he did not raise his head until he heard a heavy sigh.

"What do you—" he began in a testy tone that changed as he saw who his interrupter was. "Mimi!" he exclaimed. "I've never been more pleased to see you."

"*Vraiment* you have changed if you make me pretty compliments, monsieur!" she remarked as she curled up in a big chair and lighted a cigarette. "Or is it that you are in a pit and require my brain to help you up?"

"H'm, your English is distinctly the worse for wear, young woman," Reynolds commented.

"I am tired with trying to speak correctly. It was important to make no mistake at Vernstein's. Tell me about the hole that you are in, monsieur."

" It certainly is a hole," Reynolds admitted. "If I don't get out of it soon, I'll retire and breed Airedales."

"Don't grow dogs yet, *mon ami*. Listen to my news."

She unfolded her discoveries, with reservation concerning her arrangement with Jenkins. If Reynolds knew, he might wish to take immediate action: arrest Vernstein, Kent and the housekeeper perhaps, in the hope of averting further murders.

Mimi took a broader view. It was better to risk two lives than allow a dangerous criminal to escape justice. Therefore she did not tell the inspector the address of the probable victim for to-night's drama.

"Very well, Mimi. Two of my best men shall follow you and do nothing unless you signal. I shall be there also."

"In that case I think I will be arrested to-night," she announced after a moment's thought. "Perhaps Kent also. Of course we shall escape. That must be arranged please."

The inspector frowned.

"Arrest you and Kent and then allow you both to escape! You can't play with the law in that fashion my poor weak-minded child."

"Why not, monsieur? It will inspire confidence in Kent's heart if I am proved to be a criminal by being arrested. It will be doubled if I assist him to escape. You understand. Please arrest us both."

"Before or after the caretaker is chloroformed?" Reynolds questioned, inwardly deciding to use his own judgment concerning her suggestion.

"After, of course. Also one of your men must try to follow Zaldo to-night. Follow; nothing more."

"Why not arrest him? We know what he looks like."

Mimi leaned forward and thumped the desk. "Because, my poor weak-minded inspector, you don't know what he will look like to-night. If you arrest the wrong man, or make disturbances, Zaldo will fly."

"All right. That is logical," Reynolds agreed. "We'll merely trail any man who resembles him. Ever heard of a man called 'Dan'?"

"A man of that name delivered the apples at your house."

Reynolds's lips tightened.

"In that case," he said grimly, "it will give peculiar joy to learn a little more about, his activities." He explained what he had discover about Mr. Gillingham. "I'm going to call at Gillingham's office. Like to come?"

Mimi glanced at her watch.

"For one hour, yes, monsieur. After that—"

"I know," the inspector interrupted with chuckle. "You've a 'date' with a new sweetie."

"I am taking my dinner with Mr. Stephen Blair," Mimi corrected with icy dignity.

"And you throw up serious work with me to see a man you met once in Montmartre!" jibed the inspector. "By the way, what has become of the lovely Linda who has a mysterious past?"

"I do not know and am too worried to think" Mimi replied evasively. "Let us go quickly, monsieur." .

The offices that Mr. Gillingham had occupied were in a big building near Kingsway. Reynolds was frustrated to find that they were now tenanted by an architect who could tell him nothing about his predecessor.

The hall porter, on being questioned, rubbed his head and tried to be helpful.

"I could tell you plenty about most of the other tenants, sir, but very little of Mr. Gillingham. He was a crusty old gent who never gave me even a 'good day' when he came in, and his clerk was just as dumb."

"He was a stockbroker, I believe. Had he a large business?" Reynolds asked.

"He couldn't have had much. There was only one clerk. Never even had a typist till the last few months before he died."

"Do you know where the clerk and typist live?" The porter shook, his head.

"I believe the clerk went abroad after his boss died, sir. As for the typist, I've never heard her name and wouldn't have known she was working there except for a young man. Her sweetheart, I suppose."

"How did you come to speak to this fellow?"

"He used to hang about here in the hall in the evenings; an ugly bloke. I asked him who he wanted and he said he was waiting for his girl who was Mr. Gillingham's secretary. That was the first I'd heard of her. There's hundreds of people in and out all day and unless they speak to me I don't pay any attention to them."

"You'd recognise the clerk or the typist again I suppose, if you saw them?"

"The clerk I'd know, of course. But the girl," the porter looked doubtful. "I'm not certain. I only saw her once or twice. A smart, good-looking piece except for her hair. I hate that colour. Auburn, some folks call it; I say it's plain red. She'd got very bright blue eyes."

"What was her sweetheart like?" Mimi asked.

"A nasty bit of work, miss, if you ask me. Eyes tether in a white ferrety face. Once I heard him called 'Dan.'"

"Had Mr. Gillingham any family?" pursued Reynolds.

"He was a widower with one son abroad, sir. The old gentleman lived in Regent's Park. The house and furniture were sold just after he died." The porter sighed. "I don't believe he ever spoke to anyone in the building. Queer habit he had of coming back here alone at night to do a couple of hours' writing, the clerk said at the inquest."

"Was the outer hall door closed at that hour? "

"Yes, sir, at seven o'clock. Mr. Gillingham had his key, of course. If ever I was late cleaning I'd see him. The very night he died I saw him come in about nine and go upstairs. Kept his typist later than the clerk, for she and her bloke went out only half an hour before. I suppose the fellow had come here to fetch her."

"And the clerk found Mr. Gillingham dead the next morning?"

"That's right, sir. With a half-written business letter before him. The typist hadn't come. The clerk rang her up and told her what had happened. She never came here again to my knowledge."

"She wasn't called upon to give evidence at the inquest, according to the newspaper report," Reynolds said thoughtfully. "The sleeping tablets were found in Mr. Gillingham's overcoat pocket, I believe."

The porter pointed to an old fawn raincoat hanging inside his small office.

"That's the very coat, sir. It was left behind and I hung it up there. Never saw the old gentleman wear it, though, all the time I was here."

Reynolds exchanged an understanding glance with Mimi.

"What was he wearing the last time you saw him?" he asked, handing the man a coin.

"Black cloth coat, same as he always did," the porter replied. "Thank you, sir. Good evening."

The inspector was silent as they walked along the Strand.

"A man doesn't use an old overcoat pocket as a medicine chest, does he, Mimi?" he remarked at last. "Neither does he take stuff to make him sleep in his office and then start to write a business letter."

"Monsieur, I cannot support more complications to-night, please," Mimi begged in a tired voice.

Reynolds looked at her anxiously.

"Of course not. I had no right to drag you here. You're doing far too much as it is. Need you meet Kent to-night? He'll merely get tired of waiting and go on alone. My men could easily watch and follow him to wherever the place is."

"No, no. I must be there. It is necessary," the girl said hurriedly. "*Au 'voir*, monsieur."

"Have a good dinner and don't flirt too much with Stephen Blair," was Reynolds's advice.

It was good that she had not told the inspector of her promise to help Kent, Mimi reflected when she was alone.

Meanwhile her head was throbbing with a new and terrible fear. The porter's description of Dan, the "nasty bit of work," indicated that it was the 'Dan' she had seen. The whole circumstances resembled the vague story that Linda had told. The date agreed with her flight to Paris. Gillingham's red-haired, blue-eyed secretary may have been Linda herself!

How long, Mimi debated, ought she to keep her suspicions to herself? Was she being merely loyal to Linda by remaining silent, or was she shielding one who had concealed grave facts?

It was now twenty-five minutes past seven, the half-hour Linda was due at their rendezvous.

Mimi compromised with herself. If Linda did not keep her appointment, at once Inspector Reynolds should be told everything. If Linda came, Mimi decided to reserve decision until she had heard her friend's story.

XXII. THE UNIVITED GUEST

Friday evening

On the south side of Piccadilly Circus opposite Swan and Edgar's, Mimi paused in a doorway and looked across the road to see if Linda was already there.

In a fever of anxiety she heard a clock chime the half-hour. She would wait until a quarter to eight, and then, if Linda had not come, she would go to Scotland Yard.

The chimes had barely finished when a tall, slender girl with hair gleaming under a little green hat appeared. Mimi darted to her.

"You don't know how thankful I am to see *you*," Linda said, holding the French girl's hand in both her own.

"And you will never know how thankful I am to see you" Mimi replied fervently. "Tell me quickly, you are happy and safe, yes? And you are working? I have been uneasy about you."

"Very happy. I've missed you so much." Linda's eager voice altered as she added jerkily "The advertisement was genuine: I obtained the job. It is very pleasant work. Selling old china and things, and my elderly employer is kind and considerate."

Mimi noticed the vagueness of the explanation and the flurry with which it was given, but passed no comment.

"*La, la,* beware of old gentlemen who are kind to their pretty employees!"

"Oh, Mr. Went—" she broke off. "My employer is not of that type. He is Victorian in his manners. What have you been doing, Mimi?"

The French girl made an evasive laughing reply while her mind was busy wondering what English surnames had "Went" for the first syllable. She could only think of one. She would try that.

"Does Mr. Wentwood"—she blurred the latter part of the name—"need another assistant? I am a good *vendeuse*—how you say?—selling woman, and know a little about antiques."

"You know his name!" Linda exclaimed. "I shouldn't think that he needs anyone else. There is very little for me to do really. But I'll ask him."

"No, no. You must not so soon ask favours of your amiable employer. Also, at the moment, I have a little work and must return to Paris when it is finished."

"Then I hope your work will last a long time for my sake. Are we having dinner alone or—" Linda hesitated.

"We are dining with Mr. Blair at eight o'clock," Mimi said, filling in the blank. "It is a French restaurant. I know the proprietor so we shall eat well. We have time to walk there if you are not tired."

"How did you know Mr. Wentworth's name?" Linda inquired as they walked up Shaftesbury Avenue. "Surely you did not go to Yates too for a job?"

"Why not?" Mimi asked lightly, noticing the distasteful tone in which Linda had mentioned Yates's name.

"He's—I don't like him very much."

The French girl shrugged her shoulders.

"It is not necessary to like him. He has found you a job, *et voila tout*. You can forget him."

"Unfortunately I can't," Linda said in a low, frightened voice. "Oh, Mimi, I'm worried. I want to tell you why, and ask your advice, but I must not. Please don't ask me. I've promised."

Mimi's eyes hardened as she guessed that Yates was responsible for her friend's alarm. The fact that he evidently had power to enforce Linda's silence assured her that Yates was either threatening exposure or blackmail.

"Perhaps, Linda, I know more than you think," she said gently. "Do not be afraid of Yates or any one. Men of his class generally have worse secrets of their own to protect." She drew in her breath and prepared a chance shot. It was painful to hurt Linda, and if this shot were true she would be hurt. But a stern sense of duty was in the French girl's heart, and sentiment had to give way to it. "Have you seen Dan lately?" she asked in dear tones.

"Dan!" Linda stared at her aghast, the colour draining from her cheeks. "Mimi, you can't know about him?" she breathed.

"Yes, I know about Dan. I am sorry to startle you, *chérie,* but how else could I make it clear that you could trust me with your difficulties?" Mimi patted her friend's arm reassuringly. "You remember I told you not to be afraid of Yates or anyone. That means Dan also. He cannot hurt you."

Linda pressed her hand to her head.

"I can't imagine how you have found out. I tried to protect Dan. He'll kill me if he thinks I have told anyone," she said wildly. "Unless—Mimi, has he been arrested? Quick, tell me the worst."

"No, not yet. He does not suspect anything. It does not matter how I found out about—the Gillingham affair. Do you love Dan?"

"Love! I hate him. But I won't break my word. I ran away to save him because he said he was innocent."

"And you have returned to find out that he was guilty," was the French girl's reply. "Forget it for to-night and be happy." She glanced over her shoulder as they turned into Soho. "By the way, did you tell anyone about this dinner party?"

Linda shook her head.

"No. Why? Has Dan followed us?"

"Stupid one, of course not. Look, there is the nice Mr. Blair waiting for us outside the restaurant. Ah, monsieur, we are not late?" she asked as their host came forward to meet them.

"Wonderfully punctual, mademoiselle." Blair turned to Linda. "How are you, Miss Marchant? You don't look the same girl that I saw in Montmartre last Sunday night."

"My circumstances are much happier now," Linda told him.

"I'm delighted to see you both again," Blair remarked, "although I hope you won't be bored by having only one male escort. How have you been getting on, mademoiselle?" He studied Mimi's pale face a little anxiously.

She touched his arm with a warning pressure. "Perfectly, thank you, monsieur. Will you make me a little promise, please?"

"Of course, if I can," Blair answered readily.

"*Bon*! It is this. Do not ask Linda and me to talk of ourselves this evening. We both have our jobs, we like them and all goes well. But to talk about them, it is dull. *Alors*, for to-night, we will pretend that we have nothing to do. There you are, *tout simple*. Is it agreeable?"

"Quite agreeable and clear," Blair answered. "I've had a disturbing day and shall be glad to forget it. Changing stables. I must give you both my new address before we part to-night. If you don't like this restaurant, Miss Marchant, please blame your friend. She chose it."

" She will adore it—and the food," the French girl said with conviction. "One more small favour, monsieur, will you please call me Mimi?"

"With pleasure," he replied "In return, may I ask you to extend the same friendliness toward me?"

Mimi puckered her forehead in comical perplexity.

"My English he is a little slow to-day. But if you are asking me to call you Stephen, I will."

"That's the spirit," replied Blair.

" Ask Linda to do the same," suggested Mimi in a loud-whisper.

"'Sh. 'I'd like to but I'm afraid," Blair retorted in the same audible aside.

Linda laughed good-humouredly.

"You two are fast workers. It makes me feel slow and old fashioned. Besides, Mr. Blair may quarrel with me before dinner is over."

"One never knows," he replied, opening the door for her. "Shall we go in? I've already reserved a table."

The smile was still on Linda's lips when she entered the vestibule. It faded as she saw a tall young man standing there hatless. Grasping a large bunch of violets he came towards her.

"Oh!" she gasped in consternation. How and why had Nick Tyler come here? Was it coincidence or design?

Over her head Nick met Stephen Blair's eyes in a quick, hard stare. Then he ignored him.

"You're a little late, Linda. And I've had nothing serviceable to eat since our early luncheon," Nick said plaintively in his lazy voice. "However, you look so charming that I'll forgive you. Come along." He took her arm and attempted to lead her into the restaurant.

"There—there must be a mistake," she stammered. "I'm not dining with you. I've—I'm engaged."

Nick Tyler raised an eyebrow.

"Really! Just fixed it up?" he inquired. "My hearty congratulations. This gentleman is your fiancé, I presume. You're a lucky chap," he remarked to Blair. "And I'm the unluckiest. Tough to lose one's guest. However, in the circumstances—" He made a gesture indicating the hopelessness of the situation.

"I'm not so lucky as you imagine," Blair answered. "Miss Marchant is only my guest for dinner."

Nick seemed considerably cheered by the announcement.

"I can bear up now," he said solemnly. "Sorry I blundered. I must introduce myself since I've covered the lady in confusion. My name's Tyler. Nick Tyler."

There was a twinkle in the other man's eyes.

"Mine is Blair, Stephen Blair," he replied.

"And mine is Mimi," came a cool little voice. "I too am a friend of Linda. It is strange, this error of yours, Monsieur Tyler, for she and I made a promise days ago to dine with Mr. Blair this evening." The French girl's face was alight with amusement.

"Methinks the gentleman has too much good fortune. It's rather greedy to want two charming ladies to watch him eat," Nick remarked with unperturbed audacity. "I'm sure he'll snaffle the breast of the chicken and give you the leg. I have an idea. As I've ordered dinner for two, be an angel, mademoiselle, and share my table."

"I have a better plan," put in Blair good-naturedly. "Come and join our party, Tyler. It would indeed be greedy of me to leave you desolate, when you had expected to have Miss Marchant's company. Also you can keep an eye on my table manners."

"Spoken like a generous-hearted sportsman," Nick said with approval. "Thanks very much. In return I'll tell you which fork to use and give you hints on the management of peas. Linda is improving nicely since I took her in hand." He divided the flowers he carried and offered them to the girls.

Linda hesitated and then, with a low "Thank you" took them rather reluctantly. Mimi accepted with a gay, smile and fastened them to her coat.

"This going to be a lovely party," she said. "We will take our things to the cloakroom."

When the two girls were in the dressing-room, Mimi caught her friend's arm firmly.

"I will stick a large pin into you, Linda, if you are amiable. This Nick Tyler amuses me. I will tease him for his mistake."

"It was not a mistake," Linda replied. "It was a deliberate scheme on his part because I refused to dine with him. How he found out that we were coming here I don't know."

"I do, *chérie*. He followed us from Piccadilly Circus. I saw him. Did you go there from Mr. Wentworth's shop?"

"No. From my rooms. I went home to change first. That means he knows where I live." Linda said in dismay.

"Why not? So do I," Mimi told her calmly. "But there is no reason why either he or I should tell anyone else, is there?" Suddenly she had a flash of intuition. "Does he work for Yates?"

Linda nodded.

"Yes. Oh, Mimi, I wish I could trust Nick. I dare not think what his real work is!"

"Leave him to, me," Mimi urged. "It will intrigue me to find out. I adore his impudence. *Allons*, the chin up, please. "

The sparkle came back to Linda's eyes during the meal. She could even join in bantering Nick, backed by the quiet geniality of Blair and Mimi's vivacious chatter.

At once the French girl and Tyler had started warfare. His challenging remarks were capped by her swift repartee, cleverly designed to draw him out.

"Bah! you tell me, you, that you have not the pig's head and are not obstinate, Monsieur Tyler. Me, I can prove it," Mimi exclaimed.

"Pearls indeed before swine!" Nick chuckled. "What you label obstinacy is merely industry. When I want some thing I go after it until I get it." He looked at Linda as he spoke.

Mimi leaned across the table.

"Next time, monsieur,". she said softly. "exercise your imagination as well as your feet when you walk from Piccadilly Circus to this restaurant"

A speculative expression came to Nick's face. "Thanks. I'll remember, mademoiselle. By the way, are you working in London?"

"When I can," Mimi replied "And you, Monsieur Tyler?"

"When I must," he retorted. "I am usually free in the mornings," he added in a tone of invitation.

"Ah; but being French and of a serious mind, I am more interested in your work than your play, monsieur."

"It has its moments," Nick confessed. "Strategy can be very amusing."

"If successful," Mimi flashed back. "It is a thousand pities that it can so easily be frustrated." Nick gazed into her inscrutable eyes.

"A threat or a warning?" he asked quietly.

Mimi flicked her fingers negligently. "Both, if necessary, Monsieur Tyler."

There was a queer moment of tension. Then Nick said, "Loyal as well, as clever, aren't you?"

Mimi put her head on one side and considered the question.

"I have my moments," she replied gravely.

"If you two will stop bickering," Blair remarked, "I have a suggestion to make. lt's nearly a quarter-past ten. Will you all come and see my new bachelor quarters? They're between the Embankment and Temple."

"Don't you think I've trespassed long enough, Blair?" Nick asked. "After all, an uninvited guest has his limitations."

"You've not reached yours yet," Blair assured him. "You'll come too, won't you, Miss Marchant?"

"If Mimi will, I'd like to for a little while."

"*Certainement.* But only for the little, while," Mimi replied "At eleven o'clock I must go."

"Quite right. Nothing like early hours." Nick's tone was fatherly.

"Nothing," Mimi retorted. "You might be well advised to keep them, monsieur."

A taxi landed them in a few minutes at their destination in a rather dark street.

"This is the side entrance; it's nearer than coming in by the main door," Blair explained as he led, the way up to his flat and into a spacious room. "My man's worked very hard to-day and we're practically straight."

"I love your old furniture, Mr. Blair," Linda remarked.

"Miss Marchant likes antiques though she knows nothing about 'em," Nick interposed.

A while later Mimi glanced at her watch.

"I must go very soon," she said.

"You've time for a drink first. It's only ten minutes to eleven," Blair answered, ringing the bell.

As the summons was unanswered he went out of the room. In a few minutes he returned with a tray.

"That's funny," he said. "My man isn't in the flat. Help yourselves. I'll ring down to the hall porter to know if he left a message."

Instinct made Mimi follow Blair to the house telephone. He picked up the receiver.

"Is that you, Quayle?" he asked.

XXIII. MIMI IS ARRESTED

Friday night

It is said that a drowning man reviews his whole life in the last few seconds. It is certain that Mimi reviewed the events of the past five days in a few brief moments after she heard the name of Quayle.

She realised that Stephen Blair was one of the trio of jewel collectors! James Carr, murdered yesterday, was another. Blair, then, must know who the third was!

Blair had been in Paris last Sunday. Almost certainly he had been there to buy the jewels! Carr's charwoman had overheard that arrangement.

Kent had told her that their victim had moved to a fresh address, a first floor flat in a new building; and that the hall porter's name was Quayle!

Blair's man had evidently been enticed away this evening. The most important point of the moment was to save Stephen Blair's life. Time was racing on.

In less than half an hour she was due to meet Kent at Villiers Street.

It was far too long a story to explain everything to Blair now, even if he could be expected to believe it.

Naturally he would think that such a fantastic yarn was either imagination or—if he suspected Mimi—a trick to get him out of the flat so that his valuables might be easily stolen. Another probability was that he would call in the police.

No, Mimi decided, explanations would be useless. To-morrow would be soon enough to obtain the name of the third collector from Blair. To-night she must concentrate on how to get him out of the building.

She listened eagerly to Blair's replies over the wire, as he continued his conversation with the hall porter.

"An hour ago, eh? Did you speak to him? Richmond. No, no, nothing wrong, thank you, Quayle."

Blair replaced the receiver. The French girl was regarding him seriously.

"Hello, Mimi. I thought you were in the library. Grey, my man, seems to have gone off on a strange errand. The porter says that he went out about an hour ago carrying a small suitcase. Grey asked the quickest way to get to Richmond. The porter gave him directions and that's all."

Mimi frowned.

"You told the porter that nothing was wrong."

Blair smiled cheerfully.

"I don't suppose that anything is. But in any case I didn't want Quayle to imagine that his new tenant was queer. These are highly respectable flats."

"Is Grey highly respectable too?" Mimi inquired.

"Far more so than I am. He has been with me for ten years and is my devoted bodyguard. You would laugh had you seen him watch the furniture when they removed my iron safe last night. He never took his eyes off it and annoyed them intensely. He insisted upon riding with it in their van."

"Why should I have laughed? It was wise if you had money or valuable things inside." Mimi's tone was apparently detached but her heart was beating rapidly as she waited for Blair's answer.

"The darned thing was empty," he chuckled. "I rolled the contents in a couple of shabby parcels and took them to the bank two days ago until the 'move' was over. Tomorrow I'm having special burglar alarms fixed."

"You didn't tell your man what you had done?"

"Not until this evening. Otherwise I'm sure that nothing would have made Grey leave the flat without my permission."

So the jewels were in the bank, Mimi reflected. But Zaldo didn't know that, and he might kill first to obtain the keys and discover too late that the safe was empty!

"Come and see the thing," Blair invited. "It's a ponderous brute."

She followed him along the passage to a back room where he showed her the safe, the door of which stood open.

Mimi laid her hand on his arm.

"I have a great favour to ask. You were very kind to Linda when she was a stranger. Will you be more kind now that you know her better?"

"I'll do anything I can for her, or for you, Mimi," was Blair's answer. "What is it?"

"She is a little sad and worried to-night, and unfortunately because of my rendezvous I cannot be with her. Will you take her to a night club and make her dance and be cheerful? Don't let her go to her lonely rooms until it is quite late."

"Right. You arrange it and I promise to keep her up until the small hours if she'll agree. I know a decent club where evening-dress is not essential. What about Nick Tyler?"'

"Take him also," Mimi, urged. "Don't let him know that I cannot go with you. Stop the taxi on the Embankment, please, by Charing Cross Tube station. I'll get out."

Blair nodded.

"I've got the rest. You can depend on me."

"Thank you for your friendship," she said. "I like you so much."

"And what have you been up to?" Nick demanded in reproving tones when she and Blair went back to the library.

"Seeing the flat and coaxing Stephen to take us to a night club," was Mimi s reply. "Come quickly".

As they went downstairs she whispered to Linda: "Once in Paris I did something for you. To-night you must do something for me. You must not let Stephen Blair return here until two o'clock. You understand, Linda?

Make any silly excuse, dance even if you are too tired to breathe, but *keep him with you.*"

Her urgent tone made Linda realise that there was a deadly purpose underlying this strange request. "I'll stick to him like glue," she promised. "Mimi, darling, you look as if you had seen a ghost. What is it?"

"Something like that," Mimi said slowly. "So if I slip away," she added in her normally bright manner, "you will understand?"

"Of course."

Mimi cast a swift glance at Quayle the porter as they passed the window of his office in the main hall. He appeared to be a stupid creature, she was pleased to see, and seemed to be half asleep already. Detective-Sergeant Jenkins should not have a very difficult task.

Twenty minutes past eleven! After all, she would not be late, she thought as Stephen Blair helped her into the taxi.

At the corner of the street she caught a glimpse of Jenkins, striding along at a good speed. He too was on time.

The taxi went down to the Embankment and turned right.

Outside Charing Cross Tube the driver pulled up. Mimi jumped out and instantly the cab moved on.

For a moment she watched it wistfully. There went her chance of peace and safety. Such things were not for her. Of her own volition she had long ago set her feet on the stony paths of adventure. It was too late to turn back now.

She shrugged her shoulders, walked through the Tube station and up Villiers Street. Whatever fate awaited her, Blair was safe.

She had nearly reached the Strand when she saw Kent, his back towards her, looking about restlessly.

On the opposite side of the narrow street she observed two C.I.D. men whose faces were familiar, standing inconspicuously in a doorway. A little further away was another man, absorbed in a newspaper. Inspector Reynolds had kept his word.

Making no sign of recognition she passed him and the two detectives and went up to Kent.

"We have time to walk if you like," she remarked in a pleasant conversational manner.

He started nervously and turned a face of sickly hue towards her.

"I'm thankful you've come, Mimi. This business has scared me to death, and I'm none too sure you're playing straight with me."

"Then why am I here?" Mimi demanded. "What time do we start our job?"

"Ten minutes to twelve?' Kent's teeth were chattering.

The girl grasped his aim and shook it.

"Snap out of it!" she exclaimed, breaking into American slang. "We will walk quickly. It may warm your cold feet! Don't keep looking round in that frightened manner."

At a smart pace she forced him along the Strand and down Harrington Street. Behind them a closed car travelled slowly, keeping at a discreet distance.

"Anybody following us?" Kent asked in a shaky voice as the block of flats came into view.

"There is no one in the entire street," Mimi replied truthfully, knowing that the Yard car had stopped at the corner. "Give me the chloroform and pad of cottonwool. Leave the talking to me. Get behind him and seize his arms. I'll do the rest."

Had Jenkins managed his part of the business successfully she wondered, as they entered the hall. Through the glass window of the porter's office she saw the figure of a man, sitting with bent head as if reading.

With a feeling of relief she recognised Jenkins, with spectacles, porter's uniform, coat and peaked cap. He did not raise his head as Mimi and her companion came near, thereby giving Kent no opportunity of seeing a striking likeness to Mimi's late coster fiancé!

"If you move or scream I shall shoot," Mimi said to the "porter," pointing a small revolver at him. "Lie down on the floor. You won't be hurt if you do as you're told."

The "porter" obeyed, muttering a few threats under his breath. He made no resistance as Mimi pressed the pad over his mouth.

Kent, busily tying the man's feet in the semidarkness of the office floor, could not see that the porter's nostrils were clear and that a piece of oilskin rested between his mouth and the wet pad. Neither did Kent know that the heavy smell of chloroform came chiefly from the mat where Mimi had tipped most of it!

"Are you sure he's off?" Kent questioned as he saw the girl stand up.

Mimi nodded.

"That will keep him quiet for half an hour."

"Come on. We'll beat it," Kent said. "My orders were to be out of the place before midnight. It's five minutes to twelve. Go to the front door and see if the coast is clear."

"Hands up, you two," came in stern tones from a C.I.D. man who entered the hall suddenly.

"Quick, follow me." Mimi caught Kent's arm. "Run for it," she ordered as they reached the side door. "I'll try to hold them back a minute." In that brief time she managed to whisper one sentence to Inspector Reynolds: "Watch second flat left from top of stairs."

Kent darted out, straight into the arms of a detective who thrust him into a car with Mimi and got inside with his prisoners.

"You're a good sport," Kent whispered to the girl. "Well, the game's up. Even if I told the police the little I know of Zaldo and his infernal tool, Yates, we'd still get a stiff sentence."

"Be quiet," Mimi replied softly "We're not in prison yet. Listen carefully. Lean back and pretend to feel ill. When the detective bends over you I shall open the door on my side and run. You must sit quite still with your eyes dosed. The detective will, I am sure, shout to the chauffeur to guard you and will dash after me. Instantly the detective gets out, open the door on your side and run in the opposite direction. If we both get free, I will see you at Vernstein's to-morrow."

"Here, what are you whispering about?" demanded the C.I.D. man.

"My friend has a weak heart. He is faint," Mimi explained. "Tell the driver to go slower."

The detective leaned over Kent, whose naturally white face looked ashen by reason of his panic.

At the same second Mimi slid out of the door nearest to her. "Keep your eye on this chap," warned the detective as he dashed after the flying figure.

Before the chauffeur, with mock clumsiness, wriggled from behind the driving wheel, Kent had bolted.

XXIV. The Accident

Friday night

In a side street Mimi paused and waited for the detective who had chased her. Big Ben loudly proclaimed that it was midnight. She wondered what was happening now in Blair's flat.

"Here I am, Foster," she cried as the C.I.D. man reached her, breathing hard.

"Considering that this was a put-up job, miss, you needn't have run like a blooming hare," he grumbled. "I'm a detective and not a greyhound. Couldn't believe my ears when the inspector said I was to let that fellow who was with you slide off."

Foster snorted with indignation.

"Funniest arrest I've ever known," he went on. "No handcuffs, no noise, mustn't blow our whistles. Everything all nice and ladylike! Well, I suppose the inspector understands what he's about, which is more than I do."

Mimi's eyes flashed.

"The wise Inspector Reynolds understands perfectly. It is for you to obey and not to criticise him."

"Well, I have obeyed, him, haven't I?" Foster demanded in aggrieved accents. "If I hadn't, you wouldn't be here bullying me, and that scoundrel Kent would be inside the police station instead of laughing at the easy way he hopped it."

"The inspector knows that another crime will be committed if he cannot find out when and where it will take place," Mimi explained. "His only chance is through me. And my only chance is to make Kent believe that I am working on his side."

"I understand."

"To-night Kent, who had doubts about me, realises that I have helped him to escape. In future he will not be so afraid to trust me."

"All the same, miss," Foster observed, "there's that poor chap, the porter, all tied up in the office, and unconscious. Chloroform acts funny with some folk. Suppose he dies!"

Mimi suppressed a smile. The inspector had not the faintest idea that Jenkins had been substituted for the porter. When he learnt of it, he would certainly have something very pungent to say.

"The porter will be all right, Foster," she replied. "How far are we from the block of flats?"

The detective gave her a supercilious glance.

"You haven't got much sense of direction, miss. We've made a circular trip. There's the side entrance where we caught you and that rascal ten minutes ago." He indicated a door less than fifty yards from where they stood. "Well, now you've been arrested and have escaped, I'll get back to some real work near the front door."

Mimi's eyes were strained up towards the first floor windows, trying to trace which belonged to Blair's flat. She remembered noticing that the iron fire staircase was outside the window of the room where his safe stood. Was there a flicker of light showing in that room now?

A taxi swung past, and slowed up at the side entrance. A man stepped out quickly, and crossing the pavement, unlocked the door. It was Stephen Blair!

Mimi did not stop to think what ill luck could have brought him back at this critical moment. She rushed up and grasped his arm.

"Why have you come back?" she demanded anxiously. "Where are the others?"

"Linda and Tyler are dancing in the club to which I took them in Sloane Square." Blair explained. "Linda left her handbag upstairs; I've come back to fetch it. What on earth are you doing here, Mimi?" he asked in surprise.

"You must not go to your flat now," she said in urgent tones.

Blair frowned.

"Must not. Don't be absurd. Of course I'm going."

"I can't explain; there is no time. Please, please do not go," she implored. "It is dangerous."

"Either this is melodramatic nonsense or queer work is going on that I ought to know about." Blair's face was cold and determined. "Perhaps I've taken you a little too much on trust, Mimi"

He thrust her aside and entering, shut the self-locking door. She beat on it with her fists frantically, but no one came.

"There's a light in that first floor room now, miss," Foster exclaimed. "Shall we try to get up the escape? I'll climb over the yard gate and open it."

"Be quick. A life is at stake," Mimi said in agonised tones.

"What's the trouble, Mimi?"

The distracted girl turned to see Inspector Reynolds beside her. Never had he been more welcome than in this dreadful moment. She poured out her explanations feverishly.

"Blair is up there now, possibly being murdered by Zaldo," she added.

"There's no time to run round half the block and in by the front entrance," Reynolds declared. "The fire escape is our only hope. See! Foster has got the yard gate open."

They raced across the dark area to the foot of the fire staircase. Before Reynolds could climb the iron ladder a window above them was suddenly opened. A startled gasp from Mimi made him look up.

Outlined against the lighted room was the figure of a man holding a limp form in his arms. For one second he stood there, poised. Then he hurled his burden down into the darkness.

That second saved Stephen Blair from certain death. For the inspector and Mimi, gauging the distance, broke the full force of the fall.

Reynolds shouted to Foster for help. Mimi had fallen under the impact. Reynolds flashed his torch on to her.

"Stephen—is he dead?" she asked. "Do not think about me—look after him."

"We can do nothing yet. I've sent for assistance," Reynolds told her. "Lie still."

"Listen. He must not die. He knows who the other—" Mimi's eyes closed and her head dropped heavily against Reynolds's shoulder.

She was lying on an improvised couch in the inspector's office at Scotland Yard when she recovered consciousness. Beside her sat Dr. Tempest, the Yard pathologist.

"Feeling better?" he asked. "You'll have to lead a quieter life, young woman. Inspector Reynolds has been badly worried about you."

Mimi gave him a wan smile and turned to Reynolds with a mute questioning look of appeal.

He bent over her immediately.

"Alive, but unconscious," he replied. "He's in a private ward at Charing Cross Hospital. We shall know more soon. Take this."

Mimi drank obediently from the glass held to her lips. Presently, after stretching her limbs to test if they were damaged, she sat up.

"Why am I lying here when there is so much to be done?" she demanded with indignation. "It is ridiculous. I am entirely unbroken in the bones."

"That is fortunately true," replied Dr. Tempest. "But you are bruised and had a bad knock on the head, so you must stay where you are."

"What time is it?" she inquired. "Tell me what has happened, please," she said to the inspector when the doctor had left them.

"'It is twenty minutes past one. You've been here nearly an hour," Reynolds answered "Directly we have a telephone message from the hospital giving us news of Mr. Blair's condition, I shall take you home to my wife. I rang her up and she sends you her love."

Mimi touched her brow cautiously.

"My head aches. Perhaps it will be good to have the peaceful sleep for once," she admitted. "And now, tell me about to-night. Your man followed Zaldo, yes? I told you which was the flat of Mr. Blair."

The inspector's face clouded. Mimi had been through enough to-night without this disappointment.

"You didn't mention Mr. Blair's name, Mimi, in your hurry. Your words were: 'Watch the second flat on left from top of stairs.' I posted a man there at once. No one came out of that flat. A young couple, newly married, went in. They live there."

"But I am sure I counted carefully, monsieur."

"There are two staircases," he told her. "The main one; and one used for service that goes down to the side entrance. From the first floor landing, which winds round corners, the service staircase is out of sight and I didn't imagine that you could have known of it. There was not a second to waste in trying to find out."

Mimi nodded sadly.

"I understand, monsieur. Your man guarded the wrong flat. It was my fault."

"Just a bit of bad luck. Forget it. You did your best."

"No, no. You make a big mistake, monsieur." She clasped her hands in despair. "Me, I am a vain imbecile. I talk too little to you, and try to do too much alone. This afternoon I had discovered where the flat was, and the porter's name. Also that the victim had only just moved in."

"Those details might have made a difference," Reynolds agreed in even tones.

"They might have enabled you to follow Zaldo to his hiding place and," Mimi said soberly, "to have saved Stephen Blair from this."

"Concussion isn't necessarily fatal, you know. That is what the doctors think it is"

"Could Zaldo have suspected that detectives were in the building, monsieur?"

"Definitely not, unless he has powers of clairvoyance," Reynolds assured her with a chuckle. "Immediately after your arrest people poured in from the theatres. A couple of detectives followed the only two men who went out and resembled Zaldo even slightly. Both those men went to highly respectable homes. We have found out their names."

"There remain two hopeful chances," Mimi commented. "The best is Mr. Blair. He can tell us the name of the third collector. The other is perhaps, myself. I can go to Vernstein's to-morrow and see Kent whom I so nobly helped to escape!" She lowered an eyelid at the inspector.

"About Mr. Blair, we can say nothing at the moment. About Vernstein," Reynolds's eyes grew stern, "you shall not go back there if I can prevent it. And concerning Detective-Sergeant Jenkins there, is a small matter that needs clearing up, young woman. How did it happen that I found a useful member of my staff lying in the porter's office, looking very green about the gills?"

Mimi shot a mischievous glance at him. "Quayle could not have acted so cleverly, so I substituted Jenkins. Is he well?"

"Considering everything, yes. I'm sure he will be touched by your kind inquiries. I'm not going to scold you for your ingenious efforts, but in future, you must tell me if C.I.D. men are involved."

"You've said the mouthful," Mimi remarked ruefully. "I get you, boss. I will shoot you the works and lay off your flatties. How's that, big boy?"

"O.K. by me," the inspector, retorted in the same vein. His expression deepened to gravity as the telephone bell rang.

"News of Stephen Blair," Mimi exclaimed eagerly. "Ask if we can see him at once. Say it is urgent."

She listened with growing impatience to Reynolds's monosyllabic replies over the wire. At last he replaced the receiver and gazed at her with disturbed eyes.

"Stephen Blair is still unconscious and may remain so for days. Perhaps there will have to be an operation. He seems to be pretty bad, poor beggar." Reynolds broke off in dismay. "Why, you poor kid," he murmured as Mimi suddenly burst into tears.

"So you really are human!" he commented a few minutes later when she had recovered her composure. "I always thought that you had no heart."

"You were right, monsieur; I have not." She drew out her mirror and powdered her nose. "Tears! Poof, they are nothing. I am a little tired and—how you say?—cross. Mr. Blair gave me a nice dinner, he has information that we need. And now he has had an accident and cannot tell us. So," she waved her hand with an airy gesture, "of course I cry—with temper, you understand."

Reynolds nodded.

"I understand," he replied, "perfectly."

XXV. Nobody's Luck

Saturday, 1 a.m.

"Considering your weight, you dance fairly well," Nick Tyler informed his partner, as the music ended and they returned to their table.

Linda Marchant, secure in the knowledge of being barely eight and a half stones and a superb dancer, smiled amiably.

"And considering your profession," she retorted, "you dance well enough to be a gigolo! What time is it?"

"One o'clock. I shall charge you overtime for my services if Blair doesn't turn up soon."

Linda looked puzzled.

"I can't understand it. He went to get my handbag. He said he wouldn't be more than twenty minutes."

"Perhaps he found the contents of the bag more interesting than your company," Nick suggested. Linda gave him a scathing glance.

"It contained a few shillings, a powder puff and my handkerchief, Mr. Tyler."

She pushed back her chair and stood up.

"It's very late and I'm going home." Her tone was icy.

"With or without my company?" he asked.

"Without."

"Good! I'll be released earlier than I had dared to hope," Nick drawled. "Will you patronise a bus or a taxi?"

"A taxi."

Nick grinned cheerfully.

"How do you propose to pay the fare if you haven't got your bag?"

The girl hesitated.

"It would be kind of you to lend me a couple of shillings, please," she said.

"Ah, but I'm not kind. However, I may as well make a thorough sacrifice of my time and see you home. I'm going your way."

Linda looked uneasy. "You don't know my way."

The man raised an eyebrow.

"You don't mean to say that you've left thirty-five Kenford Street already"

"Why shouldn't I leave there" Linda asked in a low tone.

Nick ignored her question.

"You and Blair are a restless pair. He moved from the Adelphi yesterday and you apparently moved to-day."

"How do you know Mr. Blair's previous address?" Linda demanded. "You met him to-night for the first time and he didn't mention the Adelphi."

"Oh I snooped round when we were in his room to-night," Nick told her imperturbably.

"You'd be invaluable at Scotland Yard, Mr. Tyler."

"Waste of my talents, my dear girl. I do better where I am. Where did you pick up that bright little Parisienne?"

"I met her in Paris."

"Pity she didn't stay there. She's too dangerously sharp for you, Linda."

"I decline to discuss my friends with you."

"I'm not discussing 'em; I'm issuing an order, *per pro.* our dear employer, Yates. Unless you want your secrets laid bare, Linda, go easy with the cute Mimi. Blair seems a decent sort of chap; a bit dull perhaps compared with my vivid personality."

"Mr. Blair is charming and sincere, and his courtesy is delightful after your—"

"Outrageous behaviour," Nick supplied. "You're running to clichés. One day you must devote some time to brightening up your conversation. Here's the cab. Tell the driver where your new stables are."

"Since you followed me there to-night you know I've not moved from Kenford Street," she said.

"Of course I do, but papa likes his little girl to own up nicely. Jump in and we'll continue squabbling. I'd prefer a real healthy row with you, but unfortunately your temper gets out of hand too soon."

Linda gazed out of the taxi window as they drove off.

"It's strange that Mr. Blair didn't come back."

"Stranger still that your odd French friend hopped out of the cab. And strangest that Blair should have ordered the cabman to drive on and leave her! Perhaps he and she planned it all beforehand, and he's with her now."

"Mimi isn't that type," Linda asserted.

"All girls are the same type when they're attracted to a man. Blair may be quite different from what your girlish fancy has painted him. He's a mysterious bloke. Told you he was an author, didn't he?"

"Yes. Isn't he?" There was a note of alarm in the girl's voice.

Nick's face was inscrutable.

"Possibly," he admitted. "He might also be a gentleman crook, such as your humble servant, or—" he paused, "a detective."

"He can't be." The words seemed to be forced from her lips, as if she were making herself believe them.

"Well, let's hope you're right if you've told him any little secret. At any, rate, he's extremely friendly with your pal Mimi. I'm sure of that. Don't let it make you unhappy, but watch your step."

"I wish I knew if you were disinterested or merely spiteful, Nick."

"When in doubt, always think the worst of me. I'll get your bag and bring it along to-morrow morning. Here's your house. Run along to bed like a good child." He raised her bare hand and laid it against his cheek for a second. "Can't make up your mind whether you want to slap my face or kiss me, eh?" he asked, his eyes searching hers with a quizzical expression.

"Exactly that," she answered, and rang the bell.

"Choose the slap. It's wiser. Good night."

Linda's thoughts before she dropped off to sleep were disturbed by alternatively deciding that she hated Nick Tyler for his impudent self-assurance, and liked him for the bracing effect he had upon her.

She was sure that he was not the kind of man a decent girl should take for a companion, but did decent girls conceal important facts from justice concerning a scoundrel? By protecting Dan she had put herself outside the pale.

Immediately after Mr. Gillingham's death she had believed in Dan's innocence, and that she was doing the fine and honourable thing in hiding so that she might not be called at the inquest.

Now she suspected that Dan was even worse than a thief. Her duty was to tell the police all she knew.

But if she took that course, Dan would keep his word and do his best to incriminate her.

Nick had warned her against Mimi. Which could she trust? The irresponsible man, employed by Yates, who said he was a crook, or the French girl who had befriended her and yet seemed to have such an intimate knowledge of her past?

And now Nick had put doubts into her mind concerning Stephen Blair, in whom she had believed implicitly. Looking back over the dinner, the visit to his new flat, and his vanishing from the night club, she saw how strange it all was. Was there some subtle connection between Mimi's unexplained departure and Blair's non-appearance with her bag?

With a sigh she determined that in future she dare not trust him either. Her secret permitted her to take no risks. Life would be lonely, but pleasant friendships were not for her just now.

She was dreaming of Nick's mocking face when the landlady brought in her early tea.

"Morning, miss. Hope you enjoyed your party last night," the woman said, her face wreathed in smiles.

"There's a parcel come for you. Delivered a few minutes ago."

Linda looked at the packet, which was addressed in unfamiliar writing.

"I enjoyed the evening, thank you, Kate," she replied. "Turn on the bath, will you? I'm rather late."

"Yes, miss. I'll have breakfast all ready." The landlady's eyes lingered on the unopened parcel. "Smart young gent brought it. He'd got what you may call a come-hither eye. My word, I bet he's a gay spark with the girls,"

Linda recognised the description.

"You didn't approve of him, I gather, Kate?"

"Approve ain't the word, miss. He could do anything and get away with it. I'm no oil-painting at the best of times, and at half-past seven in the morning I look worse than the wreck of the 'Esperus. But, bless my soul, if your gent didn't pretend I was Garbo's twin."

"He's not my gent," Linda hastily interposed. "What happened?"

"Well, I was polishin' the doorstep when he came, along. 'Good morning, young lady,' ses he, 'would you be an angel and give this to Miss Marchant?' I said I would when you woke -up, but I was not a young lady. And that began it. A fine jot of nonsense he poured out, his blue eyes fair laughing all the time, about beauty being in the eye of the be'older, and anyhow, I was the nicest thing he'd seen that day. You know what he's like, miss."

Linda pursed her lips.

"I know, Kate. Don't let him turn your head."

Kate seemed a little confused by the advice.

"Of course not. In a way I brought it on myself," she mumbled. "I do hope you won't be offended, miss."

"What in the world are you talking about?" Linda asked in bewilderment. "What have you 'brought on' and why should I be offended if an acquaintance of mine leaves a parcel with you?"

The landlady swallowed and decided on full confession.

"Well, when he said that, I answered pert-like that I reckoned his breakfast was the nicest thing he'd seen this morning. He came all over sad and tired-like. 'That's where you're wrong, my girl,' he told me, "for I've had none and am not likely to have any. I had to deliver this parcel for Miss Marchant, breakfast wasn't ready when I left my home in the country, restaurants near here are not open yet, and I've an appointment-in an hour.' "

Kate raised her hands deprecatingly.

"He was shivering, awful. What could I do after that?"

"What he meant you to do, Kate." Linda gave an exasperated laugh. "Ask him to have breakfast here. Where is he?"

"Down in the sitting-room before a nice fire, waiting for you and reading my noospaper," Kate answered. "He must be nuts on you, miss, to come out at this hour on a cold-morning. There's hundreds of girls could jump at a young gent like him. You hurry up and put on a nice frock."

"He seems to have sandbagged you pretty thoroughly, Kate. I'll be down by eight o'clock."

She opened the packet when the landlady had gone. Inside was her handbag and a note which ran as follows:

Saturday morning, 7 a.m.
Here's your property. Unless your landlady has a heart of stone I shall probably be taking breakfast with you. Being thoroughly dishonourable and entirely without delicate scruples, I searched your bag. No letters inside, I was sorry to see. Yours, at least until the bacon and eggs arrive, when I may be horribly disillusioned if your face shows a "hang-over" from the night before.
NICK.

Linda walked downstairs with a step that matched the determination in her heart. Once and for all she would show this preposterous young man that he had exceeded the boundary of her patience.

She opened the sitting-room door. There he was, lying on a couch drawn in front of a blazing fire, as if he owned the place!

He sprang to his feet as she came in and faced her sternly.

"Of all your impossible and impertinent behaviour, Mr. Tyler," he said, fixing her with a cold eye," this is the worst. How dare you come here and blarney my landlady into allowing you to have breakfast? I flatly decline to continue your undesirable acquaintance. Will you-please go at once?"

His eyebrow shot up at a comical angle and he suddenly grinned. "Now I've got that off your chest for you, Linda, come and sit down," he suggested in his normal tone.

She fought hard to control her features. Suddenly her lips twitched and she broke into helpless laughter.

"Don't imagine that I forgive you," she gasped at last. "I'm absolutely furious and should be glad to know I'd never be bothered with you again."

"Safety first is your wise motto this morning, I see," Nick replied lightly. "It's a bit late in life, but I congratulate you."

"What do you mean?

"Having come through one streaky episode you naturally don't want to be entangled with another." His face was grave. "I shall be fairly safe if only I can get to South America, and, with the kind-hearted woman whom I shall ask to go with me, I may find happiness and safety. One has to pay sooner or later for one's mistakes, Linda," he added with a sigh.

"Are you joking, Nick?" the girl demanded in a low voice. "Are you really in danger?"

"'Sh," he warned as the landlady came in with a laden tray. "Of course I was in danger—of being starved—until this sweet angel took pity on me. Kate, how would you like to marry me and go to South America?" he asked, turning to the woman.

Kate favoured him with a fond smile.

"Don't tempt me with them glorious ideas so early in the day, sir, or, you may regret my answer, and me with an impedimenta in the shape of a worthless 'usband and all." She glanced at Linda and added darkly: "There's some folks I could name, sir, as don't know their luck till it's too late. Please ring if you'd like any more toast or coffee."

Nick was silent for a moment when the woman went out.

"She was wrong, Linda. I'm nobody's luck," he said. "By the way, I wasn't very sporting about Blair last night. He couldn't come back. He met with a bad mishap; his man told me when I called for your bag. I'm afraid this news has been a shock for you," Nick went on in a jerky tone. "I'll send you a wire when I know how Blair is; you'll probably like to go and see him. Meanwhile, I'll push off. I'm sure you'd rather be alone. For once I actually know when I'm not wanted."

"I'm sorry about Mr. Blair," Linda replied. She paused and placed a little jade elephant on the breakfast-table. "Meanwhile, Percy will take a politely boiled egg. Kindly serve him while I pour the coffee. And—don't be a fool, Nick."

XXVI. A Jade Elephant

Saturday morning

It was nearly ten o'clock when Mimi awoke. Beyond a
slight headache and a few bruises she was little the worse
for last night's misadventure. Ruthlessly she raked over
the episode that had ended in her outburst of tears when
she had heard that Blair's life was in danger.

"Tears. Bah! I'm getting sentimental," she mused.
"Weakness of that nature is not for me—unless I change
my job."

This point reminded her of the promise she had made
to Inspector Reynolds to lay all her cards on the table. To
do so would involve Linda, who trusted her, in terrible
complications. So far the inspector had no idea that Linda
had been the late Mr. Gillingham's secretary and Dan's
sweetheart.

Dan was in all probability a murderer, and Mimi had
no intention of allowing him to escape. But if she could
prove him guilty of another murder, justice would be
satisfied and Linda's name would be spared.

In fairness to the inspector she must redouble her
own efforts if she decided not to be frank with him.

That being so, a return to Vernstein's house seemed
imperative now that Blair's accident deprived them of his
help. Neither Vernstein nor Kent would suspect her of
treachery after last night, and she stood a good chance of
discovering when the next attack was contemplated.

Her face was unusually white and set in expression as
she drank the coffee that Mrs. Reynolds brought to her
bedroom.

"My husband wants you to ring him up as soon as you
can," Mrs. Reynolds said, "and explain everything as you
promised last night."

Mimi simulated a yawn.

"Me? But I have nothing more to tell him, madame," she said in accents of vague surprise. "The blow on my head made me say stupid things perhaps."

"Perhaps," Mrs. Reynolds agreed dryly. She cast a shrewd glance at the girl. "He also hoped that you would stay here and rest quietly to-day, Mimi."

"It is a good suggestion, madame. Maybe I will take the little walk this morning and then, you and I, we could visit the cinema after luncheon."

We *could*," Mrs. Reynolds emphasised, "but I've a suspicion that we shall not. I'm afraid that you might take the little walk and not return! You're not fit to run any more risks at present."

"I want to call on a dear friend, madame. It will not tire me. Please do not bother the inspector about it."

Mrs. Reynolds scorned weak sentiment as much as Mimi did, and although she had a deep affection for the French girl, her duty to her husband came first.

Making an evasive reply, she went downstairs and called him up.

"Is that you, Tom? . . . Yes, Mimi seems fairly well. She says it's a mistake and that she has nothing more to tell you. I'm convinced she is planning a move of her own. You think she will go back to Vernstein's! It's no use being angry, my dear. You can't take her out on a leash."

*   *   *   *

In his office at Scotland Yard Reynolds received his wife's message with rage in his heart. Never in the whole of his successful career had he been more completely baulked than he was now over these jewel murder cases. Gillingham, James Carr, and last night the brutal assault on Stephen Blair!

The clues and motive unmistakably pointed to Zaldo, the headquarters of his gang had been discovered by Mimi, and yet the inspector was helpless.

If he arrested the Vernstein bunch, not one of them would tell him where their ringleader was.

His one thread of hope had lain in Mimi's hands. And now she said that she had nothing more to tell him!

Once more she evidently intended to attempt a task alone that should, because of its hazardous nature, have the backing of C.I.D. men. The fiasco in Blair's flat and his accident that might prove fatal, would not have happened had she confided in Reynolds yesterday afternoon.

What in the name of fortune had changed the girl?

Vanity? She had not a streak of it in her make-up. Love? Her emotion on hearing of Blair's condition was understandable, but as he was a victim, clearly she was not shielding him. Chivalry? Mimi's strong sense of justice would never allow her to protect a miscreant. Loyalty?

At that word Reynolds halted. The question was not so easily dismissed. Mimi was intensely loyal: particularly to her own sex if they were down and out.

Down and out! He repeated the phrase reminiscently, remembering that he had teased her a few days ago for saying "out and down." It was concerning the girl Linda she had met in Montmartre and whom she had brought to London.

There was something mysterious about Linda, something in her past that Mimi, after one slip, had declared to be of no importance.

There again Mimi had bargained with him: her information concerning Zaldo in exchange for his promise not to torment her poor Linda!

Well, Mimi had broken her word and he meant to break his, Reynolds decided. Mimi's uncompleted sentence came back to him: "Perhaps if you knew that behind Linda is an unsolved—"

At the time Mimi had laughed the matter off, and the discovery of James Carr's murder early next morning had thrust it from Reynolds's mind. Suppose—

His brain leaped as be reached for the telephone and called up his wife.

"Tell Mimi to speak to me at once, Agnes, and say I'll take no excuse," he said over the wire.

Eh? Then I'll hang on until she's out of the bath."

In a few moments a dulcet voice greeted him with "Good morning, Papa Reynolds. I hope that you are in excellent health and temper."

"My temper will be as excellent as my health when I receive your accurate replies to my questions," Reynolds told her sternly. "Where is Linda and what is her full name?"

A ripple of laughter came to his ear.

"Linda Smith left for Scotland last night, monsieur," Mimi answered. "It is a thousand pities that I cannot give you her address until she writes to me. Oh, la, la, does Madame Reynolds know that you wish to meet a pretty girl?"

"And that is all you will tell me, Mimi?"

"That is all, monsieur. How is Mr. Blair?"

"Still unconscious. But," Reynolds added with meaning, "when he recovers somewhat he will be able to tell me about Linda, since he and you dined with her last night. You understand, Mimi? If you refuse to be frank I must fight this battle as I think best."

"And I, as I judge fair, monsieur," was the girl's steady answer.

Something in the bravery of her last sentence softened Reynolds's indignation. Mimi must feel that she was fighting in a just cause to turn her back on him when her help would have been so useful.

For a moment he experienced a little pang of regret at her desertion. Whenever they had worked together in disentangling the complications of a murder case, her ingenuity and gaiety had inspired his efforts. Now that gallant little figure had resolved to stand alone, hoping to trap a vicious criminal unaided rather than obtain, support and incriminate her friend.

Reynolds's first errand was in Kenford Street where the taxi had dropped Linda last Wednesday evening.

On arriving at number thirty-five he devoutly hoped that a maid would open the door and not the landlady. Maids easily succumbed to his methods; landladies were apt to be more difficult.

He was unlucky. The landlady appeared and proved extremely difficult.

"May I see Miss Linda—? I've forgotten her surname for the moment," Reynolds confessed.

"Then you'd better wait until you remember it," was Kate's instant retort. "I'm not in the habit of calling my lodgers by their Christian names."

"Of course not," Reynolds agreed genially, "but you would remember if you heard it, I'm sure. Linda is an unusual name. The lady is young and pretty."

"So are thousands of other girls," Kate retaliated, "but you won't find the one you want if you can't describe her better than that. What's she like?"

"I'm not very good at description," Reynolds fenced. Suddenly he decided on testing the suspicion that had leaped to his mind a while ago. Suppose Linda was the red-haired girl described by the caretaker as being Gillingham's secretary! "How stupid of me," he exclaimed. "Red hair and blue eyes."

"Funny you didn't remember that before," Kate replied suspiciously. "Well, there ain't no dark red Linda Anybodies in this house, mister; my lodgers are all elderly. However, I don't want to discourage you. There's over a hundred houses in this street, and you can try 'em all as far as I'm concerned. Good luck," she added and, banged the door in his face.

Delicate inquiries at adjoining houses brought no helpful result. The occupants seemed to live in the basements and mind their own business. A postman delivering letters knew of no one bearing that Christian name on his round.

The first blank, Reynolds reflected. He could have number thirty-five watched. But, the girl might have moved elsewhere.

He would try to construct things from another angle. Stephen Blair's dinner party last night, for instance. When a man invited a lady to dine with him he usually asked her to choose the restaurant. To Reynolds's knowledge Mimi had telephoned to Blair arranging the time and place. There was a possibility that she had selected the French café in Soho where she knew the proprietor and to which she had taken Reynolds and his wife three evenings ago. He would call there.

Monsieur Antoine expressed himself as being enchanted to meet the inspector again. Yes, Mademoiselle Mimi had dined here last night, he said, with two gentlemen and a lady.

Reynolds raised his eyebrows.

"Two gentlemen? The lady with mademoiselle had auburn hair and blue eyes if it is the same that I mean. Miss Linda Somebody," he added in a questioning tone.

The Frenchman's manner changed to one of reserve, as he recalled his errand on Mimi's behalf a few nights ago. He was giving nothing away for the moment.

"Monsieur knows more than I apparently. Naturally I did not hear the lady's name, and there was no reason why I should observe her particularly. One has many clients and one forgets. Monsieur will understand."

" Monsieur" did understand only too well.

The waiters who served them might have heard the lady's name mentioned," Reynolds suggested, without much hope of success, since Antoine would certainly warn them to be silent.

"They shall be called immediately," the Frenchman promised. "A thousand pardons, monsieur, but I trust nothing is wrong to cause you to make this investigation."

"The gentleman who gave the party met with an accident. Inquiries may arise," Reynolds said ambiguously, thankful for the workable excuse.

"Monsieur has not forgotten that Mademoiselle Mimi will of course know the lady's name and address."

"I have not forgotten," Reynolds replied, repressing a smile.

As he expected, the waiters' minds were a blank on the subject.

At the door he tackled the porter before Monsieur Antoine had the opportunity to muzzle him.

Here Reynolds learned that the second gentleman had appeared unexpectedly in the hall, had given the two girls some violets and had gone off with them in a taxi after ten o'clock.

The inspector reached Stephen Blair's flat feeling he had advanced a step.

One glance at the grief-stricken face of Blair's servant assured him that this individual had had no hand in last night's business.

The man explained the fake message by which he had been called away.

"If I'd stayed here, sir, it would never have happened," Grey said bitterly. "I'll never forgive myself. I'm sure it's all through that dangerous hobby of his. Collecting jewels, I mean. The only bit of luck is that the stuff was all in the bank. I'd no idea he was bringing company back here last night."

Reynolds's eyes gleamed at the news that Blair had had visitors.

"We'll go in and look round, Grey."

The man apologised for the library being untidy.

"I've had no heart to touch anything, sir."

Reynolds noticed four glasses on the tray that held the decanters and soda siphon. Three visitors, then!

On the floor a few dead violets were lying! Evidently his guests at dinner had returned here with him.

"I found some violets in the little room where the empty safe is, sir," Grey mentioned.

"Any idea who your master's guests were?"

"None whatever, sir. Mr. Blair is very popular and has scores of friends. But no ladies come to his flat, except his friends' wives."

"Any elderly gentlemen visit here? Perhaps to see his collection of gems?"

"Not what you might call elderly, sir. Whether they came to see the jewels I couldn't say. My master knew that I hated the blessed things, and rarely spoke of them to me. Every night of my life I was terrified of burglary. His uncle left him pots of money and a lot of valuables a few years ago, and that began this craze."

"Well, Mr. Blair is no worse this morning. If any reporters come, you know nothing. By a lucky chance there is only a small paragraph in the late editions of the morning newspapers saying that Mr. Stephen Blair was found unconscious in the yard of this building last night. It is presumed that he accidentally fell from the window of his first floor flat. That's all the publicity I want about the affair."

"I understand, sir," Grey replied. "Good day."

Downstairs in the hall the inspector paused for a few words with the porter.

"Ah, Quayle, you're back, I see. You weren't on duty at midnight, were you?"

The porter rubbed his chin.

"Well, sir, I was and I wasn't, so to speak," he replied heavily. "At about half-past eleven last night the manager of the flats came along and said I was to take an urgent note at once to an Inspector Reynolds at Highgate."

"How long have you worked here?" asked Reynolds, now understanding for the first time why he had found a blank sheet of paper in an envelope addressed to himself, in the letter box at Highgate.

"I'm new to the job, sir."

"Ah! Go on."

"Well, I took the letter, not seeing any objection. I hope it was on the level, sir. I don't want to get into any trouble. You're one of the directors, perhaps."

Reynolds suppressed a smile.

"No, I'm not a director, Quayle, but I don't think you'll get into any trouble. Only, another time, stay at your post."

He turned away to find Blair's manservant waiting for him.

"I ran down to tell you about the handbag, sir. One of the lady guests must have left it behind last night."

Reynolds wheeled round eagerly.

"I'd better see it before it's claimed, Grey."

"I'm sorry if I did wrong in letting the gentleman have it early this morning."

"Did he give his name or the lady's name?" Grey seemed a little uneasy at the question. "Neither, sir. He said a lady guest of Mr. Blair's had left her bag and might he have it at once. He mentioned the articles it contained."

Disappointed as Reynolds was, there remained still a gleam of hope.

"What was in the bag? Any letters?"

"No, sir. A small green handkerchief, a powder puff, lip-stick and a little money."

"Nothing else?"

"Nothing but a queer little green elephant about four inches long. It might have been made of jade or ordinary green stone for all I know."

A red-haired girl with blue eyes called Linda who owned a green elephant! Reynolds smiled to himself cynically. And that was all the clues he had with which to trace her in a city that contained millions of women!

XXVII. The Secret of the Cabinets

Saturday morning

Linda moved about the antique shop that morning in a strangely peaceful mood.

Occasionally she smiled to herself as she recalled the uninvited guest who had taken breakfast with her a few hours ago. Nick Tyler's persistence was becoming a joke. At times his self-assurance was irritating, but nevertheless he certainly made her forget her anxieties. One couldn't be introspective in that young man's presence.

If only she could feel convinced that he was not a crook, she would be much happier.

There was the damning evidence that he was employed by Yates who was undoubtedly a blackmailing scoundrel.

For the moment she decided to dismiss tiresome problems. Here in this pleasant retreat under her kindly employer she could forget the troubled past. She glanced at him now with warm gratitude, as he sat writing at a table under the glass dome at the back of the shop.

"Miss Marchant, would it trouble you to deliver this small packet for me?" he asked. The address is not far from here and the packet is urgent and valuable."

"I'll go at once, Mr. Wentworth," she agreed willingly.

"I hope you are happy here, Miss Marchant." There was a whimsical expression in his eyes that even the horn-rimmed spectacles could not conceal. "It must be a dull existence for a young woman to spend her time among antiquities of which I'm afraid I am one."

"You're not at all old," she replied with warmth. "Your brain is far keener than that of most men, and you have a knowledge and experience of things that really matter. I'm terribly happy here, and happiest of all when I hear you discussing antiques with clients."

He raised his eyebrows in amusement.

"With that gay young man Mr. Tyler, for instance?" he inquired.

"By no means with him in particular. It is you whom I find interesting to listen to."

"So, beard and spectacles and all, I can-compete favourably in your eyes with youth! Well, it's comforting to my vanity to have so loyal a partisan. I promise not to let your flattery spoil me unduly."

Under her breath Linda whispered to herself "You sweet old darling. You're too old world to live in these times of rogues."

Aloud, she said as she took the packet from his hands: "I shall be back within half an hour, Mr. Wentworth."

"By the way," he remarked as he gave her a sealed envelope, "I should like you to have your salary and commission now. Over the week-end you may be glad of a little cash."

"It's most thoughtful of you. But I've only been here two and a half days. How do you know that I shall turn up on Monday morning?" she inquired.

"If I were a gambler, young woman, I would willingly bet the entire contents of this shop, which are more valuable than you imagine, that you would return unless prevented by death or accident, which heaven forbid," was his calm reply.

She bit her lip. There was something she had to say to him and it was difficult.

"Mr. Wentworth, forgive me if I am being impertinent, but I must tell you again that you are too trustful. It worries me. Please, please be careful. I'm sure you only laugh at me for being a nervous fool."

"You are neither nervous nor foolish," he replied. "On the contrary, I am grateful for your regard for my interests. But," he added with a quiet chuckle, "who can have designs on me or my property? Do you suspect anyone in particular?"

"Every man or woman who enters this shop," Linda answered swiftly, "until I can satisfy myself that each one is an honourable client and nothing else."

"Indeed, I must be cautious in inviting visitors here!" Mr. Wentworth commented. "I thank you for your frankness, Miss Marchant. You are a good watch-dog."

A few yards from the shop a woman overtook her. Linda was surprised to see that it was her landlady. "What's wrong, Kate?"

"Thank goodness I've caught you, miss. I sincerely 'ope that nothing's wrong. I've slipped along here to warn you that if ever I saw a 'flattie' in my life I saw one at my house half an hour ago. Snooping round for a Miss Linda whose surname he didn't know and I took good care not to tell him."

Linda stared aghast.

"Do you mean that a detective called and asked questions about me?"

"That's what I've been telling you, miss. I handed him the same yarn that I told the bloke last Wednesday night."

The girl pressed the woman's aim gratefully. "Thank you, Kate. Where am I to go? I can't have you dragged into trouble."

"You'll stay with me and use the side door and the back lane,' Kate said decisively. "They've filed my house twice and had no luck, so maybe they'll leave it alone for a bit. As for trouble," she gave a contemptuous snort, "I hid my 'usbaud for two months when the cops wanted 'im, and I shan't forget how you gave me money to pack the scamp off to America. Don't you fret. Scotland Yard flatties won't find you in my home unless they call out the militia and make 'em form fours all round it."

"How could anyone know I was there?"

"That's for you to say, miss. Them friends you went out to dinner with last night, could they have split on

you? Or," the woman's face fell, "even that smart young
gent who came this morning? Though I'd never have
believed it of him."

"I don't know, Kate. I'm frightened," Linda told her.
"It was good of you to come and tell me. It's my half-day
off. I won't comeback until it's dark. I must hurry now to
do an errand. Good-bye."

Returning a little later she found the shop door open.

On entering she heard a man's voice raised in heated
argument with her employer at the far end under the
dome.

"Your threats don't frighten me," Mr. Wentworth was
saying. "You're a wastrel. Not one penny of my money
will you get now or at any time, whether I'm alive or
dead."

"Don't forget that you've other things just as
valuable," sneered the younger man. "I must have some
cash, uncle. I'm desperate. I could do you in easily now,
take what I wanted and get out before anyone knew it."

"Could you?" Mr. Wentworth smiled significantly and
glanced down the shop.

Towards them Linda was advancing, a duster in her
hand, her attention apparently engrossed with wiping
specks from the furniture. Not once did she look in the
men's direction, but her face was rigid with
determination.

"You have heard all that I have to say," Mr.
Wentworth said clearly. "Get out and don't come here
again or you may be sorry for it."

The younger man strode down the shop, muttering as
he brushed past the girl, and went out.

"You wait until to-night," she heard him say.

"And that," remarked Mr. Wentworth in his quiet
tones, "was my nephew, Miss Marchant."

"So I gathered," Linda replied briefly. She noticed
with concern that her employer's hands were trembling.
"May I make you a cup of tea?" she asked.

"A very pleasant suggestion. Perhaps you will join me. I should like to show you some of my real treasures afterwards." His eyes twinkled. "My watch-dog should know what she is guarding."

He chatted easily on the merits of jade while he drank the tea. Linda was preoccupied with the threat she had heard the young man make as he passed her. Should she inform her employer of it, or would he disregard the danger, and think she was interfering?

She had just decided on a course of silence and increased watchfulness when a phrase caught her ear.

"Yes," came her employer's voice. "Mr. Tyler's judgment is as remarkable as his honesty. It was a rare piece for colour and quality?'

"You mean the little jade elephant that he bought for two guineas?" she asked, a little puzzled. "If it was rare, the price was ridiculously cheap. He may be a good judge but he's not honest. If he knew it was rare and under priced, he ought to have paid more," she added stoutly.

"He did, Miss Marchant," Mr. Wentworth replied. "The price was twenty-two pounds, not two guineas. A simple mistake on your part, that was quite pardonable in a novice. He realised this and insisted upon paying the difference. I did not want to take it, but he forced me to do so with the urgent request that you should not hear of it." His lip twitched amusedly. "I should not have broken my word, only it occurs to me that you are uncommonly hard upon that young man. I want you to wipe him off your list of suspected callers here."

An old adage flashed into Linda's mind. "Throw a sprat to catch a mackerel." Could Nick be trying to impress Mr. Wentworth with his honesty for some ulterior purpose?

The thought persisted as her employer unlocked the black cabinets that had aroused Nick's curiosity and drew out shallow trays covered with black velvet. Raising the wrappers, he invited Linda to look at the contents.

She gave a startled gasp. Superb jewels in various settings gleamed from their sombre background. Before her lay diamonds of a size that even her inexperience told her must be worth a fortune. Rubies, emeralds, sapphires shone in tiaras, necklaces and rings. Ropes of pearls that might have adorned a royal breast shed their pale soft lustre of beauty.

"It's like some exquisite fairy tale," she exclaimed. "They ought to be kept in a bank. It's dangerous to have them here."

Mr. Wentworth's hands touched them almost caressingly.

"Does a man keep a pet dog that he loves shut in cellar for fear that it might be stolen?" he asked "These are *my* pets. I love to see and handle them when I will. As for burglars," he flicked his finger "my jewels could not easily be disposed of. They are world famous; even a single stone would be recognised."

"The stones might be cut," Linda objected.

"That is true. It hurts me to think of such vandalism." He replaced a velvet covering with the delicate tenderness of a mother tucking up her infant. "I am proud that you like my beloved treasures. One of the great joys a connoisseur experiences is in exhibiting his collection to an appreciative audience. You have never seen any gems so wonderful, I am sure."

"Never," Linda replied, and then added unthinkingly. "Once before I was shown a collection. Some of the jewels and the settings resembled these, but there were not so many and they were not so fine."

"Really" Mr. Wentworth did not appear to be over-pleased at the news "This is very interesting, Miss Marchant. We collectors have one unpleasant vice in common: secrecy. Who is my rival?"

Too late Linda wished that she had not mentioned the subject. Still there could be no harm in revealing the incident to Mr. Wentworth. He was not the type of man who read sensational news. Mr. Gillingham's death was

more than six months ago and there had been no mention
of jewels in the report of the inquest.

"He was my employer. I was his secretary and left
when he died," she answered. "He was a business man
and I had no idea that he was a connoisseur of gems until
one day he opened a safe and showed me his hoard."

"If it contained anything better than I own I shall be
thoroughly envious," was Mr. Wentworth's rueful
comment. "Can you remember what was there, Miss
Marchant? Try to show me what kind of things he had."
Indicating the trays before her he added: "Arrange them
as you like."

Thankful that her employer seemed more interested
in the other man's jewels than in the name of the owner,
Linda applied herself willingly to the task. Her memory
was excellent, and she could even recollect the order in
which Mr. Gillingham's treasures had been arranged on
the different trays.

She stood back in a little while with a touch of pride
and surveyed her efforts.

"Like this," she said. "The top tray had a crown with a
tiara on either side. The second held rings arranged in a
circle around four massive bracelets. Another tray was
filled with pendants and brooches. I'm not very sure of
these as they were small articles. The last tray I
remember best of all; it contained four magnificent
necklaces." She smiled up at him. "And women love a
necklace. There was, I remember in particularly, a pearl
rope, very like yours, but I think of a slightly deeper
shade; and one necklace of immense diamonds. I've
placed your emerald one in place of it here."

Mr. Wentworth regarded the trays sadly.

"I suppose the collection went to my late rival's
family. Certainly it has not come into the market or I
should have heard of it." He sighed as he replaced the
trays in the cabinets. "Well, you've broken my vain old
heart, Miss Marchant, and made me both covetous and
jealous, but I thank you for the trouble you have taken.

It's nearly one o'clock and Saturday is your free afternoon. I must not delay you."

"I'm in no hurry. My life is happier here than anywhere else," the girl declared with a trace of bitterness in her tone. "You will close the shop for the day now, won't you?"

"To customers, I hope." Mr. Wentworth's face had the mischievous expression of a boy who was slipping away from school to play marbles. "I'm going to stay here and play with my toys." He nodded towards the cabinets.

Linda caught her breath in dismay. She could not let this old man stay here alone, with the memory of the menacing words his nephew had uttered ringing in her ears.

"I'll stay too and polish the Waterford glass," she said. "Please let me. I've nothing else to do."

"No engagements with friends to offer you more amusement than dull work of that kind?" His gentle voice held a quizzical note.

Linda shook her head.

"I've no friends, Mr. Wentworth."

He put the bunch of keys in his pocket and rose.

"In that case," he remarked with a smile, "we must see if an old gentleman with an envious mind for jewels can provide something more entertaining. Will you take luncheon with me, Miss Marchant? I suggest the Berkeley. Afterwards perhaps you will allow me to escort you to a matinee of your own choice."

Seeing her hesitation he went on: "It's the only way you can be sure that I don't play truant and return here alone."

"I would do a great deal to prevent that," Linda said firmly. "It is extremely kind of you. I shall love to come, thank you."

Suddenly she remembered her promise to Yates to take him her salary the moment that she received it. One day soon she determined to make a full confession to Mr.

Wentworth, and if he would forgive her, shake off Yates for ever.

"I have an errand that I must do," she added. "I'll meet you at the restaurant in half an hour."

XXVIII. Zaldo Issues Orders

Saturday, 1 p.m.

Dan gave a bored yawn, looked at his watch, and rose from the bed upon which he had been lying fully dressed. It was one o'clock and he wanted a meal and a drink in which water would play no part if he could help it.

Already he was regretting the impulse that had made him suggest staying in Yates's flat. Yates had locked up his liquor, and ate at a restaurant.

Also twice, yesterday, on returning unexpectedly, Dan had found Yates in his bedroom, suspiciously near his suitcases. So far a parcel, hidden behind the chimney flap, was safe, but at any minute Yates might discover it, and then indeed blackmail would begin in earnest.

The parcel was becoming a millstone around Dan's neck. Apart from its value, it was too bulky to be carried in his pocket, and he knew no peace of mind if he went out without it.

To dispose of any of the contents was impossible in this country. Vernstein was the only fairly honest "fence" that he knew, and the Jew was a member of Zaldo's gang.

Meanwhile Dan's supply of cash—depleted further by the notes Yates had extorted yesterday—was far too low to enable him to get abroad and realise on his unlawful assets. He'd been a fool to have those two expensive suits made. One would have to be pawned at once to give him a little money to go on with.

Wrapping up some garments, he opened his door cautiously and peeped out into the small hall. Yates was apparently shut in his office. Possibly that sidey blighter Nick Tyler was with him.

Dan was never sure whether Nick was pulling his leg or not, and he had no wish to find out now. Yates had

made it clear that Nick Tyler knew nothing about Zaldo
and was employed for casual work.

As Dan had been refused the privilege of having a
key, he left the flat door open a few inches on going out
now. If Yates heard it shut he would seize the
opportunity to search the bedroom again.

Parcel under his arm, Dan set out for a pawnbroker
who had "obliged" him on previous occasions of similar
embarrassment.

A few minutes after his departure Linda reached
Yates's flat. She was about to press the bell when she
noticed that the front door was a little ajar.

Pushing it open she looked inside the dingy hall which
contained nothing but a table on one side and a large wall
cupboard on the other.

The girl paused a moment and listened, in case Yates
was engaged with a client. Everything was silent,
however.

Suddenly she heard the jangle of a telephone bell and
Yates's voice answering it irritably. She didn't. want to be
late for her appointment with Mr. Wentworth, but
obviously must wait until this call was finished.

Before she could retreat out of earshot Yates's tone
had changed to one of cringing deference. Something in
the context of his reply over the wire arrested her
attention.

"Yes, sir, the red-headed girl arrived and got the job
at once," she heard. "Not since, but she'll call here soon. . .
Well, sir, I—er—thought it was wise to keep in touch
with her." Yates's voice sounded as if he had received a
sharp reprimand.

"Exactly what you told me to say about her parents,"
he continued. "No, I wouldn't say she was suspicious but
she'll need firm handling. I had to pretend I knew a bit
about her past to frighten her. Of course I know nothing
really, but I guessed there was something queer or you
wouldn't have planned to get her into that post."

The girl pressed a trembling hand to a pulse that throbbed in her forehead. In what dreadful predicament had she landed herself by answering that advertisement? "Very good, sir," Yates went on. "I understand. Monday night, eleven-thirty. I'll warn Kent. It ought to be easy. The old man doesn't sleep there, his nephew says, and is never there late at night. Perfectly, sir. The nephew, Kent and—" The name was inaudible, though she fancied it began with "D." "If you insist. But I've never done that kind of job." Yates sounded uneasy and reluctant. "All right, sir," he said after an interval. "I've got it clear. All four of us, Monday night. The old man's nephew will get the keys of the shop. I'm to bring everything here afterwards and await your further orders."

There was a click; the conversation was evidently over. The next instant a flood of violent language burst from Yates who was evidently voicing his displeasure at the instructions he had received from his unseen caller.

Linda tiptoed outside, and allowed him a few moments to cool off before she rang the front door bell. She had only one desire; that was, to get away from this place as quickly as possible and try to forget what she had heard for a few hours. In her present panic-stricken state she could not think calmly. To-morrow she must attempt to reconstruct that one-sided conversation and fill in the blanks.

"What the—Oh, it's you, Miss Marchant."

Yates, rather less clean than on her former visit, stood before her. "Come in," he invited, smoothing his angry expression to a bland smile of welcome.

Linda drew an envelope from her bag and gave it to him.

"Mr. Wentworth wished to pay me to-day," she said in frigid tones.

Yates fingered the envelope and, leered up at her.

"You seem to be getting on with him very nicely. How much has he given you?"

"I neither know nor care, since you will receive it and not I," she retorted. "I've not opened it."

The man tore the envelope open and pulled out a five-pound note. Attached was a message stating that it was for a week's salary and commission on sales for two days.

Pocketing the money, Yates attempted to introduce a social element into the chilly atmosphere.

"Run in any time, Miss Marchant. What about a drink and a spot of grub with me now?"

"No thanks," she refused. She went out, dosing the office door behind her.

In the hall a tall man stepped from the wall cupboard and raising his finger to enjoin silence, followed her out to the staircase.

"Been listening-in for long, Mr. Tyler?" she inquired with mild scorn.

Nick nodded cheerfully.

"Quite a while," he admitted. "I was here before you came. We both seem to have overheard friend Yates say quite a lot of interesting things on the telephone. Little girls shouldn't listen outside doors. It's really not done by the best people."

"You're an amazing person," Linda told him. "Shameless in some things, over-scrupulous in others. How dare you let me make that ridiculous mistake about the jade elephant and then pay the twenty pounds difference to Mr. Wentworth with a proviso that he should-not tell me?"

"And the sneaking old, scoundrel promptly did so!"

"Only to prove to me that you were both honest and chivalrous."

"It's worth the money to make you believe in my sterling qualities, Linda."

"On the other hand it is money wasted if I remain unconvinced," was her answer.

Nick's mouth twisted to an odd smile.

"I must put in some good word on my behalf during dinner to-night. Let me see," he reflected. "I think I'll take you to the Trocadero grill room. Your table manners are coming along, so well that I can risk a really good restaurant now. After that, you may hold my hand for a little while at the movies. I'll look up a good film. Don't be late. Trocadero, seven o'clock."

He darted back into the flat and shut the door before she could reply.

A quarter of an hour later a taxi put her down at the Berkeley.

"I do hope that I have not kept you waiting," she said a little breathlessly as Mr. Wentworth came forward to meet her.

"You have been barely the half hour you requested," he told her. "Join me in a glass of sherry."

During luncheon Linda's thoughts wandered back to the inscrutable personality of Nick Tyler. Nothing would induce her to dine with him to-night, she decided. And caught herself wondering where he was now.

At that moment he was sitting in Yates's office exhibiting a very different facet of his character.

"The trouble with you, Yates," Nick was drawling, "is that you work too hard and under-rate my intelligence."

"What do you mean?" his employer demanded suspiciously.

"You do all the hard, brainy stunts and give me stupid little jobs that are child's play to one as gifted as I am," Nick complained. "You should take me into your confidence over big matters where my valuable powers of observation and deduction might be of great service to you."

"Pity you ain't at Scotland Yard," sneered Yates. "Only a little matter of a forgery prevents you from being England's first detective, eh?"

Nick looked pained at the jibe.

"You needn't remind me of that. However, to show my deductive powers, I'd favour you with three instances, Yates, gratuitously. One, you have a man staying here; his habits are not nice and you don't trust him. Two, you've recently come into money. Three, you're extremely, worried and perhaps scared about something. Am I right, sir?" he demanded with the blithe air of a showman.

"Any fool can make silly statements, but—" his employer began.

"It takes a wise man to prove 'em," Nick finished for him. "I will now do so. One: a chair and a table are missing from this room since yesterday; they're not in the kitchen or your bedroom, so presumably they're in the spare bedroom. Ergo: a guest. Male species and of nasty habits, because in the kitchen I noticed a soiled breakfast cup smelling of tea and brandy, and containing several chewed cigarette ends of a strong brand. I don't blame you for not trusting him or locking away the whisky that you usually leave about. The answer to number two is the healthy pile of money that you were counting when I came in. Number three—"

"That'll do," Yates said hastily. "We all get worried at times but don't want to blat about it."

"As you will," Nick agreed with indifference.

"Out of loving kindness I offered you my manly bosom in case you might like to lay your head on it—quite metaphorically—and pour your troubles out to my soft heart and not-so-soft brain."

Yates glared at him.

"I should hate to. What you're driving at I don't know, Tyler." His tone had something of the snarl of a dog at bay. "I've had enough of your funny stuff for one day. You can clear out."

"Keep cool, my pretty one. Temper's bad for your blood pressure." Nick flicked a speck of dust from his sleeve. "By the way, speaking of funny stuff, don't try to involve Miss Marchant in anything—er—awkward. I can be most unpleasant as an enemy, Yates." Behind the indolent composure of Nick's voice was a hint of steel, and his blue eyes were hard and inflexible.

"Bluff doesn't frighten me, Tyler."

"No? Then I suppose that something serious has occurred to turn you into the pasty-faced craven that you appear to be now. You're afraid, Yates; badly afraid. I knew it the moment I saw you. Well, get on with your foul little schemes, but—leave that girl or any girl out of them."

Yates's lip curled.

"Quite the gentleman, ain't you?" he taunted. "Don't forget you may one day be a convict."

"Employed by a crook and a blackmailer," Nick supplemented with a broad grin. "Don't get run over by a bus, sweetheart. You're destined for a career where clothes and meals are provided free. My love to your profitable lodger."

XXIX. The Trap

Saturday afternoon

Reynolds walked up the hospital steps and into the wide quiet hall.

"Is Dr. Tempest here?" he inquired of the porter. "I am Inspector Reynolds. He is expecting me."

"Yes, sir. He is still with Mr. Blair in consultation with the other doctors. I'll tell him that you are here directly he comes down."

Reynolds stared gloomily out of the window of the small waiting-room to which he had been conducted. Work, even at the highest pressure, he loved when it showed results. But work, plus sleepless nights and anxious tension with no spark of hope in sight, was wearing him down.

Somewhere, perhaps even within a mile radius, was a red-haired girl called Linda, who could tell him a lot about "Dan." Dan, who had probably caused the death of Gillingham.

And upstairs in a ward lay Stephen Blair, who could by a word possibly prevent another crime from being committed. Reynolds was now waiting to know when that word might be spoken.

"Ah, here you are, inspector. Sorry to keep you waiting."

Reynolds jumped at the sound of Dr. Tempest's voice and pivoted sharply to face him.

"Well, doctor?" he asked in a shaky, hoarse tone.

"Not too encouraging a report, I'm afraid," the pathologist replied. "Blair is still unconscious." Reynolds gave a weary sigh.

"Thank You, It's good of you to have given me your opinion on the case."

"Sorry. I've no better news for you." Dr. Tempest put his hand on the C.I.D. man's shoulder and swung him round towards the light. "What's the matter, inspector? You look all in. Worrying about these confounded murder cases? Have you had any food lately?" he demanded, holding out his cigarette-case.

"I had some breakfast." Reynolds took a cigarette and gazed at it with blank eyes.

"You put that in your mouth and apply a lighted match," the doctor said dryly. "Also, as it's nearly four o'clock you will come and have some food at my club with me. My luncheon was little more than a dog biscuit. By the way, the porter showed me a bunch of violets that he said a young lady had left for Mr. Blair this afternoon. There was a card attached on which was written: 'With the best wishes from Linda."

"Linda!" Reynolds exclaimed. "Curious wording for an English girl to use."

The porter described the young lady as being dressed in black; a tiny, black-haired, slip of a girl with dark eyes, he said."

"That's an exact picture of Mimi," Reynolds said in puzzled tones. "I don't understand."

"Never try to understand the ways and wiles, of a woman," advised the medical man. "Come along. Let's go and eat."

Over a meal that was badly needed the strain in Reynolds's face relaxed.

"I believe I was hungry," he remarked with a grin, surveying the empty dishes.

"I had the same impression," agreed the doctor. "At the sober age of forty-one, one expects to find a little horse sense in the head of one of England's famous sleuths."

"Famous! Call me a prize idiot instead. Think of it, doctor. Two murders have been committed. If Blair pegs out, that will make a third. And yet another may be perpetrated at any moment. I know the cause and the name of the criminal and I can do nothing. Nothing! I've raked London for a clue to him. How would you feel if you were in my position?"

"Pretty much as you do, I expect, though my philosophy in life is to do your utmost and then, if it fails, to stop worrying." Dr. Tempest was silent for a moment. "By the cause and criminal, you mean 'jewels' and 'Zaldo?'"

Reynolds nodded.

"Yes. It doesn't help my peace of mind to know that I could lay my hands on two or three of his band at this moment," he groaned. "I feel desperate enough to rope in everyone inside Vernstein's house to-day. At least it would bust up the crowd."

"And allow the ringleader to escape and form a fresh gang at his leisure," the doctor reminded. "Where's your devoted Jenkins these days?"

"He has been keeping in reach of Mimi in Whitechapel. He'll be at the Yard now. That girl is running incredible risks, doctor."

"She wriggles out of tight corners because she keeps a cool head. About your end of it, inspector, isn't there some fresh angle from which you could tackle this affair?"

"There is one," Reynolds replied. "The chance of success is remote. Also it would mean a visit to Paris and that would take up valuable time."

"You could go by air, and to-morrow, being Sunday, isn't of much use to you here, is it? Hop into my car," Dr. Tempest suggested, "and I'll drive you to the Yard while you think over the idea."

A few minutes later they walked along the corridor to the inspector's office.

At the door Reynolds paused.

"It's a tempting gamble, doctor; I wish I could feel that it was justifiable."

"Bigger bets than that have come off. Nothing like travel to cure depression. Good luck."

Something of his old enthusiasm returned to the inspector. Entering his office he saw his assistant waiting for him.

"Ring up Croydon and book two seats on tonight's air service," he ordered. "You and I are going to Paris.".

The arrangements for their trip were speedily made and, with an hour to spare, Reynolds sat down at his desk to do a little solid thinking.

"Let's weigh up all the known facts, Jenkins."

Drawing a sheet of paper towards him he wrote down the names of the victims.

GILLINGHAM. Found dead in office in April. Sleeping drug. Porter saw his red-haired secretary and her young man called Dan leave shortly before Gillingham entered on night of his death. Motive unknown but suspect jewels. Is the mysterious Linda the secretary? Are she and Dan members of Zaldo's gang? And is she now acting as a decoy for them?

JAMES CARR. Found dead in library three days ago. Took Fleming's tincture in mistake for sherry. Undoubtedly put in decanter by fake charwoman. Motive proved to be robbery. Clocks stopped at midnight, jewels stolen. Carr one of three men who purchased Euralian jewels.

STEPHEN BLAIR. Brutally assaulted at midnight yesterday. Motive, robbery. Safe empty; jewels in Blair's bank. Blair recently went to Paris. Was probably the purchaser of Euralian jewels. Zaldo ordered caretaker to be chloroformed. Linda in Blair's flat earlier in evening; also Mimi and unknown young man who dined with them.

"If Linda was Gillingham's secretary, she may be one of Zaldo's accomplices," Reynolds mused.

"Did Mimi say that Linda met Stephen Blair in the Montmartre café by accident?" Jenkins inquired.

"Mimi told me very little but I gathered that impression," was the inspector's reply. "Also Blair called on me last Tuesday to make a few inquiries concerning Mimi in whose charge, he explained, was a friendless and penniless English girl he had encountered by chance."

Jenkins smiled.

"It's a rich jest, sir, to think that Mr. Blair wanted Mimi's reference to know if she was fit to act as nursemaid to Linda, who is probably the worst type of adventuress! Of course our visit to Pans is in order to find out a bit about Linda's life."

"Something like that, my boy," Reynolds admitted. "We're going to beat the record for swift 'snooping' while we're there. I must be back again by Monday morning at the latest." His forehead puckered. "You saw, the old Jew Vernstein when you went to his house with Mimi. What was he like?"

Jenkins pondered the question for a minute.

"Thick-set build, medium height, keen eyes, beard that I'm certain was grown on his face, guttural accent, age about sixty," he reeled off.

Reynolds tapped on the desk reflectively.

"Will you tell me," he asked, "why a list of the Euralian jewels was in Vernstein's possession *before* they were all stolen?"

"That point never occurred to me, sir. I see what you mean. Vernstein is a 'fence.' He would naturally make a list of stolen goods that he has been given to dispose of, but, unless he is very much in Zaldo's confidence, how can he know of thefts that are contemplated?"

"You're getting close to the idea." Reynolds flung down his pen restlessly. "I'd give a great deal to know what Mimi is doing now."

"She turned up at Gunner's Court just before I came away," Jenkins told him.

*　　*　　*　　*　　*

Mimi returned to Vernstein's fold that Saturday afternoon with an unaccustomed sensation of numbness in her heart. It was as though a door through which she had glimpsed a vista of warm beauty had been banged in her face. She reviewed herself impartially.

Last night she had acted like an emotional fool after Bair's accident. Ringing in her ears were the last words he had said to her, before he thrust her aside and went up to his flat. "Perhaps I've taken you a little too much on trust, Mimi."

Even if he lived to know that he was mistaken, the memory of those words would remain. The peculiar nature of her work demanded secrecy, and sent her into dangerous places with questionable characters. Long ago she had decided that romance must play no part in her life, unless she was willing to give up perilous adventure for household ties.

She was not willing to do so. Years had elapsed since a bunch of Apaches had murdered her young brother in Paris, but the passing of time had only strengthened the vow she had made to track down criminals. No one had asked the reason, and few would have understood why this gallant little creature strove so fiercely to attain the ends of justice. Some thought it was for the money she gained; some for the thrill she experienced.

Only her friend Inspector Reynolds knew her story and, once mentioned, it had never been referred to between them since.

On her way that afternoon, still a little dazed from the blow on her head, she had paused at the hospital to which Blair had been taken. If he were well enough to speak, he could reveal the name of the future victim, and there would be no necessity for her to go to Vernstein's.

The bulletin from the porter, to whom she had given the violets in Linda's name, settled that question. Further delay might be dangerous. Since she had elected to act alone and tell the inspector nothing, her only honourable course was to do all that lay in her power. It must be Vernstein's at once.

She knocked at Vernstein's door and received a warm welcome from the Jew, with whom were Kent and the housekeeper.

"Let's play poker," Kent suggested, "and try to forget our troubles."

The quartette sat round the table with apparently no other thought than the game. Mimi kept up a ripple of tantalising chatter, hurled at Kent with the object of provoking him to some angry admission that would be of use.

Labouring perhaps under a sense of gratitude for her help in his escape from arrest last night, Kent controlled his temper.

It was much later when a visitor arrived for Vernstein. He put his head round the door and signalled to the Jew, who left the card party and went into the passage.

Mimi recognised the newcomer. It was Dan, the man who had delivered the case of "apples." Straining her ears, she caught broken snatches of his conversation with Vernstein. "Yates has had a message," Dan was saying. "Everyone but you . . . eleven-thirty. . . . He'll have the keys of the shop. . . . Yates is to keep stuff . . . further instructions."

Then in vehement tones Dan added: "I don't like it. Zaldo's never arranged things this way before. I tell you I'm scared and so is Yates. No, I won't stay now, thanks. I'm going to have a couple of nights' good sleep before the job. Tell Kent what he's got to do. I asked Yates about that French girl. He says Zaldo's never spoken of her. Are you sure she's O.K.?"

Mimi cast a side glance at Vernstein as he resumed his seat at the table. His face was bland and inscrutable when he picked up the cards that Kent had dealt during his absence.

"What did he want?" Kent asked in an uneasy undertone.

The Jew studied his band and ignored the question. "Three cards, please," he demanded calmly.

The game proceeded with no word or hint from Vernstein as to the reason for Dan's visit.

The silence was ominous. The Jew suspected that she was a spy and not an ally.

She had pieced together what she had overheard. Eleven-thirty was the time; the two nights' sleep that Dan said he needed before the job indicated Monday as the day. A shop was the objective and Zaldo's men were to deputise for him apparently.

But *where* was the job going to take place, and who was to be the victim?

Without that information Mimi dare not leave this house. Yet how could she manage to stay here without appearing to be too eager?

Vernstein unexpectedly solved that problem for her as she yawned and pressed a hand to her head.

"You look very tired, Mimi. Why not stay here to-night?" he suggested.

She affected surprise at the invitation and a little diffidence in accepting it.

"Nonsense, of course you won't be in the way," he replied. Adding slowly: "Don't hurry off to-morrow. It would be better if you remained here until Tuesday at least. You are safe in this house. Whereas, after last night's adventure, who knows what may happen?"

Was there a hidden menace in his words? she wondered. Did he mean to keep her a prisoner until Tuesday?

For the first time she realised the danger of the trap into which she had walked deliberately. Just now it was open. But one false step and it would shut closely upon her.

XXX, THE PRISONER'S VICTORY

Saturday night

Detective-Sergeant Jenkins's face wore a rather disappointed expression as he followed the inspector along the brilliantly-lighted boulevard in Montmartre.

"So this is the Place Blanche!" he remarked moodily.

"Yes. What's the matter with it?" Reynolds inquired, noticing the disparaging tone.

"Reminds me of the Edgware Road on a Saturday night, sir. This place doesn't smell of fish and chip shops. Otherwise I don't see much difference. I've seen arc lamps before, and there are crowds and 'loud speakers' in London."

"A thoroughly insular Britisher, aren't you?" Reynolds commented. "Keep your prejudices to yourself. French people are very quick to see antagonism and I want to get at least one of 'em to become chatty to-night. Here's the Grey Rat Café where Mimi lives."

Pushing open the door, the inspector led the way to a corner table and looked round.

"That's the fellow I want," he said to Jenkins. "I fancy that you'll hear me tell more untruths in the next ten minutes than you dreamed I was capable of. Here he comes."

Reynolds looked up with a smile of recognition as a middle-aged waiter with a morose face approached them expectantly.

"Why, if it isn't Mademoiselle Mimi's old friend," he exclaimed. "She sends you her best wishes, Jules. You remember me?"

"Perfectly, monsieur," the waiter replied. "You came here last year to see mademoiselle. I trust she is well."

Reynolds shook his head sadly.

"Not too well, Jules. She is staying with my wife for a short rest. Mademoiselle works too hard and," he lowered his voice to a confidential tone, "is far too generous to strangers. That English girl she took to England for instance. But perhaps you never met her?"

Jules indulged in a knowing wink.

"Did I not know her? Mademoiselle Mimi is indeed too warm-hearted. I am not surprised that that red-haired girl has robbed her."

"You and I, Jules, may yet get something back for mademoiselle if you will tell me anything you know. Meanwhile," Reynolds pressed a note of substantial value in francs into the waiters hand, "get us a couple of cognacs."

The tip galvanized Jules's brain into mental efforts which surpassed the inspector's wildest hopes.

Eagerly he poured out the history of last Sunday night's incidents, describing Linda's visit and the unknown young man who had brought the news paper for her.

"Mademoiselle Mimi asked me about this stranger. At the time I knew nothing," Jules continued. "Since then a client who was in the café and saw him told me that the stranger had lodged at an hotel near here. He was English and young; his name was Wentworth. The English girl sang under the name of 'Lola' at the cabaret across the road."

"Can you tell me the English girl's full name?" Reynolds's voice was tense with excitement.

"One moment, sir."

Jules returned presently with a large book "Here is the hotel register."

Reynolds bent over the list of names and thanked Providence for the laws of France that compel every alien to answer in writing a catechism of questions.

At last! Linda Marchant.

The details did not interest him. He closed the book and handed it back to the waiter.

But Jules had a trump card. His dislike of Linda for being an unprofitable customer had intensified now that he imagined she had abused Mimi's generosity.

"And this," he said proudly, laying a newspaper on the table, "is a copy of the journal that the stranger left for her. See! it was marked up in blue pencil here." His finger indicated the small advertisement column.

The inspector glanced down the printed matter, observing immediately the advertisement that requested the services of an auburn-haired girl with blue eyes.

"Apply to F. Yates, 27 Silver Square, London, W.1."

"We've a lot to do before we go to bed to-night," the inspector said. "I must ascertain how long Linda Marchant was in Paris. If she was here before Gillingham died, we're on the wrong track. We'll try the manager of the cabaret first."

From him Reynolds obtained the address of the girl whom he had known as "Lola."

It was nearly one o'clock in the morning when Reynolds satisfied himself that Linda had arrived in Paris from London just six months ago.

"To-morrow morning," Reynolds observed to Jenkins, "we'll deal with the stranger who delivered the marked newspaper to her, one Wentworth by name, who was staying in some hotel near the Place Blanche."

An icy rain descending in torrents next day added discomfort to the difficulties of their search.

Less than an hour before they were due at Le Bourget aerodrome their quest was rewarded.

A Frederick Wentworth of London had spent a week recently at the Hotel de Lycée. His visit had ended last Wednesday, the day on which Linda and Mimi had travelled to London.

The hotel proprietor was able to give an intelligent description of his late client. Twenty-five years of age, medium height, thin small face with dark eyes and long nose.

"That's the bag, Jenkins," Reynolds observed as he hailed a cab and told the driver to go to the aerodrome. "We've got nothing definite against the Wentworth bird, but his appearance tallies with that of Linda's unknown donor of the news-paper."

"There's only one point troubling me," he went on. "Supposing that Yates and Wentworth are crooks and the fair Linda was also in the same line of business, why had she to be tricked by this advertisement into re-joining her old profession? It takes a bit of thinking out."

"I shan't have any time for thinking, I'm afraid, on the flight back," Jenkins answered with an unhappy glance at the stormy sky.

His face was rather wan when he and the inspector landed at Croydon that night.

"It's wonderful what an aeroplane can do, Jenkins," Reynolds remarked as they drove away by taxi.

"It's wonderful what it can do to me!" retorted the afflicted passenger. "A penny tram over Westminster Bridge is all the travelling I ever want to do across water, sir."

Reynolds called at the Yard to see whether Mimi had turned up or telephoned. She had done neither, he learned, nor when he reached his home had Mrs. Reynolds any better news to give him of the French girl.

Had the inspector been granted second sight, he would perhaps not have slept so peacefully.

Early that Sunday morning Mimi had been conscious of stealthy movements from the bed wherein Vernstein's housekeeper had slept.

Peeping through half-closed lids, the girl feigned sleep and watched proceedings. The woman collected her clothing in her arms, tiptoed to the door and locked it behind her.

Mimi lay still, puzzling over this new development. Evidently she was to be held a prisoner. At all costs she must not let them know that she realised it.

Her mouth set to a fighting line. Vernstein meant her to stay in this room, did he? Well, she would let him see that she was staying here by her wish and not his. Taking out her mirror, she gave her face an unusual "make-up." Satisfied with the result, she lay back on her pillow and waited.

Twice she heard the woman come upstairs, listen outside the door and go away again. The third time the lock was softly turned, someone walked across the room and stood beside her bed. Mimi did not move nor open her eyes

"Mademoiselle," the woman said, placing her hand on the girl's shoulder, "you are sleeping late. Here is your breakfast. It is ten o'clock."

Mimi looked at her with wide dazed eyes, produced a hoarse cough and shivered violently. Then she allowed her lids to close again.

The woman placed the tray beside the bed and bent over her. Then leaving the door open, she ran downstairs.

"She is ill, I tell you," Mimi heard the housekeeper say in frightened tones. "Her face is ghastly and her eyes have dark circles. It is a fever."

"I'll go and see," was the answer in Vernstein's voice.

Mimi, expecting that, had prepared accordingly by the simple ruse of dipping her hand into the jug of hot coffee and wiping it quickly.

She opened her eyes and gave a pathetic smile as the Jew came near. He took the hot hand lying conspicuously on the sheet and laid it down with a grave nod at his housekeeper.

"I am so sorry to be a trouble," Mimi whispered, "but I fear I must remain in bed. When one has had malaria these attacks of fever come suddenly."

She had not told anyone of the blow she had received in breaking Blair's fall. Now seemed a good time to make use of it. "Perhaps also in my struggle to hold the detective while Kent escaped, I was hurt a little." She pushed back the thick fringe, that covered her forehead and revealed a huge bruise on her temple.

The Jew's face melted with compassion, "My poor brave child, I had no idea you had been hurt!" he exclaimed in tones of compunction. "Kent was not worthy, of such pluck."

For the rest of the day the door was unlocked and tender care was lavished upon the invalid.

Towards evening she announced that the fever had abated. Might she try to walk downstairs?

Vernstein wrapped her carefully in a warm rug and carried her down to a couch which he had drawn before the fire.

The suspect and prisoner had become a heroine she reflected with amusement She had regained with interest the confidence that she had lost, and now perhaps stood a good chance of discovering the plot that was prepared.

"Talk quietly. I won't have her disturbed," the Jew ordered "Why are you so scared of to-morrow night's job, Kent? Neither the old man nor the girl will be in the shop at that hour, and you'll have Yates, Dan and the old man's nephew there to help you."

XXXI, A Trip by Proxy

Monday

During the long hours of that night Mimi pieced together the scheme that was brewing. By the morning she had worked it out clearly. "The girl" of whom Dan had spoken was undoubtedly Linda, and "the old man" must be her employer. It should not be difficult to trace the address of a connoisseur named Wentworth with the aid of a London directory.

In her heart she knew that her duty was to acquaint Inspector Reynolds at once with the information that she had acquired and let him act as he wished. Linda was the obstacle. Her silence and flight after the Gillingham affair were innocent. But if it were discovered that twice she was involved even indirectly in a jewel robbery organised by Zaldo, her complicity would be suspected, and heavy punishment might follow.

If by some means she could get Linda out of London, Mimi decided that she would tell the inspector everything.

The next item was to invent a plausible reason for getting out of this house. It might be wise to let Vernstein imagine that she was leaving London.

"It is good that I am almost well," she announced at breakfast. "I have business to-day that may take me to Liverpool. By the way, monsieur, can you dispose of cocaine if I bring some back?"

Vernstein appeared relieved. So that was this clever girl's job! He was pleased to hear it.

"Perhaps," he replied. "Liverpool is a long way. I fear you cannot return to-night."

Mimi shrugged her shoulders.

"There is always to-morrow," she replied indifferently.

The Jew raised no demur to her departure from the house, in which he seemed to be alone that morning.

"Take care of yourself," he urged.

Mimi sped along the streets in the keyed-up elation which she and Inspector Reynolds both experienced when a course of action was plainly indicated. The address of Mr. Wentworth, art dealer, was easily found in the directory. He was not a telephone subscriber, she noticed.

Walking past the shop after a swift glance through the window showed her three things: Linda, dusting the furniture; an elderly man with a beard, clad in hat and overcoat, standing at the far end of the shop; and a woman on her knees, scrubbing.

All doubt was removed. This was without question to be the scene for to-night's robbery, for the charwoman was Vernstein's housekeeper!

Mimi walked to the end of the street thoughtfully. How could she get at Linda without entering the shop and being recognised by the woman who was scrubbing?

"If it isn't the elusive little Mademoiselle Mimi," exclaimed a debonair voice at her elbow.

Mimi looked up into Nick Tyler's blue eyes and wondered if his presence was a godsend or a nuisance. She decided to be wary and let him do the talking.

"I was just about to call on our mutual friend Miss Marchant, and tell her that Mr. Blair's condition is unchanged," Nick remarked. "That is, he is still unconscious but his general health has improved."

"She will be glad to receive your news, monsieur."

"I often call in to brighten her life when the old blighter is out," Nick answered.

Mimi wrinkled her nose to a quaint smile.

"The old blighter! That is a nice new word form, If you mean Mr. Wentworth, he is there now. I have just passed the shop."

"H'm. I think I'll wait until he goes out. When I do see Linda shall I give her any message from you mademoiselle?"

"Thank you, yes. Please ask her to have luncheon with me over there." Mimi indicated a small restaurant.

"I'll come back in an hour. She shall have your message," Nick promised. "Are you going to invite me also?"

The French girl put her head on one side and studied him.

"Not to-day, monsieur. Another time perhaps, when," she paused, "when I know you better."

"I'm worth knowing," Nick asserted. "There's a lot of hidden good in me."

"One day I will hunt the treasure, monsieur. *Au 'voir.*"

Soon afterwards Nick Tyler opened the door of Yates's flat quietly with his key, and stepping into the hall, listened.

From inside the office came sounds of a heated argument in full blast.

"Do as I order, Dan," Yates was saying. "One word from me to Zaldo about the stones you stole from Gillingham's safe and your friends can order wreaths."

"I'll give you half if you'll let me off this affair to-night," the other man offered.

"Pshaw!" Yates exclaimed "What's that compared with the chance we've got staring us in the face? Here I'm offering you the opportunity to rope in a fortune and get out of the country. Kent and I are all set for South America. You'd better come with us. There's a boat sailing—"

"I've got a hunch that it will sail without us, Yates. You're proposing to double-cross Zaldo. I believe he suspects us."

"What makes you get that crazy notion?" Yates asked with a laugh.

"In all the other cases," said Dan, "Kent and I have got everything ready, but never once have we ever touched a safe or handled the jewels."

"Excepting when you robbed half of Gillingham's hoard!"

"Wasn't I entitled to it?" Dan demanded. "I had to put the veranox in his bottle. It makes me sweat when I wonder if Zaldo knows I helped myself to a tidy packet before he got there. Yates, tell me you've seen him. Kent and I never have. What's he like?"

"The only time I saw him he was dolled up like a mummy and sat in the shadow! Don't get the wind up, Dan. Maybe he thinks to-night's job is such a soft one that he ain't needed. You see, there won't be any killing. Zaldo only commits murder for two reasons: to get the keys of the safe or prevent the victim from identifying him. Well, young Wentworth is going to get hold of his uncle's keys to-day and the old man doesn't sleep on the premises. I tell you, boy, it's a cinch for us. We bring back the valuables here and then—"

"You and Kent and I hop it," Dan cut in. "What about Vernstein and the old housekeeper and young Wentworth?"

"The Jew's a fence and can stick to his own job and his housekeeper. Young Wentworth's a fool. You can forget him."

"How much does Nick Tyler know?" Dan it inquired.

"Nix about Zaldo. He thinks I do shady work, but nothing criminal. I'm sending him out of the way to-day. Feel easier in your mind?"

"Yes. Only one other question, Yates. Why does Zaldo label his jobs by the mad trick of stopping the clocks at midnight? Is it vanity?"

"Vanity be hanged," Yates retorted. "That's the cleverest alibi he could have. He works any time between half-past eleven at night and four in the morning, as best suits him. Whereas the police are looking for a man who hasn't a good alibi for midnight!"

"That's washed out my worries," Dan said.

"Fine," Yates answered. "Let's have a drink on the strength of it. We won't talk any more about the business now."

Nick went outside and closing the door silently, rang the bell. His summons was answered by Yates.

"It's you, is it, Tyler?" he growled. "Forgotten your key again. Do you ever remember anything?"

"Very little," Nick said with a disarming smile. "I've a slight cold so I won't kiss you, lovey." He walked ahead of Yates into the office where Dan was standing, glass in hand. "Hello, you're the new lodger, I fancy."

"Dunno where you get that idea," Dan snapped.

"They come to me easily," Nick said. "It's eleven o'clock in the morning and you're wearing no collar or tie and have not yet shaved. So I conclude that you've stopped in the midst of your toilet to have a drink with Yates. Don't let me keep you."

Dan glared at him and went out of the room.

"You're a bit too fresh, Tyler," was Yates's irritable comment.

"I'm always like that in the morning," Nick informed him cheerfully. "A clear conscience and sound sleep works the trick. You ought to try the recipe. Baggy eyes are singularly unbecoming to your rugged style of beauty. Well, sir, any esteemed orders for your faithful servant to-day?"

"Yes, two of 'em, and you'll obey without any back-chat," Yates returned with undisguised venom in his tone. "Go round and tell the Marchant girl to come here at two o'clock this afternoon. She's got to come, mind."

"I'll lay your polite message before her with the pleased certainty that she'll have a suitable reply. And then?"

"Pack a bag and catch the next train to Nottingham," Yates ordered. "Wire me the name of your hotel and await my instructions by letter."

Nick raised his eyebrows.

"Sealed orders, eh? I don't know anybody. in Nottingham. Sure you can't make it Leicester? I know a nice girl there."

Yates hesitated for the fraction of a second.

"No, you'll go where I say, Tyler. That's all. Get out. I'm busy."

Nick paused on the landing outside the door. The empty room opposite Yates's flat was occupied, he noticed, and men in shirt sleeves were busily arranging furniture.

The door was open and the room already roughly arranged. Nick strolled inside and asked one of the men for a match. The man complied, accepting a cigarette from Nick's case with a gruff "Thank 'ee, sir."

"You've made a quick job of settling in," Nick remarked. He leaned against the door with a casual air and closed it. "I didn't know this room was let. Only arrived this morning, didn't you?"

That's right, sir," agreed the man. "Can't afford to waste time these days when rent is high and trade slack."

"What business do you propose running here?" Nick inquired, offering his cigarette-case to the second man.

"Cleaning and pressing suits, sir," was the answer. "We shall be grateful for orders. If you live on these premises we can press garments for you in an hour."

"Thanks, but I don't live here," Nick told him. "I've merely been paying a business call on the man who lives opposite."

"If he's an amiable sort of gentleman perhaps we could arrange to share his telephone, sir," the older man suggested.

"The gentleman across the landing has a telephone but is not always amiable."

"May we use your name, sir?" the younger man asked in eager tones. "It might help"

"It would probably hinder," Nick replied with a grin. "Good morning. You ought to do well here."

At the foot of the stairs he looked up. The door of the new tenants' room had been opened again.

There was a speculative glint in Nick's eyes as he went to deliver Yates's message. No one was in the shop but Linda when he reached there. Having given her

Mimi's message he repeated Yates's words exactly, expecting an indignant retort from her.

"I can't think what he wants. Must I go, Nick?" she surprised him by asking in tremulous tones.

He thought for a moment.

"Yes, I think you should. It's wiser to risk danger and find out what the *enemy*," he emphasised the word, "is up to than to hide safely and know nothing. If Yates gets tiresome, yell at the top of your voice. There are some new tenants in the room opposite his, at work with the door open. I fancy they'll rush to your rescue."

"You won't be there?" Her voice had a disappointed tone.

"I? My dear child I can't be tied to your apron strings always. I've a date in Nottingham this evening—with a blonde."

"You're absolutely heartless."

"Did I ever profess to possess that organ save for blood-pumping purposes?" Nick inquired. "Since your tender soul is filled with thoughts of Stephen Blair—and by the way, I feel sure that he will recover—you must, stand on your own, young woman. Mimi at one o'clock, Yates at two o'clock, remember. Don't forget to yell loudly."

Nick strolled along, humming an air from the latest revue, until he came to a district messengers office.

He wrote a telegram and after a little conversation handed it and a five-pound note to the manager.

"I'll call for the change later on when you worked out the cost," he said. "Choose a bright youngster and don't let him make a mistake or miss the train. I wouldn't have my uncle disappointed by not receiving his birthday telegram. Good day."

The manager selected a smart youth and explained the job. "Take the next rain to Nottingham, book a room at a hotel near the station, fill in the name of the hotel on this telegraph form in the blank space, send it off and take the next train back. And don't ask me why!"

XXXII, REYNOLDS ON THE TRACK

Monday morning

Before nine o'clock that morning Reynolds went to 27 Silver Square with his assistant.

He and Jenkins inspected the exterior of the building, which had a card attached to the railings announcing that there was a large room to let. Shortly after, they interviewed the landlord at an address supplied by the caretaker.

Being made aware of the professional status of his callers, the landlord acceded to their unusual request for the immediate and temporary tenancy of the empty room on the first floor.

"I trust that nothing is wrong with my other tenants, gentlemen," he remarked nervously.

Reynolds parried a reply by a mild inquiry concerning their neighbour-to-be.

"Ah, you mean Mr. Yates. He runs the Select Employment Bureau and I fancy a private inquiry agency also. You know the kind of thing, providing evidence for divorce."

Reynolds reflected grimly that indeed he knew the kind of thing.

"Where next, sir?" asked Jenkins, as they emerged with the keys of their new residence and the inspector hailed a taxi.

"Tottenham Court Road. Second-hand shop. Tell the man to drive like blazes. Every minute is precious. Didn't you tell me that as a boy you worked in a tailor's shop for three months, pressing clothes?"

Jenkins appeared bewildered.

"Yes, sir. But what's that—?"

"You're going back to your old trade, my lad." the inspector chuckled.

By ten o'clock they were back in Silver Square with their assortment of furnishings which include the loan—for a consideration—of, a table, some flat irons, and a couple of chairs.

"Now," Reynolds ordered, surveying the room with a pleased smile, "off with our coats, and let's get this place into shape. Just a minute, we must settle the delicate affair of names in case we're asked. Miles and Sloan. How's that? You're Sloan."

"Let's hope nobody comes in to have a suit pressed. I'm out of practice."

"On the contrary I mean to tout for orders in the building," the inspector said decisively, "especially across the landing."

"I'd better get my hand in on your overcoat then", Jenkins stated, placing the irons on the gas ring.

By half-past ten the new establishment had a business-like appearance, and the front door—which was left open—bore a hastily, written card announcing that "Miles and Sloan" were open to receive orders.

Posting himself where he had a clear view of the door of Yates's flat, Reynolds was delighted to see the morning bottle of milk being lifted from the mat.

"He's a late bird, so we've missed nothing yet," he observed.. "If anyone leaves the flat I shall probably follow him. You keep watch here."

Reynolds was very interested when Nick Tyler arrived, opened Yates's door with a key, and ten minutes later slid outside and rang the bell as if he had just arrived. He was still more interested when Tyler called on them.

"Going to trail him, sir?" Jenkins asked when their caller left.

"I think not. That's a very astute young gentleman and Silver Square is too empty for me to risk being seen. There may be bigger fish. Jenkins, our caller was remarkably like the man who dined with Blair, Linda and Mimi. The porter at the Soho restaurant described him to me."

There were no more visitors that morning, but just before one o'clock a surly looking young man came out of Yates's flat. At the door he paused to call back a question.

"How many cigarettes do you want, Yates?"

"Fifty," came the reply. "Hurry up, Dan. I want to go out and get a meal. We can't both leave the flat to-day. I must be here again by two o'clock."

Dan! The inspector fastened on to the name as avidly as a ravenous dog on a bone. If the root of Zaldo's gang was in Gunner's Court, certainly the branches were here, he thought, as he followed the young man on his errand to the tobacconist's and back again.

"I'd like to squeeze Dan's neck until he confesses to the Gillingham murder and tells me where Linda Marchant is," Reynolds muttered as he and Jenkins ate a scrappy luncheon. "There goes Yates to get his nourishment. I won't raise suspicion by tracking him."

Before two o'clock Yates returned. A minute later Dan went out, calling back a message to the effect that he would only be gone for half an hour.

"I think it may be more important for me to stay here than to follow him," Reynolds decided.

At two o'clock he heard light footsteps on the stairs and a girl dressed in dark green appeared and rang Yates's bell.

Reynolds held his breath with excitement. The girl had hair of a vivid auburn hue. All possibility of a mistake was dispelled by Yates's first words to her as, he opened the door.

"Come in, Miss Marchant. I'm all alone and we can have a cosy chat."

The girl drew back haughtily.

"I don't want a cosy chat, thanks. I must go back to my work at once. Why did you send for me?"

"I'll tell you when we're inside," was Yates's reply.

The girl turned and gave a nervous glance toward the half-open door of the room that Nick had spoke of and behind which Reynolds was concealed. Then she followed Yates in and his door was closed.

"Watch the stairs, Jenkins, and warn me if Dan is coming," Reynolds ordered. "I'll try, to listen through Yates's letter box."

He reaped nothing but a draught in his ear and retired disappointedly.

"I'm going outside to wait in the Square," he told his assistant, "and shall follow her to China if necessary."

The interview was short.

"It's hard if you can't answer a few simple questions," Yates said at his door. "You'd have been penniless if I hadn't got you a job."

"I've no illusions about your philanthropy, Mr. Yates," was the girl's icy reply. "I refuse to tell you anything about my employer's habits or goods. If I have any more threats from you I shall make a clean breast of everything to him and warn him against you."

Yates's teeth parted to an angry snarl.

" Oh, you will, eh? I'd deal with you long before that, my pretty dear, and in a way you—" He broke off and frowned at the half-open door opposite.

While Linda hurried down the stairs Yates walked across to see who his new neighbours were. He saw a man bending over a gas ring, in the act of lifting off a hot iron.

Jenkins, fully aware of his visitor, tested the heat of the iron by spitting upon it in a professional manner.

"Who d'you think you are?" demanded Yates in belligerent tones.

Jenkins drew forward a chair and beamed upon him.

"Good afternoon, sir. Did you want something pressed at once? I must finish this overcoat that a customer needs urgently and then I am at your disposal. My partner has just gone out about an important order."

"No, I don't want anything pressed and had no idea you were starting a business here. What's the meaning of your door being left open?"

"Business, sir," Jenkins explained glibly, banging the iron on Reynolds's overcoat. "People see a closed door and pass on, whereas if it's open they pop in—like yourself—to see what's going on. I think we ought to do well. We're in a good position with flats all around us."

"You'll keep your confounded door shut or I'll make the landlord clear you out," Yates snapped. "The draught comes across to my flat."

Jenkins looked pained.

"I am sorry about that, sir. I'll get my partner to have glass panels put in. That would suit you and us, wouldn't it?"

There was no answer to the suggestion that Yates could think of. He walked out angrily and slammed the door behind him. Before Yates had crossed the landing Jenkins had opened it again.

" Sorry, sir," he remarked pleasantly. "My partner's orders. I'll get him to come across and talk with you about it presently."

Yates mentioned a place to which the pair might go and went into his flat.

From Silver Square the inspector trailed Linda with zeal but less discretion than he usually displayed, so fearful was he of losing her.

Fortunately she was too engrossed in her affairs to recognise that a man who had boarded a bus on her heels walked into the antique shop ten minutes after she had unlocked it.

She seemed as if she were in a dream, he observed, as she came forward.

"I should like to see some tapestries," he said, noticing that they were hung at the far end of the shop.

Linda preceded him, while Reynolds's alert eyes took in every detail. The black cabinets under the dome intrigued him. Those cabinets were of painted metal and very strong, unless he was mistaken, and probably held precious articles.

The tapestries were not very attractive.

"We have sold the best ones," Linda told him. "I'm so sorry."

"Jade would do just as well, if you have any small, well-carved pieces." Reynolds smiled genially. "I've a birthday very soon and thought I'd buy a present, from myself to thyself with much love."

Her blue eyes flashed with amusement.

"You'll be sure of receiving one gift that you like," she replied. Suddenly a thought crossed her mind. If she could sell the jade elephant that Nick had given to her she could refund the money to him. Taking the curio from her handbag she placed it amongst some china vases. Presently her customer observed it.

"H'm, it's more than I intended to pay," he replied upon hearing the price. "May I think it over until to-morrow?"

A boy entered at that moment to fetch a parcel which Linda had to pack. Reynolds wished her good day.

On his way to the door he slid behind a tall-boy in a recess, considerably interested in a young man who, having peered cautiously through the window, came in and walked straight up the shop, without seeing Reynolds.

"Is my uncle here?" he demanded.

"No. Mr. Wentworth is out," Linda replied.

"Good. I'll wait for a few minutes," the newcomer said. Sitting down at the desk under the dome, he lighted a cigarette and slipped his hand quickly into one of the drawers.

Reynolds noticed that the girl, having sent the boy away with the parcel, hovered round the young man uneasily.

"I'll call in again," he told her. "You needn't bother to tell my uncle I was here."

"I shall most certainly inform Mr. Wentworth of your visit," she answered coldly.

The door being open, Reynolds hurried out and waited until the young man appeared. Two taxis presently sped in the same direction. The first one bearing the young man, stopped at 27 Silver Square.

Reynolds got out at the corner and hurrying along reached the foot of the stairs in time to see Wentworth's nephew vanish into Yates's flat.

Recklessly the inspector raised the flap of Yates's, letter box and heard a few precious words from the two men who were inside the hall.

"Here are the old man's keys, Yates. That redheaded girl hates me like poison."

They went into a room and Reynolds's luck ended.

"Nothing happened here, sir," Jenkins reported. "Dan returned, and then this chap came."

"He's Wentworth, the art dealer's nephew, Reynolds explained, "and is apparently planning to rob his uncle at the shop where Linda Marchant is employed. I'm puzzled, my lad. Men keep keys in their pockets and not inside a drawer. Either young Wentworth is a fool, or else he meant his uncle's assistant to see him take the keys! The girl seemed straight and loyal to her employer. Well, what's the next move, I wonder?"

XXXIII. NICK MAKES A CONFESSION

Monday afternoon

The next move surprised the C.I.D. men. It took the form of a second visit from the cheery blue-eyed man who had called on them that morning.

He was inside their room before Reynolds was aware that anyone had come upstairs.

"Sh," he whispered with a grin on his face. "I'm supposed to be on my way to Nottingham. Tell me, have there been any visitors to the opposite flat? A charming girl, for instance?"

"A lady with auburn hair called at two o'clock," Reynolds replied slowly. "She stayed only a few minutes."

"No S.O.S. from her, or any disturbance?" Nick Tyler asked anxiously.

"The lady came and went quietly," Reynolds replied. "A young man, a Mr. Wentworth, is there now."

Nick glanced at him whimsically.

"You get hold of names quickly, don't you. I say," he remarked to Jenkins, "you'll ruin that overcoat. You were pressing it this morning. Well, you've done me an excellent turn about that girl, really, I'm in your debt. Will you press my coat if I take it off?"

"With pleasure, sir," Jenkins said eagerly. "I'll do the entire suit if you like, and you can wait behind the curtain."

"Fine." Nick emptied his pockets and placing the contents on the mantelpiece, slung the coat across to Jenkins. "You shall have the slacks in a minute." Taking Reynolds' coat from the ironing board, he added, "I'll borrow this to put around me. It's a bit chilly", and retired behind the curtain.

Jenkins put his hands on his hips and looked questioningly at the inspector, who shrugged.

Reynolds fetched the waistcoat and trousers from their client who was contentedly smoking a cigarette and reading a newspaper.

The pressing went on in silence. Presently Jenkins pointed to the mantelpiece. The inspector nodded and looked over the articles that the man had left there.

Both men jumped as their client suddenly chuckled and addressed them.

"How are you getting on, *inspector*? Don't singe my pants, I beg of you."

Reynolds drew the curtain aside. On the customer's knees was Reynolds' overcoat and upon the overcoat was laid the entire collection of items that Nick had found in the pockets.

Reynolds eyed the culprit severely.

"What's the meaning of this?" he enquired.

"I thought one good turn deserved another, inspector. Though I'm really in your debt. My set of junk wasn't half so interesting as yours."

The gay impudence brought a twinkle to the inspector's eyes.

"What's your game, Mr. Tyler?" he asked.

"I'm in deadly earnest, inspector. By the way, never liked the name of Tyler."

"Meaning that it is not your real name?"

"Meaning that even a C.I.D. man occasionally calls himself Miles or Sloan. I don't know which of you is supposed to be Miles, and I doubt if you do."

'You're not far out," agreed Reynolds. "Well, Mr. Tyler, are you going to help or hinder us?"

"That depends. It's each for himself, perhaps. I'll decide when I see how your pal treats my clothes."

The situation had become both amusing and profitable, reflected Reynolds.

"Go carefully, Jenkins," he called out. "A whole lot rests on Mr. Tyler's suit being pressed nicely." He turned to Nick with a smile. "Do you know anything about Yates?" he asked.

"A whale of a lot, inspector. He's an unpleasant beast and—my dear employer! I may get the sack for playing Don Quixote to a fair damsel to-day."

"I fancy that wouldn't disturb you, Mr.—" Reynolds paused. "Shall we each lay a few cards on the table?"

"I'll show you my entire hand on one condition," Nick offered. "You first give me your word honour that Miss Linda Marchant's name is kept clear and that she is not worried in any way."

"I will if you can prove to me that she has acted innocently," was Reynolds's answer.

"You mean over the Gillingham affair?"

Reynolds nodded.

"If she were guilty no one would be more ready than I to have her convicted." Nick's voice was grave. "She had no idea that Dan was making love to her in order to rob Mr. Gillingham. She ran away solely to save that rascal. Half-starving in Paris, she was enticed here by a crew of scoundrels. She is now working honourably and loyally for Mr. Wentworth, and terrified for the safety of his life and possessions. She regards me with strong suspicion. Ever heard of Zaldo?" be demanded.

"I have," Reynolds replied, "but if you are going to tell me that you are Zaldo, I'm afraid I shall not believe you."

"Mimi is a good little scout," Nick said with irrelevance. "She and Linda had luncheon together to-day. Blair's distinctly better, I heard an hour ago. Got a cigarette?"

"Just when did you first meet Mr. Blair?" Reynolds inquired, offering his cigarette-case.

"In the cradle, I should think Stephen and I were kids together, school and college mates and lifelong friends." Nick leaned closer to Reynolds. "Yates holds a cheque I forged in Blair's name! I had to do that to qualify for a job with Yates."

"If anything happens to Mr. Blair, it might be awkward for you," Reynolds remarked.

"Not a bit. The old lad thought of that and deposited a full explanation with his solicitor at the time."

"You did this merely because you suspected that Mr. Gillingham—who was probably an old friend of yours—did not die a natural death?"

Nick clenched his fist until the knuckles were white.

"No, inspector; not because I merely suspected, but because I knew it was not a natural death, Mr. Gillingham hated drugs of all kinds. He had valvular disease of the heart and never took hypnotics to induce sleep. The only stuff he ever touched was harmless soda-mint tablets. Who could know better than I, his only son? I am Nicholas Tyler Gillingham."

There was silence. Then Reynolds nodded slowly.

"So rather than call in the police you decided to solve the problem of your father's murder by yourself, Mr. Gillingham?"

"The police hadn't been much use, had they?" Nick asked candidly. "I landed in England a week after my father died and was staggered to hear that an open verdict had been given at the inquest. Well, inspector, do I open my mouth further or do you refuse to keep Linda out of the mess that is imminent?"

"I give you my word," Reynolds answered.

Jenkins put his head round the curtain.

"That young chap Wentworth is just leaving Yates's flat," he said. "Shall I follow him?" He glanced at Nick. "Here's your suit, sir. I've done my best."

"Save your time, sergeant," advised Nick. "Young Wentworth's only a pawn in this game. He's played his part in getting his uncle's keys. Let me dress and we'll put our heads together on this business. I've done no end of listening at keyholes lately and have learnt a lot that may help you."

"It certainly appears that Zaldo is setting a trap to catch his double-crossing associates," Reynolds commented a while later. "We shall have a ticklish job to prove we're right. If I only had one real piece of evidence!" "We may get it," Nick said confidently. "The day's young if we're not. I'll wait here if you don't mind until Yates receives my wire from Nottingham. I'd love to see his face when he reads it."

The daylight had faded by the time that Nick and the inspector had compared their joint knowledge.

"Miss Marchant will resent it bitterly, I'm afraid," Reynolds said ruefully.

"It's the only possible way to prevent her from being mixed up in it to the hilt" Nick declared. "Ah ha, a telegram for Yates. Like to know what I said, inspector? I kept a copy."

Reynolds unfolded the form and read it.

Yates, 27 Silver Square, London, W.1.

Here I am darling at Terminus Hotel am missing you terribly ever your loving Nicky.

"It cost a bit, but it was worth it," Nick remarked with feeling.

"Here's Mimi, sir," warned Jenkins's voice from the door.

The French girl rushed in, breathless and eager.

"They gave me your address at the Yard. I've trailed Vernstein and the housekeeper from Gunner's Court," she said quickly. "They are in a café in Oxford Street. I have a taxi waiting. Come at once and see who is with them. Young Wentworth has just joined them but that is not all. Who do you think is there? Zaldo himself! He looks different, but I recognized his eyes. I am *sure!*"

"May I come too, inspector?" Nick inquired.

"Yes. Step on it, young man," he said.

XXXIV, LINDA AT THE YARD

Monday evening

It was nearly six o'clock when Mr. Wentworth entered his shop. Linda ran towards him with visible relief.

"Oh, I am glad—I've been so anxious—" she began incoherently and stopped in confusion. Her employer would think she was mad.

Mimi's urgent request during luncheon that she should leave London at once had alarmed her. Mimi must be a crook who wanted to get her out of the way.

On top of that had come the interview with Yates, followed by the visit here of her employer's nephew. She was sure now that a horrible plan was afoot for that night.

Mr. Wentworth patted her shoulder.

"I'm sorry I am late," he said in his calm voice "My weakness for chess is incurable, and I'm a slow player. I won three games" he announced with solemn triumph. "Tell me what the trouble is. Did you break a teacup or forget to buy a shillings worth of stamps?"

His gentle raillery dispersed the girl's fears in a measure; she determined to put the matter before him.

"Mr. Wentworth, your nephew called early this afternoon. He only waited a few moments and said that I need not tell you of his visit. I informed him that I should do so."

"A most unpleasant young man," her employer admitted, "but far too much of a fool for one to worry about him."

"I'm not so sure that he is such a fool as you imagine. He sat at your desk and I feel certain that he took something from one of the drawers. Please go and look. I've been terribly unhappy."

Mr. Wentworth went to the desk and searched for a moment. His face was grave as he turned to the girl.

"You are right, Miss Marchant. He took my keys. I must try to foil any plans that my nephew may be making. Thank you for your care and don't be anxious any more."

The knowledge that he was concerned about her broke down the girl's resistance. She burst into helpless tears.

"I can't go on with this deceit, Mr. Wentworth," she sobbed. "I don't care what happens to me; you shall know everything."

Breathlessly she poured out the history of her employment with the late Mr. Gillingham; of Dan's share in that strange death and her flight to Paris; of Yates's advertisement and the contract she had signed to hand over to him all that Mr. Wentworth gave her; of the fable concerning her parentage; ending with Yates's request to-day for details concerning the time the shop would be closed tonight.

"And now you know just what kind of a desperate creature I am," she finished, and wondered why she had not mentioned Nick Tyler's name.

"On the contrary, Miss Marchant, you are one of the most honest and honourable of women," he assured her, "and I cannot thank you sufficiently for your confidence. In return I will make you a little confession. The red-haired girl I am supposed to have loved is a myth. My nephew invented her for Yates's benefit and boasted of it to me for a joke on the day that I engaged you. To test your honesty I brought up the subject of your parents and am afraid that I drew on the fiction of my lost love! You did not lie; you evaded the question. I have no words to express my great admiration for your conduct."

He held out his hand and took hers in a firm clasp.

"I feel happier than I've been for months," she said.

"I'm very glad. Now I must arrange for police protection, I'm afraid," her employer said sadly. "It's not very pleasant to know that one's own nephew is involved."

"I'm terribly sorry, Mr. Wentworth. Good night."

"Good night, Miss Marchant. I think I shall keep guard myself here to-night."

Linda walked up the street with a firm resolve in her mind. She had her own keys to the shop. Tonight she also would go there and keep watch. At least she could scream for help if anyone attacked Mr. Wentworth.

At her side two men appeared. One of them spoke to her in low, grave tones.

"I am from Scotland Yard, Miss Marchant. I must ask you to come with me at once."

She gazed at him, wide-eyed.

"Why?" she asked.

"Concerning the death of Mr. Gillingham," the officer told her. The girl stumbled into the car and sat silent during the short journey.

"This way, please," the officer said, leading her along a corridor. "As Inspector Reynolds is engaged you may be detained for some time."

Inspector Reynolds! That was the name of the C.I.D. man whom Mimi knew. Had the French girl betrayed her?

A constable was on duty outside the room into which she was ushered. She heard the door closed behind her and realised that she was a prisoner.

Someone else was to share her captivity apparently. A tall young man rose from a chair and came towards her. It was Nick Tyler!

"Hello, Linda. You too! It's what the old 'lags' call a 'fair cop,' isn't it?"

"Was it Mimi who did this?" Linda asked in a husky whisper.

Nick drew a chair near the fire and forced her into it.

"Of course not. It's just fate," he said cheerfully. "Let's make the best of it. There's some food coming soon, the inspector keeps a good brand of cigarettes and," he added, watching her face carefully, "Stephen Blair is better. He'll be pleased to get your flowers. You may be able to see him soon."

"Why should I?" she asked dully. "I'm glad he's better, of course." Her brow puckered. "I never sent him any flowers; I'm sorry to say that I never thought of it. Nick, about you. Is it serious? Will you be arrested?"

"I may get a life sentence!" He pinched her pale cheek. "Cheer up. You must be sick of my conceit and bullying."

"I—I loved it," she admitted. "It braced me up when I was spineless, and full of bitterness and self-pity."

He caught her hands in his.

"Linda Marchant, if we get out of this mess, and I feel sure we shall, will, you marry me?"

"Yes—but it would be nice to hear that you loved me."

"You priceless fool-angel, why do you think that I've pestered you to death ever since I met you in Yates's office? Love you? I adore you, woman, and in spite of Scotland Yard I'm going to kiss you."

The door opened and Inspector Reynolds came in and coughed loudly. Over Linda's shoulder Nick winked and then murmured meekly: "Sorry, sir. I was trying to comfort the lady."

"Please let me speak to you about Mr. Wentworth, inspector. It is—" Linda stopped abruptly. "Why, you're the man who came to the shop this afternoon and asked to see tapestries."

"And green jade," put in Nick sternly. "How dare you try to palm off my poor Percy?"

"That will do, young man,' Reynolds said with a warning smile. "I think you both have a few explanations to make to each other. I've only run in for the keys of the shop that you have, Miss Marchant. Mr. Wentworth has this moment called to see me," he added.

Taking the keys that Linda handed over, he left the pair alone.

Downstairs, Mr. Wentworth introduced himself and put the situation briefly to the inspector.

"It may be nervousness on Miss Marchant's part, and bluff on the part of my nephew," he explained; "but perhaps a little supervision to-night would be advisable. I hope I did right in coming to you," He gave an apologetic smile. "Miss Marchant threatened to do so if I did not."

"You leave everything to us, Mr. Wentworth," Reynolds said soothingly. "We'll look after your interests. That is what we are here for. Good night."

Jenkins was standing in the hall as Mr. Wentworth went out.

"Quite a distinguished-looking man, sir," he commented as the inspector joined him. "That little trim pointed beard suits him."

Reynolds nodded thoughtfully.

"Yes. By the way, describe Vernstein again to me. I didn't have your luck in seeing him."

Jenkins screwed up his face in disdain.

"He's a little taller and broader than Mr. Wentworth, and a few years older probably. Vernstein also has a beard and moustache, but the beard is decidedly longer and greyer and more shaggy."

"And both grow on the premises," Reynolds supplemented.

"Old Vernstein's fungus does, I'm certain," his assistant replied "One can always detect an artificial beard."

Reynolds looked at his watch

"Go and get outside a hearty supper, my lad. You'll need it. You know where we're to meet"

"Yes, sir. What about Mimi? She may expect to be in at the death after all her work, though it would be better to keep her out of it."

Reynolds smiled

"She's done her part nobly. To-night she is going to the movies with my wife."

Upstairs in the inspector a office Nick and Linda found the time passed very quickly in filling in the gaps that needed explanation. After a good supper, and Nick's assurance that their present detention did not herald a term of penal servitude, the girl's spirits revived.

"And now," said Nick at length, "I want you to stay here quietly while I go on an errand with the inspector. I'm meeting him at eleven o'clock."

XXXV, The Final Round

Monday night

At eleven o'clock that night the inspector unlocked the door of the antique shop and cautiously entered. He was followed by Jenkins and Nick.

Within all was silence and darkness, save for the distant light of a street lamp which gleamed on objects near the window.

"Disconnect the door bell," Reynolds ordered.

"No one is here yet. I'm going to look around."

"There's no back exit," he said presently. "The front door is all we need to watch. Don't precipitate matters, Jenkins. I want to get 'em red-handed. Where's the Yard van?"

"Parked round the corner, sir. They'll drive nearer the shop after our birds arrive."

"I have just left Stephen Blair," Reynolds told Nick. "He is conscious and was able to tell me that he bought the jewels in Paris for the late James Carr, himself and Keble Wentworth. By the way Blair, is rather more than interested in Mimi!"

"How does she feel about him?" Nick asked.

"A bit more that she admits even to herself," was Reynolds's reply. "I told her it would be kind if she went to see Blair and she answered 'Monsieur, I cannot afford to be kind. To-morrow I return to my beloved Montmartre where much happens.' But her voice was shaky and I've a suspicion that Blair is not an utter fool and will soon hunt her up in Paris. Ah! Here's Mr. Wentworth. He said he'd come along."

They held their breath while the art dealer walked up the shop and secreted himself behind a heavy screen close to the cabinets.

It was exactly eleven-thirty when the shop door was opened silently and four men came in.

One of them—young Wentworth—remained just outside the door.

The other three—Yates, Dan and Kent—crept up to the far end of the shop. With the aid of a torch they unlocked the cabinets and transferred the contents to a canvas bags.

The inspector waited until they had finished. Then he pressed the electric switch and the upper portion of the shop was flooded with light.

"Quick, Jenkins!" Reynolds said, advancing towards the startled men.

Yates put his hand to his hip, but withdrew it as Nick called out, "I have you covered, Yates. Hands up, all of you."

The three men stood there in dazed silence while Reynolds and Jenkins linked their wrists with handcuffs.

Outside the door stood a van, with sturdy looking police officials holding the door open.

"Get in," ordered Reynolds to his prisoners. "You've let that young skunk Wentworth escape!" Yates snarled as the doors were slammed.

"That's over, sir," Reynolds remarked, returning to Mr. Wentworth in the shop. "Your nephew seems to have got away. Perhaps that is as you would wish."

Mr. Wentworth gave a sigh of relief.

"Thank you, inspector—for your consideration. I was relieved to see that the young scamp did not come in here to take part in the robbery. What would you advise me to do with this?" He pointed to the bag which now contained the jewels.

"Take it to the Yard if you wish. Or, better still, take it home with you," Reynolds advised. "Jenkins, get Mr. Wentworth a taxi."

"I suppose, sir," Reynolds said to the art dealer as they walked towards the door, "that your young woman assistant could have played no part as accomplice in this matter?"

"Absolutely none, inspector," Mr. Wentworth answered with emphasis. "Miss Marchant has proved herself to be of the highest integrity. It is entirely due to her warning that I became aware of all this. Promise me," he added earnestly, "that you will dismiss from your mind any suspicion concerning her. It would be unkind to doubt her in any way."

"I promise, Mr. Wentworth," replied Reynolds, helping him into a taxi with the bag of jewels.

"Good night, inspector, and many thanks."

"This isn't good night," replied Reynolds grimly, getting into the taxi. In his hand a revolver gleamed. "You and I are going together just as far as the nearest police station, Zaldo."

*   *   *   *   *

It was nearly three o'clock in the morning when the inspector glanced round the little party assembled in his office at Scotland Yard.

Nick was sitting on the arm of Linda's chair. Jenkins was stowing two revolvers away in a drawer.

"We've got the whole bunch safely in the bag," Reynolds said. "That's the main thing."

"Inspector, what made you first suspect that old Mr. Wentworth was Zaldo?" asked Linda. "It was a great shock to me."

Reynolds leaned back in his chair.

"When thieves fall out, and that is what has happened in this case, detectives get a fighting chance. Some of the bunch have talked to-night and that, together with information which was already in our possession, now enables one to string the facts to-together.

"A connoisseur named Gillingham was murdered by Dan under Zaldo's instructions six months ago. Dan double-crossed him and stole part of the jewels. Linda Marchant fled to Paris. We all know why.

"Zaldo suspected Dan of double-crossing him and wanted those jewels. Acting through Yates, Zaldo got Linda Marchant—Gillingham's late secretary—back in the hope that she knew what Gillingham's jewels had consisted of, and to find out if she had shared in Dan's plunder."

"Now I understand," Linda broke in, "why Mr. Wentworth, I mean Zaldo, got me to tell him exactly what Mr. Gillingham's collection was like! I even used Zaldo's jewels, arranging them on trays, to make my explanation clear."

"Quite," observed Reynolds. "That showed Zaldo that Dan had cheated him. Just one point," he said, turning to Nick, "how did you come to link up with Yates?"

"My old pal, Stephen Blair, who is also a connoisseur, told me months ago that he had grown suspicious of a man named Yates who had called on him with some cock and bull story about jewels."

"I get the rest," Reynolds said. "You, with Blair's cognisance, got in touch with Yates to keep tabs on him. Now," he went on, "we come to the next main incident. Blair went to Paris and bought the Euralian jewels, one third for himself, one third for James Carr, and one third for Zaldo who passed under the name of Wentworth.

"'Wentworth' paid honestly for his portion but wanted the rest for nothing! Under his instructions Vernstein's housekeeper poisoned James Carr, and Zaldo emptied his safe.

"There remained only the third portion in Stephen Blair's possession. Zaldo arranged for Kent to chloroform the caretaker—a little effort that was frustrated." He glanced at Jenkins with a smile.

"On this occasion Zaldo was unsuccessful. Blair had lodged his jewels in a bank. But he stunned Blair and threw him out of the window. By the way, at the police station to-night, Zaldo rather boasted of his strength and prowess in wrestling. He is fifty-eight. Without his beard he would probably, look fifteen years younger."

"That mops up the past," Nick agreed.

"And," said Reynolds, "brings us to a startling revelation which Mimi made twelve hours ago. She tracked Vernstein and his housekeeper to a cafe and hurried to fetch me, as the man whom she thought was Zaldo had joined them"

"When Mimi pointed out Zaldo to us," Nick interposed, and I recognised him as Mr. Wentworth, Linda's respectable old employer, well; that did rather put the lid on it"

"Then the nephew who stole Mr. Wentworth's keys from his desk was in league with him!" Linda exclaimed.

"Yes, Miss Marchant," acquiesced Reynolds.

"That was part of his trap. Young Wentworth, Vernstein and the latter's housekeeper were all loyal to Zaldo On the other hand, Yates, Dan and Kent had double-crossed him so he planned to have them caught red-handed at the antique shop. They were. We have since rounded up Vernstein and the housekeeper."

"Where were they?" asked Nick

"In Yates's flat, searching for the jewels that Dan had stolen. We found the parcel up the chimney." Reynolds turned to Linda with a smile in his tired grey eyes. "Your troubles are ended, Miss Marchant. I hope you have a great deal of happiness coming to make up for what you have suffered."

"Be a real sport, inspector," Nick urged, "and act as my best man! After my atrocious behaviour it would clear my character in Linda's eyes."

"In that case, of course I must agree," Reynolds said. He raised the receiver of his telephone and rang up his wife.

"Tell Mimi that we've got Zaldo and the whole bunch," he said.

Across the wire a girl's tremulous voice answered him.

"My congratulations, monsieur. Please tell me when people can see sick people in a hospital?"

"I fancy," Reynolds replied with a chuckle, "you can visit Stephen Blair in Charing early in the afternoon. I thought you'd find out sooner or later that you were human, young woman."

THE END

Other Resurrected Press Books in *The Chief Inspector Pointer Mystery* Series

Murder at Bridge

When an afternoon bridge party attended by some of Hamilton's leading citizens ends with the hostess being murdered in her boudoir, Special Investigator Dundee of the District Attorney's office is called in. But one of the attendees is guilty? There are plenty of suspects: the victim's former lover, her current suitor, the retired judge who is being blackmailed, the victim's maid who had been horribly disfigured accidentally by the murdered woman, or any of the women who's husbands had flirted with the victim. Or was she murdered by an outsider whose motive had nothing to do with the town of Hamilton. Find the answer in... **Murder at Bridge**

One Drop of Blood

When Dr. Koenig, head of Mayfield Sanitarium is murdered, the District Attorney's Special Investigator, "Bonnie" Dundee must go undercover to find the killer. Were any of the inmates of the asylum insane enough to have committed the crime? Or, was it one of the staff, motivated by jealousy? And what was is the secret in the murdered man's past. Find the answer in... **One Drop of Blood**

AVAILABLE FROM RESURRECTED PRESS!

GEMS OF MYSTERY
LOST JEWELS FROM A MORE ELEGANT AGE

Three wonderful tales of mystery from some of the best known writers of the period before the First World War -

A foggy London night, a Russian princess who steals jewels, a corpse; a mysterious murder, an opera singer, and stolen pearls; two young people who crash a masked ball only to find themselves caught up in a daring theft of jewels; these are the subjects of this collection of entertaining tales of love, jewels, and mystery. This collection includes:

- **In the Fog - by Richard Harding Davis's**

- **The Affair at the Hotel Semiramis - by A.E.W. Mason**

- **Hearts and Masks - Harold MacGrath**

AVAILABLE FROM RESURRECTED PRESS!

THE EDWARDIAN DETECTIVES
LITERARY SLEUTHS OF THE EDWARDIAN ERA

The exploits of the great Victorian Detectives, Poe's C. Auguste Dupin, Gaboriau's Lecoq, and most famously, Arthur Conan Doyle's Sherlock Holmes, are well known. But what of those fictional detectives that came after, those of the Edwardian Age? The period between the death of Queen Victoria and the First World War had been called the Golden Age of the detective short story, but how familiar is the modern reader with the sleuths of this era? And such an extraordinary group they were, including in their numbers an unassuming English priest, a blind man, a master of disguises, a lecturer in medical jurisprudence, a noble woman working for Scotland Yard, and a savant so brilliant he was known as "The Thinking Machine."

To introduce readers to these detectives, Resurrected Press has assembled a collection of stories featuring these and other remarkable sleuths in The Edwardian Detectives.

- The Case of Laker, Absconded by Arthur Morrison
- The Fenchurch Street Mystery by Baroness Orczy
- The Crime of the French Café by Nick Carter
- The Man with Nailed Shoes by R Austin Freeman
- The Blue Cross by G. K. Chesterton
- The Case of the Pocket Diary Found in the Snow by Augusta Groner
- The Ninescore Mystery by Baroness Orczy
- The Riddle of the Ninth Finger by Thomas W. Hanshew
- The Knight's Cross Signal Problem by Ernest Bramah

- The Problem of Cell 13 by Jacques Futrelle
- The Conundrum of the Golf Links by Percy James Brebner
- The Silkworms of Florence by Clifford Ashdown
- The Gateway of the Monster by William Hope Hodgson
- The Affair at the Semiramis Hotel by A. E. W. Mason
- The Affair of the Avalanche Bicycle & Tyre Co., LTD by Arthur Morrison

RESURRECTED PRESS CLASSIC MYSTERY CATALOGUE

Journeys into Mystery
Travel and Mystery in a More Elegant Time

The Edwardian Detectives
Literary Sleuths of the Edwardian Era

Gems of Mystery
Lost Jewels from a More Elegant Age

E. C. Bentley
Trent's Last Case: The Woman in Black

Ernest Bramah
Max Carrados Resurrected:
The Detective Stories of Max Carrados

Agatha Christie
The Secret Adversary
The Mysterious Affair at Styles

Octavus Roy Cohen
Midnight

Freeman Wills Croft
The Ponson Case
The Pit Prop Syndicate

J. S. Fletcher
The Herapath Property
The Rayner-Slade Amalgamation
The Chestermarke Instinct
The Paradise Mystery
Dead Men's Money

The Middle of Things
Ravensdene Court
Scarhaven Keep
The Orange-Yellow Diamond
The Middle Temple Murder
The Tallyrand Maxim
The Borough Treasurer
In the Mayor's Parlour
The Saftey Pin

R. Austin Freeman
The Mystery of 31 New Inn from the Dr. Thorndyke
Series
John Thorndyke's Cases from the Dr. Thorndyke
Series
The Red Thumb Mark from The Dr. Thorndyke Series
The Eye of Osiris from The Dr. Thorndyke Series
A Silent Witness from the Dr. John Thorndyke Series
The Cat's Eye from the Dr. John Thorndyke Series
Helen Vardon's Confession: A Dr. John Thorndyke
Story
As a Thief in the Night: A Dr. John Thorndyke Story
Mr. Pottermack's Oversight: A Dr. John Thorndyke
Story
Dr. Thorndyke Intervenes: A Dr. John Thorndyke
Story
The Singing Bone: The Adventures of Dr. Thorndyke
The Stoneware Monkey: A Dr. John Thorndyke Story
The Great Portrait Mystery, and Other Stories: A
Collection of Dr. John Thorndyke and Other Stories
The Penrose Mystery: A Dr. John Thorndyke Story
The Uttermost Farthing: A Savant's Vendetta

Arthur Griffiths
The Passenger From Calais
The Rome Express

Fergus Hume
The Mystery of a Hansom Cab
The Green Mummy
The Silent House
The Secret Passage

Edgar Jepson
The Loudwater Mystery

A. E. W. Mason
At the Villa Rose

A. A. Milne
The Red House Mystery
Baroness Emma Orczy
The Old Man in the Corner

Edgar Allan Poe
The Detective Stories of Edgar Allan Poe

Arthur J. Rees
The Hampstead Mystery
The Shrieking Pit
The Hand In The Dark
The Moon Rock
The Mystery of the Downs

Mary Roberts Rinehart
Sight Unseen and The Confession

Dorothy L. Sayers
Whose Body?

Sir William Magnay
The Hunt Ball Mystery

Mabel and Paul Thorne
The Sheridan Road Mystery

Louis Tracy
The Strange Case of Mortimer Fenley
The Albert Gate Mystery
The Bartlett Mystery
The Postmaster's Daughter
The House of Peril
The Sandling Case: What Would You Have Done?
Charles Edmonds Walk
The Paternoster Ruby

John R. Watson
The Mystery of the Downs
The Hampstead Mystery

Edgar Wallace
The Daffodil Mystery
The Crimson Circle

Carolyn Wells
Vicky Van
The Man Who Fell Through the Earth
In the Onyx Lobby
Raspberry Jam
The Clue
The Room with the Tassels
The Vanishing of Betty Varian
The Mystery Girl
The White Alley
The Curved Blades
Anybody but Anne
The Bride of a Moment
Faulkner's Folly
The Diamond Pin
The Gold Bag
The Mystery of the Sycamore
The Come Backy

Raoul Whitfield
Death in a Bowl

And much more!
Visit ResurrectedPress.com
for our complete catalogue

About Resurrected Press

A division of Intrepid Ink, LLC, Resurrected Press is dedicated to bringing high quality, vintage books back into publication. See our entire catalogue and find out more at www.ResurrectedPress.com.

About Intrepid Ink, LLC

Intrepid Ink, LLC provides full publishing services to authors of fiction and non-fiction books, eBooks and websites. From editing to formatting, from publishing to marketing, Intrepid Ink gets your creative works into the hands of the people who want to read them. Find out more at www.IntrepidInk.com.